CITY of PROMISE

CITY of PROMISE

Dawn Prough

By Light Unseen Media
Pepperell, Massachusetts

City of Promise

Cover and interior design by Vyrdolak, By Light Unseen Media.

This is a work of fiction. Names, characters, places and incidents are either the products of the author's imagination or are used fictitiously, and any resemblence to actual persons, living or dead, business establishments, events or locales is entirely coincidental.

Perfect Paperback Edition

ISBN-10: 1-935303-41-4
ISBN-13: 978-1-935303-41-1
LCCN: 2012941551

Published by
By Light Unseen Media
PO Box 1233
Pepperell, Massachusetts 01463-3233

Our Mission:
By Light Unseen Media presents the best of quality fiction and non-fiction on the theme of vampires and vampirism. We offer fictional works with original imagination and style, as well as non-fiction of academic calibre.

For additional information, visit:
http://bylightunseenmedia.com/

Printed in the United States of America

0 9 8 7 6 5 4 3 2 1

CHAPTER 1

There are nights I appreciate my life. And there are also nights like this, when the wind howls off the ocean and Gideon isn't the "City of Promise," but a cage of safety. Sounds messed up, but when you can't leave somewhere for fear of your life, it is a cage. That depressing thought spawns another: *Does the caged vampire sing?* I can answer that: not really.

Around my dangling feet, seawater splashed and churned. I could just see the uppermost of the massive hydraulic fans gently rotating under about twenty feet of ocean, but the dark water hid everything else. Normally, it would be utterly black down there, but the maintenance lights were on. Even I need some light to see underwater at night.

Gideon's turbine fans spin in their tunnels below the city, propelled by the ocean's currents. The energy they generate helps run the City of Promise, powering all the necessities for life. Normally, the fans would be damaged by contact with debris, but each fan was wreathed by defensive nets. I'm not sure what they're made of, but the nets protect the fans from biologics and trash. They keep the fans clean, but the nets have to be cleared out and repaired on a regular basis. Tonight, that was my job. Lucky me.

Usually, it's just a matter of cleaning off the barnacles and other sea life that build up, but occasionally you'll find a surprise. While frames hold the nets taut so that creatures can't get wrapped up in them, sometimes a fish or dolphin manages to get entangled. It's considered one of the more emotionally draining jobs to continually clean carcasses out of the webbing, or at least I've heard my human coworkers say so. They talk about how depressed they feel after finding a dead dolphin. I've never felt that sentiment, but I don't clean the nets all the time. Or feel a particular emotional connection to dolphins.

Usually, my job is to repair and maintain the pillars that hold Gideon in the center of the Atlantic Ocean. Not dead center, of course—the saying is mostly poetic. We actually sit on the spine of the Atlantic, where the South Atlantic Ridge lies hidden under the waves. Less than two hundred feet beneath us, the mountains reach upward, providing an anchor for Gideon. The area is a seismic nightmare which precluded the possibility of building on the ocean floor. Because of that, Gideon floats despite being made of concrete and metal, and the anchors and pillars serve as moorings to keep the city in place without using power-hungry engines.

For the last two days, GWE had gotten enough call-outs to create staffing problems, and we'd had to juggle duties around so that everything got done. GWE is short for Gideon Water and Energy, called "Gooey" by those with a lack of respect for authority—like anyone employed by them. The bureaucracy governs all the utilities for the city, and employs many of the city's vampires. There are things that would kill a human that don't faze a vampire, so it's a great deal for the city.

For example, there's less chance that they'll have to pay compensation if the injured worker is already dead.

I tipped my head back and sighed heavily as I stared at the stars. I love Gideon, or at least what it represents, but would I be here if I didn't have to be? Here, I'm a free member of society, but I'm trapped by the fear that grips the rest of the world. Only in this city am I safe; everywhere else hunts for my kind. Outside Gideon, I'd be hunted as an animal, but I would be free. Some people are never happy.

"Hey, girl." Malcolm dropped inelegantly into a sitting position on the catwalk next to me, a sandwich in his hand. "You look like you rolled out of the wrong side of the coffin."

I grimaced and sighed at the curly-haired man, not bothering to hide my fond irritation. Malcolm is a nice guy, but he has a really annoying habit of making bad vampire jokes around me. Occasionally, he tells a good one, which I do laugh at. If I really wanted him to stop, I wouldn't laugh at any of them.

"Very funny, Mal," I chuckled weakly. Malcolm is the only

person at work that I get along with at all. He's not even afraid of me, which is surprising. The founders of Gideon may have declared that vampires were people, but most regular folks don't believe it. I can't blame them. If I were a lamb, I wouldn't want to work with a wolf. "Got a blonde joke? Those are always good."

"Those are only funny when a blonde is around." He grinned, snaking out a hand to flick one of my dark curls. His grin only widened as he bit into his sandwich.

I watched him eat; he comically over-chewed, trying to get a rise out of me. I've told him that I don't find food appealing anymore, and I certainly don't miss it, but he doesn't seem to believe me. Even if I can remember a time I loved ham on white, I want one like a lion wants a bucket of oats.

"So, I saw we're cleaning the nets tonight," Malcolm added after a moment of chewing. "Who'd you piss off? I know it wasn't me—everyone loves me."

"You mean they don't love me, too?" I grinned before giving a serious answer. "Gabe said the day and evening shifts were short-handed, so they didn't get to clean the nets in Tile Thirty-Two or Thirty-Four." The tiles were the building blocks of Gideon; each one could float on its own. The city was built of hundreds of these concrete blocks strung together to stabilize them. Only part of the tile was visible above water; the rest was a long air-filled tube that provided buoyancy. These tiles were formed into two rings surrounding a central core. The Inner Ring and the Core were a mixture of residential and business. Why have another ring and a separate core? The official line is that it provides further stabili-zation. I'm convinced that the truth is simpler: the Core is for the wealthy, and having a separate ring keeps the riff-raff away. The Outer Ring shielded the city from the ocean and was the platform where most of the "dirty" work of keeping the city going was done. The fans were part of that effort, generating energy to make life easy for the residents. "The good news is that it's only two nets, and once they're clean, we can go."

It wasn't company generosity; once we were done with the nets, there wouldn't be time left to make the dive to a pillar or anchor line before the end of our shift. GWE couldn't legally require me to work once the sun was up so they couldn't make Mal stay either; they'd never hear the end of it if a vampire got a special privilege that a human didn't.

"Well, then," Malcolm said and stuffed the rest of the sand-wich into his mouth. "Leff's go."

I had to laugh at him with his cheeks puffed out like a rodent's as he tried to choke down his sandwich. Top his already round face with the mass of curly hair and he really did look like a squirrel or some other rodent.

"Why does Sarah put up with you?" I asked him as I bounced to my feet with the perfect poise of the dead.

Malcolm grinned, giving me a grotesque view of his partially-mauled dinner, as he answered, "Sfe saifs I make her lauff."

He moved over to the tile's control panel as I followed him, double-checking my dive suit.

"So does a cat with tape on its paws," I grunted, tightening my tool belt. "I still wouldn't want to date one."

Malcolm gulped noisily one last time as he bent over the fan control panel; I could hear his grin as he replied, "Well, I give better—"

"La-la-la!" I sang out as I clamped my hands over my ears. "I don't want to hear what you give better than a cat!"

"I was going to say 'back rubs,' you dirty-minded little girl." Malcolm grinned, but I knew from his evil smirk that wasn't what he was going to say. He glanced down at the panel and his smile faded. "Well, crap."

"What?" I asked as I slid in next to him. He put his arm over my shoulder, making room so that I could see too. The workspace is designed for the heroin chic, with just enough room for the operator between it and the concrete wall. There are no two people on the planet small enough to work at the panel together without violations of personal space and possibly physics. Space here is at a premium, but I don't know how the truly obese members of Gideon society manage all the close quarters.

"The bottom camera is out," Malcolm growled, pointing to the panel. It should have been showing its section of net, but tonight it only showed a blue screen. He glanced at the e-board with tonight's assignments, sighing. "The day crew didn't note it. They probably didn't even check to see what's wrong. Sorry, Misty, you'll have to look and see if it's come undone or if it's broken."

"Part of the job." I shrugged and wiggled out from behind the panel. Naturally, it was the worst camera to check, as it rested at the bottom-most point in the net. Fun, fun. I checked my equipment one last time, unused to the lighter weight of this gear. My normal job maintaining the pillars requires pliers, wrenches, and any number of heavy tools.

As Mal prepared to monitor my dive, I pulled the hood up, feeling my stomach tighten. I made sure that my hair was all tucked in before I finished pulling the zipper shut under my chin. Last, I secured the goggles, making sure they were set comfortably and that I could see. It was time for the least pleasant aspect of this job.

"I'm ready. Don't forget to shut off the fans."

"Don't worry," Malcolm said. "First thing I did. They should be stopped by now."

I fought the urge to glare at him for being efficient. But it would be upsetting for Malcolm to know just how much this part of my job sucked, so I stepped to the ladder and began the climb down. The temperature of the water was neutral to me. I've been told that it's damn cold this time of year, but I didn't notice. I could feel that it was colder than usual, but vampires are no longer sensitive to temperature extremes.

The ocean holds another unpleasantness for me, one that I can't seem to get used to.

I reached the end of the ladder and did one final check to make sure I had all my gear on me. It was a pain to have to swim back up to the top of the pen if I forgot something, and I only wanted to do this one time. Once I was sure I had everything I might need, I stepped off the ladder.

I didn't let myself hesitate; I might not do it if I tried to psyche myself for it. I just did it. I plunged into the salty water and twisted myself so that I was facing down. With a sharp kick I began to descend, and as I did, I released the residual air in my lungs. The bubbles caressed my exposed face, running along the edge of my goggles before disappearing above me. The sensation and sight pulled up unpleasant memories of fleeing America, trapped in a shark cage under the water with six other vampires. It had been the only way to get smuggled out of America and it was terrible: the fear of being caught by officials while nearly starving because of the lack of blood supply. The fish had eaten at us, taking nips of flesh while we were packed so tightly into the cage we couldn't move. Long-term exposure to seawater ruined our tough flesh, loosening and degrading it until it sloughed off. No one in the cage was surprised when one of us lost it; when he started to tear into us, we bent the bars and shoved him out. He disappeared into the infinite depths below us, unable to scream because his lungs and vocal cords were infused with water.

I inhaled water. Even dead, the body remembers that this is wrong. I struggled to remain calm, to let the water in rather than choke it out. That stirred memories, too, even older than the cage under water. Before they were taken, my sires and I had hidden in a sewer treatment plant, in one of the tanks. I'd hated that so much—choking down the filthy water and avoiding any intake pipes that would suck me deeper into the system. We'd emerged only to eat and look for somewhere else safe. There had been nowhere else.

See? It's a wonder I can get into the water at all.

Back to work, I chided myself. *You're in Gideon, you're safe. Get going.* That admonishment got me past the ghosts and moving. With my lungs filled with water, I kicked for the bottom of the net. I'd start there and work up.

The fan blades hung like ghosts in the dark water; the security lights stationed periodically around the nets didn't pierce the darkness so much as accent it. I left my powerful flashlight off. If I didn't see a problem, I didn't have to fix it.

Mentally, I ran down the checklist of things to do. No signs of a barnacle infestation, which was good. Usually, they're more common close to large land-masses but it was still minutely possible for them to travel out here and take up residence. I thought checking was mostly a waste of time and busy-work since Gideon's scientists had devised ways to keep the pests' populations and growth low. I caught flashes of fish moving outside the net—none inside tonight, thankfully. Trying to catch living fish that have snuck through is more annoying than picking their rotting corpses from the nets. It also meant that I didn't have to search for the hole they got in through, the very definition of looking for a task.

So far, so good. The camera was still below me, and I kicked downward powerfully, eager to get this done. As I approached the bottom of the net, I saw a shadow floating in the water, backlit by the bottom light. It was large, large enough to be a dolphin. There was no movement beyond the sway of the ocean, and it looked like I had a corpse to clean out after all. But as I got closer, I realized that this wasn't a fish. I snapped on my flashlight to get a better look at it, flooding the water with blindingly bright light.

A woman floated gracefully in the murky water, her head tilted back as if she were watching me approach. That was unlikely; she was clearly dead. I locked eyes with her, surprised by the intimacy of her lifeless gaze. I had to fight to tear my eyes away from her dark ones.

She was in her early twenties, with a delicate, Asian face. She looked like she laughed a lot; there were smile lines around her eyes, and she had lips that seemed inclined to expressions of joy. Her straight, thick hair drifted in a black cloud around her face and body; it looked long enough to reach the middle of her back. She was wearing a cute yellow dress that I wouldn't have worn, and a denim jacket that made me miss my old fringed jacket, bought while I was still alive and lost somewhere in New Orleans after I died. You can take the girl out of the '80s, but the love of denim jackets and hot pink leg warmers is forever.

I can't communicate with Mal verbally; my larynx was filled with water, so I didn't have a communicator on me. GWE doesn't waste resources on unnecessary support for their undead workers, like air tanks or life vests. It makes sense; it's not like I could get into any trouble that would kill me, not unless someone turns on the fans. All I had was the touchpad on my arm; a slender keyboard with a screen that sent messages up to the control panel.

I quickly typed, *Mal, found body.*

His reply was unhelpful. *Fish it out. Do I need to tell u how to do ur job? ;)*

No, I punched into the pad, *a human body. Call the police & any1 else who NTK.*

There was a long silence. *Don't touch anything. Get out.*

I agreed but I had to give a full report. *Yes,* I told him but I didn't start up. Instead, I swam underneath the woman, trying to see if she was the reason that the camera wasn't working.

She wasn't, but the cinder block that was tied to her feet was. It had landed on the camera, busting the casing and half-ripping it free of the support beam that housed it. It would need to be replaced completely, but that would have to wait for her body to be removed.

I began to head up, but a flash of color caught my eye. A pink ribbon was wound around the fingers of her left hand. It was thin and short, and the color didn't match her current outfit. I floated closer, careful not to brush the hand as I stared. It reminded me of a child's hair ribbon, and had I not found it around her fingers I wouldn't have given it another thought. It seemed too important, as if the woman was trying to say something from beyond the grave. But her message eluded me, and I pushed away from her and began to swim to the surface. Strangely, the image of that ribbon remained with me, a delicate touch of beauty in the face of death.

CHAPTER 2

My nights aren't usually this interesting, I thought as I looked down at the woman. She was in a body bag, but I remembered how she looked when they pulled her out. She'd been pale and gray, though she hadn't been in the water long enough to destroy her skin. I knew all about salt water effects on dead skin. Her black hair had hung limp and stringy; her face was dragged down into an empty mask by gravity's pull on her loose muscles. The once-bright yellow dress had been wrinkled and lank against the concrete floor.

I couldn't reconcile that limp creature with the floating angel I had found under the cold waters of the South Atlantic. It made me a little sad, like I'd done her a disservice to find her.

Malcolm had been separated from me by the police when they arrived. I'm sure they were questioning him, and I wondered if his inquisitor was as annoying as mine.

"Misty Sauval?" I turned at the question. A tall man was approaching, his height and medium build emphasized in a good way by his long coat. He would have looked good without the coat, honestly. The word for him was *swarthy:* dark hair, eyes and nut-brown skin all put together in a nice package. The flaw to his appearance was the eyeglasses; no one should have to wear them with all the laser surgery, so they were cosmetic. They looked good on his face, but they made him stand out in a crowd.

"Yeah?" I asked. It was both confirmation and question. My voice was tired and more than a little surly.

"I'm Elias Haase, *Gideon Daily.*" The reporter pulled out a recorder. "I'm covering this story—"

My eyebrows rose and I looked around before interrupting. "Really? The cops let you in?"

He grinned mischievously, a very sexy expression. "Well, *let* isn't the word I'd use, to be honest."

I didn't smile back; I wasn't in the mood despite my appreciation for flaunting authority. "Nice." I glanced at the cops milling around. "Hope you wore your running shoes or have a good lawyer."

"Don't worry about me," That cocky grin was still on his handsome face.

"Oh, I don't," I assured him, crossing my arms.

"So I understand you found the body?" Elias glanced down at the body bag as if trying to see through the opaque material.

"I shouldn't talk to you." My statement was delivered without inflection.

"C'mon." Elias stepped closer. His voice dropped to a friendly murmur; everything about him implied that we were buddies. "Help a guy out here."

"Fine." I turned and pointed the way he'd come. "You can leave through that gate."

He had a sense of humor; he laughed despite my refusal to help. "Cute. Look I'm just looking for some info here—I don't even have to name you as the source. Misty, I protect my sources, so the police won't—"

"Hey!" A voice rang out and I turned to face the newest thorn in my side. I groaned as the tall, thin man with blond hair stormed toward me, his long coat snapping around him like an angry bird. In the last few hours, I had become very familiar with the angular, fey features of the man scowling at me. He was Peter Benoit, Gideon detective and all-around tough guy, in his own mind. I'm sure that's what he wanted people to think about him. His delicate features were more suited to an artist or a dancer than a cop, and I had no doubt that worked against him in his profession. That's probably why he was such a jerk. Must be hard to intimidate a perp when he can easily picture you on stage in full *Cats* regalia. "Get away from the body!"

"Yer offica left me here," I said, my thick New Orleans accent flowing out. I hid a wince; I hate it when others can pinpoint my heritage. I'm Creole, born in New Orleans in the mid-nineteen seventies, and I look it with dusky skin that had confused a lot of people trying to peg my race. It had given me a look that others called exotic, as I had the dark complexion with light eyes, but it had given me an annoying accent, too. People hear that sugar-sweet accent and make stupid assumptions. Sixty years is a long time to lose an accent if you really try at it but I hadn't been completely successful. When I get upset or sad or angry, it can creep out. Guess which one I was right now?

Behind Benoit, another man in a suit approached. He was a darker form compared to the blond Benoit, short black hair and cinnamon skin. He was not as tall as Benoit or as handsome but there was something appealing about him. While I'd instinctively disliked Benoit, I instinctively liked his partner, Oliver Criado. He was Latino like the reporter, but where Elias was smokin', Criado was more ordinary. His attraction was largely personality.

I think that Benoit took the sudden accent as a sign of incrimination; his thin face haughtily assumed a dark scowl. Ignoring my statement, he asked, "Getting another look at your handiwork?" Benoit had been hot to pin this death on me since he got here. Without waiting for my reply, he grabbed my arm and dragged me away from the body. I bit back a growl at that, knowing that even if I was justified in taking offense at the handling, it'd only be used against me later.

Elias' eyes were wide as he glanced at me for my reaction. I swallowed, counted to ten and pointed at Elias. "Do you always let reporters on your crime scenes?"

Two sets of eyes snapped to Elias; two expressions of consternation crossed male faces. Elias rolled his eyes and scowled at me. I realized that they'd been so focused on me that they hadn't really seen Elias. "Officer!" Benoit's voice cracked like a whip. A young man standing nearby hustled over. "Get this man off the crime scene."

I smirked as the cop gestured Elias to the exit I'd just pointed out to him. My superior good mood didn't last; Benoit caught my arm and spun me around, marching me away from the dead woman. Criado trailed us, quiet and calm. He was definitely going for the "good cop" vibe in this conversation. The Southern Atlantic wind blew my dark, tightly curled hair wildly around my head, half-covering my face as we staggered to a stop a short distance away. "There're no bite marks on her." I was as calm as I could be while wrestling my wet hair out of my mouth and eyes. I have some patience for this kind of game, but his constant accusations were irritating. I had accepted his first accusation with grace and his second with patience, but I was running out of both. And I was still wrestling with my accent. "If ya find one, get a warrant for a radius check."

"How about we get one now?" Benoit leaned forward to intimidate me. Immediately, I imagined him dancing and singing about catching mice and bit back a laugh. I doubted that would help me, so I set my jaw and stared up into his fair face with its classic, Franco-aristocratic lines. I made sure to keep my face straight; no point in making things worse. I know my rights; I didn't have to give them a radius check even if they found a bite. I could insist on a warrant, and was within my rights to do so. I'd cut them a lot of slack up until now because I understood that they were freaked out by my presence. The cops don't generally handle us well. We are parasites living off the people they swear to defend. Oil and water, and it showed in all our interactions.

My salvation showed up in the form of Rick Foreman, my case worker.

"How 'bout we... Oh, thank god. Rick!" I waved at him, relief relaxing my hardened expression.

He waddled over, smiling uncertainly at the detectives and me, his coat turned up against the cold wind cutting off the ocean. He was clutching a plastic insulated mug of coffee in his hand and looked miserable. He's the stereotypical mid-level bureaucrat; overworked and underpaid, overweight and poorly dressed. "Hey, Rick," I said, nodding to him. "If you're going to keep your hair that short, you really need a hat in this weather."

"Misty." He mirrored my nod, ignoring the hat comment. His eyes flicked toward the ocean anxiously; he must stick to the central part of the city if seeing the open water was this nerve-wracking. Some people become really comfortable with the idea that they lived on a giant, stationary, concrete raft moored to the ocean floor by pillars; some didn't. Or it could be the fact that a dead body was not a twenty feet away from us.

"Rick, this is Detective Peter Benoit. He would *really* like me to be guilty of murder. The other guy is Detective Oliver Criado. I'm not sure about him yet. He seems decent, which is confusing me."

Criado smirked as Benoit scowled at me; Rick choked on the sip of coffee he was taking. I loved flustering my case worker, and I really needed to amuse myself right now. It's easy since he's so straight-laced; he's always surprised by off-the-wall statements. He's also a good case worker, one of the few who actually cares about his clients. I heard stories from the other vampires about caseworkers who won't do anything to help or worse, actively work against the vampires they're supposed to help. I got lucky with Rick and I know it. As soon as I'd reminded myself of that, it occurred to me belatedly that tonight might not be the night to try to agitate him.

Rick had no doubt dealt with this before; even in Gideon, vampires were easy targets for the cops. It was sad that we were supposed to have all this power—that we were these creatures that were so feared—but we had to have caseworkers to protect us from the authorities of Gideon. Sure, the Unity of Gideon, the governing body, passed laws that gave us protections, but those warm feelings hadn't quite worked their way down through the rank and file. We'd protect ourselves, but most of the elders had been killed in the early days of the Great Hunt, leaving us babies relatively defenseless. Yes, we're still stronger than humans, but there are a lot more of them. We can't really rebuild our numbers, since only the elders are strong enough to create more vampires. We have to survive until some of us reach "breeding-age," which is not as easy as it sounds. A lot can happen to someone over the course of three centuries, which is the minimum age for attempting the creation of "babies." Daffyad advised me not to worry about it before my fifth century, to increase the probability of change. So we have about a century to wait for the oldest members of our race to start reliably turning more vampires. That's a long time and unless there were elders hiding out somewhere, off the grid, we were looking at an uphill battle.

"What's your evidence against my client?" Rick asked in his soft, casual way as he took another sip of his coffee. Apparently, he'd recovered from my big mouth.

"She called in the crime." Benoit's voice was intense as slender fingers rose to tick off his points. "She has access and motive. She—"

"Motive?" Rick broke in, and Benoit's eyes narrowed at

being interrupted. I gleefully took note of his irritation. "What's her motive?"

Benoit was now cornered and everyone knew it. If he said that my motive was that I was a vampire, I had the legal right to press a discrimination suit against the Gideon police force. And I know he didn't have any evidence on me, because I didn't kill this woman. I didn't even know *who* she was. Sure, I found her, but it was just bad luck that it was me. It could have been any one of the GWE divers.

"We're still ascertaining what happened." Criado spoke in a soft voice that suited him well. "Ms. Sauval is a suspect, until we clear her."

"Saying too much would impede the investigation." Benoit's nostrils flared. Oh yes, there was aristocracy in ol' Petey's family tree. It seemed hard to believe that he could be this naturally arrogant as a civil servant in Gideon. I could be wrong, but I didn't think I was.

"Are you arresting my client, then?" Rick asked as he took another sip of coffee. He was outwardly casual and calm, but I could see that nervous tick of his eye that meant he was fighting some extreme reaction. I was personally hoping for righteous fury.

"Not at this point." The words hurt Benoit to say; you could see it in his pretty blue eyes. I'm a sucker for attractive eyes. Normally, I don't like blonds, but Benoit was handsome enough to be an exception, were I interested in dating. Like most vampires, I have zero sexual interest in humans except in unusual circumstances. I could still feel disappointment that with a face like that, he was a bigoted jerk. Why are the pretty ones always the ones we should avoid?

"So is Ms. Sauval free to go then?" Rick pressed.

At Benoit's sharp, reluctant nod, Rick took me by the arm and led me away. I was spared the "don't leave town" cliché, since I *couldn't* leave for my own safety. As we walked, I glanced over and saw they were loading the woman's body onto the stretcher.

As soon as we were out of earshot, Rick sighed, "So, tell me what happened."

I really didn't like his tone, but given the problems that would spring from having a client who was the prime suspect in a murder case, I could give him *some* slack. But not much—I'd had a bad night too. As clearly as I could, I told him how I'd found the body. Rick listened with his usual quiet demeanor, nodding occasionally, but he was clearly unnerved.

"This isn't good, Misty." Rick looked tired.

"Really, ya think?" I snapped, my temper giving way finally. "But they're not gonna find anything, Rick, not a damned thing. I didn't have anything to do with this! I don't even know her!"

My voice had risen to a shout, and some of the officers turned to watch me with cold eyes.

"Misty, calm down. Sit." Rick directed me to the far edge of the pool. He knew that I liked to dangle my feet in the water, and that was clearly what he wanted. I complied with his request only because I'd dragged him out of his office and out to the edge of the city, and he was on my side. Other than Mal, still somewhere being questioned, he was probably the only person here on my side. "I need you to stay calm. The last thing the cops need to see is an angry Tick."

I felt my fists clench and I forced them to relax rather than punching Rick. I knew why he'd used the derogatory term; he'd wanted to remind me how the cops were seeing me. I was a Tick, here on the scene when a body hit the ground, and I had access and motive. The motive was a lie and *I* knew that, but until the tests showed no exsanguination, I was their first suspect. I remembered that much from my criminal justice classes so long ago.

"Fine." I gripped the concrete edge of the fan-pool. "I'm calm. Happy as a lark."

"Good." He put a hand on my shoulder. "Now stay here, and stay out of trouble, ok?"

My only answer was a short nod. Rick wandered away to work his magic, and I had nothing to do except watch the dark ocean roll under a star-filled sky and hope that Rick's talk with the cops was successful.

❅　❅　❅

I hate the police. Don't get me wrong; they're probably great people when at home, around their grills or watching the game. They're probably fine parents, siblings or friends. But I remember the Great Hunt in America during the 2020s, which was led by the police and the clergy working hand in hand. I remember being chased through the street by the police, being driven to the waiting clergy with their "holy fire" and their wooden stakes. I'd nearly died at the hands of the law; I've had to kill police to remain alive. It's not something easily forgotten. And I'm sure that the GPD has heard those stories.

When I got here, I had to list all my crimes. I was given amnesty, under Gideon's Necessary Desperation Act, but I'd killed before, and I was sure that the cops had pulled my record when I'd identified myself tonight. As a citizen of Gideon, I was legally obligated to aid them as much as I could, but my skin crawled the entire time. The predator in me knew that I was in trouble, and it wanted me to act, not wait for others to act for me.

"Ma'am?" The voice pulled me out of my reverie and I looked up to see one of the other Detectives, Morrison or something, approaching.

I glanced past him to see Benoit glaring at me. Things must have gone my way, because he was scowling.

"We have your statement, but we would like to know if you have anything further before we send you home." The man's eyes wouldn't focus on me; he kept looking past me, his expression almost perfectly neutral. I say almost because the fear was still apparent in his eyes.

"I guess you discovered she has all her blood, then?" I'd been afraid that she had been drained and dumped, though I probably shouldn't think of her that way. It made her sound like bad plumbing.

"I can't discuss particulars of the case with you, ma'am." The detective's brown eyes were wary. I could smell dried blood on him, and he had a bandage on his finger. He paled when he saw me glance at it, and his right hand twitched toward his gun. Did he think I was going to eat him right here? "Do you have something to add to your previous statement?"

"No, sir," I answered, trying to keep the anger out of my voice. I didn't think I was successful, but the detective just nodded at me.

"If you think of anything else, anything that would help, just let us know." He extended a card to me with shaking fingers. He should have been worried. Were I hungry and flaunting the laws of Gideon, he was too close a temptation to ignore. It'd be too easy to grab him with arms stronger than any he'd ever felt and pull him close, whispering soothing noises to ease his struggles before biting down and claiming his blood for my own.

I let the fantasy go. I liked being free and safe; eating a cop in front of other cops would reverse that. They wouldn't bother with deportation; I'd likely be executed. Vampires are hard to contain, so the policy was deportation or execution. I'd heard that the Unity was filled with "regret" that things couldn't be different. I'm sure they lost sleep over it all the time.

I glanced at the card, as if reading it, but I didn't try to retain the information. The card would be "lost" in the first trashcan that I found, if not sooner—saltwater would destroy it pretty quickly, too.

"Sure," I said and climbed to my feet. The detective backed up, giving me room and getting out of my reach. "Can I go back to work?"

"Eh, sure, but not on this net," he said, waving at the water below us. "No one will be given access to this tank until we're done with our investigations."

❋ ❋ ❋

We moved to the nets in Tile Thirty-Four and found Gabe waiting. My boss is a heavy man, mostly from the tire around his gut. Another victim of the sedentary bureaucratic lifestyle, Gabe was also losing his brown hair. Mal called him when we found the body; for a moment I thought he was going to tell us to fish it out of the pen and dump it into the ocean. As the general manager of the third shift of GWE, he was responsible for things happening on the shift, good and bad. Having one of the fans tied up in an investigation would generate a *lot* of paperwork and a lot of heat from above to get the fan operational again. Meanwhile, the police would do their thing on their own schedule and Gabe was likely to be caught in the middle.

"So what's going on over there?" he asked us, his large form blocking access to the control panel.

"You can ask the cops," Malcolm snapped. "They weren't exactly forthcoming with us. Maybe you'd have more luck."

"No, I mean about the fan." As Malcolm scowled, Gabe focused on me. "Misty, what could you see down there? How did the fan look? Any thoughts on when we could have it operational again?"

I shrugged. "Gabe, I don't work the fans, normally. I have no idea. Get someone down there who's had more than the basic training. All I can say is you'll need to completely replace the camera."

Gabe sighed. "All right, sorry." If you gave Gabe any lip or attitude, he immediately backed down and apologized. It meant he wasn't a good manager from the upper echelon's point of view, but he was great to work for most of the time. I'd heard stories about how he was always being bowled over by other GWE employees. I tried not to push him too much; I didn't want to break him before I really needed to.

"Well, I'll go over there and wait for them to clear out, I guess." He stepped away only to pause and look back. "Misty, be careful, all right?"

I stared at him, confused. "Uh, sure. Yeah. Careful." I watched him nod and leave before I turned to Malcolm. "Was it just me, or was that weird?" All I got in response was a grunt from my normally talkative coworker. It must have been "Everyone Act Weird Night" and I missed the memo.

Work was blessedly normal compared to the last tile. I did my dive and cleaned the nets, fishing out three small sardines and then patching the hole they'd used to enter. Throughout, Malcolm remained quiet and subdued. Around the end of the shift, I couldn't take the prolonged silence anymore. We were in the finishing steps; Malcolm was updating the maintenance logs and I was cleaning and stowing the equipment. "What's up? You've been awfully quiet. I'm a little worried that the cops confiscated your tongue for crimes against humanity." I grinned.

He didn't take my bait. "I'm not used to finding bodies," he said in a hushed tone. "I keep thinking about her, wondering who she was, who's at home waiting for her. I think about her and wonder—what if that were Sarah? What would I do if I waited forever for her to come home, and they found her at the bottom of the nets?"

I blinked at him. I hadn't given her another thought, really; my concern had been for my own safety, since the police seemed to want to pin this one on me. The woman was just a body—I had seen and caused a number of them in my days in America. I hadn't stopped to think that she was a person who had a family or loved ones. To be honest, I'd learned not to think that way pretty quickly. When you feed off a creature, you do what you must to separate dinner from being. Humans buy meat pre-packaged and never think about the animal it comes from. Most of them don't talk to their food source, smell it and live with it. I have to face my prey every night, look into its knowing eyes and acknowledge to myself that I am their monster. Am I proud of that? Not particularly, but it wasn't a matter for pride. It was a matter of survival.

But I would feel outrage if Sarah had been down there. She wasn't a human I would feed off of, even if the laws allowed me to feed. Most humans I didn't feel anything for; they were food. But I cared about Malcolm; he'd been the first person at GWE to treat me with any respect. And since I liked Mal, I wouldn't hurt Sarah, and wouldn't be real happy about others hurting her either. It was a double standard, and I supposed that should bother me, but it didn't, not really. Sarah and Mal were mine to protect and my vampire family was long dead; no other humans or vampires mattered to me.

But Mal still looked at me with haunted eyes. I tried to console him. "Malcolm, it wasn't Sarah. Don't go borrowing trouble."

"Trouble?" he asked, frowning. "A woman is dead, and that's just trouble?"

"I meant," I said, trying to pick my words carefully, "that she's not Sarah, and you don't need to worry about it. Sarah is fine. You didn't know that woman, did you?"

"It didn't matter whether I knew her." Mal's pleading gaze shifted to anger. "You don't care," he spat. "A woman is dead and you just don't care!"

"I don't know her," I answered, confused and feeling the first stirrings of my own anger. What was the big deal? She was no one to me, and as far as I knew, no one to Mal. "What is there to care about? If it had been Sarah, I'd be risking imprisonment or worse to find out who had hurt her."

Mal stared angrily at me. I wasn't sure what I'd done to deserve his anger, but I was starting to get pissed. His next statement didn't help. "Maybe all those people who say you guys are just monsters are right. Maybe you guys shouldn't be allowed to live and work here."

I restrained my temper—barely. "You're upset," I said carefully, emphasizing each word. "I can see that. I may not understand why you feel pain for a woman you don't know, but that does not make me a monster. I have no one to put her face to, like you do. So *back off,* Malcolm." The last was little more than a growl. I didn't want to growl or talk. I wouldn't eat Malcolm, but that didn't stop the instinct that demanded he recognize me as his possible killer. I wanted to grab him, slam him to the ground and demand his respect. I also wanted him to stop looking at me like that, to go back to just being my friend. The two desires warred and I think it showed.

His face was pale as I restrained my violent urge to dominate him. This was the sort of scenario that made me wonder if we had any business trying to live with humans at all. They didn't understand us or our drives and in their arrogance demanded that we conform to their values. They found us to be bestial. Maybe they were right. "Misty," he started, but I waved him off.

"Not right now, Mal. I'm not in the mood for a fight."

I hurried away, eager to put some space between us. When I heard him call my name again, I took a shortcut.

The pool was roughly hexagonal with a catwalk that ran across it. I didn't go around the pool; instead I jumped over the water to land on the catwalk. As Mal cursed and started to cross the outside of the pool, I leapt again and landed by the exit. Well before my human friend was a quarter of the way around the pool, I was gone.

CHAPTER 3

I avoided Mal by hiding in the girls' room. I needed to go there anyway, to change clothes. The dive suit protected me from salt water, but it was still good to take a quick rinse. While it helped my hair and skin, it did nothing for my anger. I was still fuming when I stepped out of the shower, all the seawater off my body and down the drain. The hour was a little late; most other people were already done with their shifts. So I was alone in the room. I took advantage of the privacy to let myself act out, throwing things and disregarding their structural integrity. It was only after I nearly ripped buttons off my shirt that I forced myself to calm down.

I exited the shower room in my street clothes. People sometimes expect something glamorous, but I usually wear jeans, simple shirts and ankle boots. Most of them resemble '80s fashions, but I don't actively seek replicas. I like what I like, and what I like happens to be what was popular when I was alive.

There were two options for getting home: the public transport system or my own feet. Taking the suspended cable trolley that ran over the Inner Sea of Gideon would be faster, but I felt like a walk. Keeping an eye out for ambushing Mals, I passed by the elevated trolley station and headed for Curie Bridge that ran between the Outer Ring and the Inner Ring. The bridge served to keep the outer ring of tiles the proper distance from the Inner Ring, but a covered walkway was built on top of it. As with everything in the city, it served two purposes because of the space constraints.

Behind me, someone yelled my name. I tensed and looked back, frowning when I saw the man running toward me. His name was Basil, the Russian kind of Basil. It had been no surprise to learn that he was part of the Russian Mafia. Unlike some of the other organized crime syndicates, the *Volga bratva* wasn't a splinter from the main gang. They were full members of the mother gang, and worked in concert with her.

I knew all this because he'd told me, with no small amount of pride. And he'd told me because they really wanted to recruit me. Russia had a particularly bad history with vampires. I mean, all countries besides Gideon had bad reactions, but the stories coming out of Russia were particularly hair-raising. They had a lot of myths about ways to kill vampires, but not all of them worked. They were all painful, from what I'd heard. They didn't just kill us, they tortured us. As a result, vampires harbored a profound unfriendliness toward that nation.

That had left the *Volga bratva* in an awkward position. Most of the other crime syndicates were recruiting vampires, but because of the way we were treated in their homeland, we didn't want much to do with them. So they were always creeping around, trying to find someone willing to join up. Or someone desperate enough. For some reason, they thought I was willing or desperate. "No," I said before his mouth was open.

"Misty, I wait for you by the trolley," he said in his accented English, following me onto the bridge.

"And I've told you," I said sharply, "I'm not interested."

"I didn't even know this bridge was...walkable. To be walked on," he said. I eyed him, wondering again who had given them my name. He was not a light man: not fat, but built solidly. Sandy blond hair and beard whipped around his face as he smiled at me. "Did you know?"

"Yes, Basil, since I'm walking here," I shot back, scowling. It didn't faze him.

"I would think to take the trolley," he said, and looked down. I saw him pale as he saw open water under us. I looked down too, noting the water for the first time. "I do not like to come to the Outer Ring," Basil said, his voice a little shaky.

I wondered what he'd think of going all the way out to the edge of the ring. I'd gone there once, because I'd heard it was something to see. The outer edges of these tiles were long slopes, which dispersed the force of the currents that would otherwise tear Gideon apart. It looked like giant hundred foot long slip-n-slides all the way down into the ocean. They didn't appear strong enough to withstand waves, much less storms, and they weren't; nothing on Earth was. But they did divert most of the force of the storms. The ocean even ran up the top of the long slope, making waves that mimicked a real beach. So the designers of the city designated some of the areas public beaches and let the citizens enjoy them, though there were complaints it wasn't the same without sand. It was one more example of Gideon's duality: just when you thought this place was all sterile functionality, people managed to find some creature comforts. Of course, some things were lost on people, especially people like Rick and Basil. Living on a chunk of floating concrete can really mess with humans, and I wonder about the kind of humans who think that building a floating island is not only a good idea, but build it and move their families out there.

But I have to admit, the scientists who built this place did it well. I'd heard about some bad storms that came through about forty years ago and did some real damage, but that was before construction finished. In the thirty years I'd been here, there had never been a major catastrophe as a result of the weather or the ocean. There had been some man-made disasters, and not all accidents; there are some unscrupulous people with power who don't like scientists running around unchecked. Despite them, Gideon is still around.

"Then don't come," I offered as sage advice after realizing I hadn't said anything. I probably shouldn't say anything, but some habits die hard. He was still there, moving slower and gripping the railing. I didn't change my pace; maybe I could leave him behind.

Normally, the long walk back to the Inner Ring would have allowed me to calm down and start to think again. With Basil tagging along, it didn't do much. He kept trying to talk to me, somehow keeping up despite his nervousness. I tuned him out, trying to think—specifically, about why Mal was so upset. I thought back to my humanity, but the old emotions aren't there anymore. I had been fundamentally changed by my turning. I could conceptualize the fact that it bothered Mal to find the woman, because it made him consider losing Sarah. He was able to empathize with someone he didn't know, and I couldn't. It was

27

part of the problem with human-vampire relationships.

It had hurt when Mal called me a monster. I was a monster, but Mal had never treated me like one before. He'd been the first person I'd called friend since dying and I'd gotten used to that. For him to see me as something else made me sad and angry, like I'd lost something I didn't know was there. It had been a long time since someone was in a position to hurt me like that. Not since my sires had been burned in New Orleans had I allowed someone so close.

The problem was that I liked him, and I liked him enough that I didn't want him mad at me. I had been honest about the woman and what she meant to me: nothing. Grunting, I decided I'd just apologize next time I saw Malcolm. Not about the woman; I'd upset him, and that's what the apology would be for. He was my friend, and if that helped him feel better, I could do that.

The steel bridge, encrusted with salt and rust, melded into concrete walkways as I reached the ring. Behind me, Basil was still talking, his voice becoming much more even now that we were back on "dry land." I turned to him, causing his words to trail off suddenly. "Basil, I don't care. In fact, I don't care enough that I have no idea what you've said for the last twenty minutes. I haven't paid attention." His smile didn't fade but it became hard and brittle; I'd angered him.

"Someday, you will care, Misty," he told me, and I felt a shiver of unease. There was something true and sincere in his words, as if he would make sure that I would care. "Here," he said, handing me a small wand. "Take it." Unnerved, I did. The moment it was in my hand, I knew what it was: a phone jacker. If you plugged it into your phone, it would do all sorts of neat things, like auto-dial a number, scramble calls or even fry your SIM card. "If you need me, just use this. Good morning, Misty." He nodded and turned, walking off.

I watched him leave, puzzled. I wasn't sure what to make of his statement, but I realized that I couldn't delay much longer. Dawn was on its way, and I needed to go shopping. A glance at the watch told me I had less time then I had thought, and I broke into a run.

The Inner Ring is mostly mixed residential and commercial; stores were usually on the first few floors with the levels above that being living spaces. In this section, the sidewalks were filled with people just starting their day. Most of the store fronts were still dark; they'd open in the mid-morning. A few restaurants were open, serving breakfast and coffee to sleepy humans. Green areas bordered the buildings, offering flowers and decorative plants for the eyes, though the pre-dawn gloom hid most of their glory. My feet thudded repetitively on pale, almost white, concrete, a shell covering the ferroconcrete. Everything here was kept clean and bright with great effort, alive and thriving to keep the humans living here happy.

But when I crossed over onto the next tile, the change was distinct. It was another world on the other side of that thick line of black padding between the tiles. This tile was for the dead.

Gideon tried to keep humans from forming culturally or racially segregated communities, but they didn't try so hard with us. The Bunkers, the less-than-fond name many had for the style of building designed for us, offered apartments to the humans, too. But the Bunkers were concrete boxes—no windows or exterior designs, and most humans found them too depressing. Some gardens might have helped, but we didn't merit that kind of decoration. Trash was more prevalent, as well as a fine layer of gritty sea salt that bleached the color out of everything. It was unavoidable in Gideon, but the street crews took more effort to keep other tiles clean.

The stores here were fewer but they catered to us: blood shops were the most common. It was one of these stores I hurried toward now, Brad's Blood Bank, or just Brad's to the regulars. Brad was a certified blood dealer, and while he wasn't the closest one to my house, I trusted him. He'd never watered down his stock with animal blood, which we don't synthesize very well, and I'd never caught him trying to cheat me out of blood credits.

He was about to lock his door when I planted my palm on the glass and shoved it open. "You're cutting it close, Misty," Brad remarked, but he stepped back and let me in. Like anyone in the blood business, he was good at not arguing when a vampire showed up in a hurry looking for food.

The shop was small, just a counter and a fridge, and room for a couple of people to stand in front. A secured steel door behind the counter guarded a massive walk-in cooler, filled with blood. The fridge only held a few bags of each blood type, a blood store's equivalent to convenience store signs declaring, "The cashier only has $100 in his drawer."

The black market for blood, called the Crimson Market by those who thought they were clever, was populated by vampires who didn't play by Gideon's rules. There were a few individuals who didn't like to be on the books, and they needed to eat, too. Collecting illegal blood sometimes meant stealing it and sometimes meant someone died. Because of the danger of someone stealing legally-distributed blood, none of the blood stores could keep access to the blood open constantly, as a deterrent against theft. Instead, the coolers were only opened when a city Blood Administration Representative was there with a heavily guarded delivery.

Brad circled around the counter while I hunted in my bag for my ration card; he was already digging my preferred type from the fridge before I had it out. "How many?" he inquired, as he punched some numbers into his computer and started the purchase.

"Just one." I handed him the card as he shook his head and dropped the bag of cold blood on the polished steel counter.

"If you bought more than a day ahead," he advised as he swiped my card, "then you wouldn't have to stop here every day."

"I like it fresh," I muttered, even knowing he was right. I peered at the draw date. "Is this the freshest you have in O-negative?" Meanwhile, the view screen flashed a confirmation, verifying that I had enough credits to last the rest of the month. Nodding to myself, I entered my pin number and glanced at the clock, waiting for the transaction to be completed. Brad was right; I *had* cut it close, and it only took one worried look over my shoulder at the slowly brightening sky to confirm that. I should have taken the trolley over; the investigation and my angry shower had taken more time than I had thought.

"Yes, it is the freshest I have," Brad said shortly. He logged the receipt into my account without asking for the numbers, a true sign that I was a regular customer. "Get out of here. Go home."

"Night!" I called as I grabbed tomorrow's dinner and hustled

30

out the door, stuffing the bag into the backpack I preferred over a purse.

"You mean, morning, Misty!" he shouted after me. I barely heard him over the door closing and the pounding of my own feet as I dashed for home, but his words were further fuel for me.

A few people I passed stared at the young, dark-skinned woman running flat out in boots, but the smarter ones knew what was going on, and they got out of my way. I was almost to my block when the wind shifted, bringing the aroma of fresh blood.

That stopped me in my tracks as my nostrils flared to catch more of the scent. I'd heard scientists compare a vampire's ability to smell blood to the shark's same ability. Unlike a shark, we need more than a drop; it has to be a significant amount, more than a cup, and relatively fresh. We have similar ranges though; I can recognize blood in the air miles from the source.

This blood was so fresh I could almost sense the heat and wet that went with it. I knew I should ignore it. But I didn't want to. I wanted to follow the blood to the source and drink it down.

A vampire enjoys feeding. A lot of people will tell you it's a sex thing. They're either blood-sticks—people who willingly donate to vampires—or vampires using a line to get a meal. Some people get off on being bitten and fed from; I try not to judge. Some vampires find feeding a suitable replacement for the intimacy of sex. For me, it's not a sex thing, it's an all-thing. Blood is everything; it's the first day of spring, the first bite of a good meal—anything that revitalizes and refreshes you feels like blood.

It's illegal for a vampire to drink from a human donor, even indirectly. Gideon saw a lot of over-feedings in the first few years after they opened their borders to vampires, so they initiated a system where donors were paid to donate blood for vampires, and vampires worked for wages and a blood allowance. The system was boring for the vampires, but it stopped the accidental over-feeding. The punishment was deportation to your country of origin, straight into the hands of whatever authority had been charged to deal with the "vampire problem." America still hunted vampires. That was ordinarily incentive enough to keep me out of trouble.

I knew that I should go home. But my feet turned toward

the source and my legs moved faster. I followed it relentlessly; by the strength of the smell, it was nearby. Hunger for hot, fresh food propelled me forward; the instinctive need to get there before other vampires drove me faster. My frenzied brain remembered the rising sun, but only to decide that it meant other vampires were less likely to find the food.

Stepping into an alley, I spotted a ribbon of blood on the pale concrete wall of a Bunker, the ruby liquid dripping down the wall. I looked up, and saw a ledge thirty feet above me. Mouth watering, I scanned the side of the building, but it was a Bunker, and I didn't see a good way up. Buildings that house vampires don't have exterior fire escapes or windows, though most of the buildings do have faux windows, and empty ledges sticking out in a pointless imitation of human housing.

Leaping as high as I could, I grasped one of the fake window sills. My fingers found a purchase that a human's couldn't, forcing a grip through stubbornness and strength. I pushed myself up with my feet, scrabbling up the side of the building. I couldn't really find permanent traction, but the cumulative efforts created forward progress. I managed to get a foot up on the ledge with one hand locked around the fake window frame, and I kicked upward again, catching the next sill. I was rewarded with a gust of wind, bringing another mouth-watering scent.

I pulled and pushed harder, doing feats a human would have been hard pressed to repeat. When I reached the blood trail on the wall, I was compelled to stop, one thought in my head: *blood!* I licked at the dripping fluid with a hungry whimper. The liquid was cold, and I could taste the concrete underneath it, but nothing mattered as I savored fresh blood again. I groaned with pleasure; it had been decades since I'd had it this fresh—it was better than my memories of my mother's gumbo. My instincts coaxed me to forget everything else, save that garnet path glittering inches from my nose. And I answered that call, climbing and licking, feeling the pure *life* in the blood.

My eyes reached the ledge and I saw red-coated fingers just inches from my face. The fingers were dry, but I could smell fresher blood. A tremble shot through my body, and I almost lost my grip on the wall. I had enough self-preservation to finish my climb and pull myself over the edge.

The source of my free drink was an injured man, lying on his stomach and bleeding from numerous cuts. He was Asian, at least in part, with an unruly haircut and a lean frame. Said frame was clearly visible as he didn't have a shirt on; given the profusion of cuts on his body, it may have been shredded. Thick jeans had offered his legs more protection. The only blood on them was what had rolled down his skin from cuts on his torso. Bruises danced over his angular face, which seemed to be set in a permanent frown.

I bent over him and in that moment, I was lost to instinct. His shoulder wound was still seeping blood, and I bent my head down, my lips trembling with desire for that crimson stream. Perhaps I brushed his skin; perhaps I exhaled a sigh of mad desire, sending a gust of cool air over his body. His visible eye fluttered open, dark and compelling.

"Help me," he whispered, his voice tense and shaky. "Please, help me."

CHAPTER 4

I was trapped by the gaze in that single visible eye. I could still smell him, but he didn't smell like food anymore. My lust for blood sang to me, but I didn't want his. I battled brief shame that I had thought about it.

God, what was wrong with me? I pressed a shaking hand to my face, trying to gather my swirling thoughts. What had happened to me, to drive me with this madness? I had once held a coworker's leg still with my superior strength, while he had thrashed and bled and screamed. I'd had the scent of fresh blood and the feel of fighting prey under my hands, and I had held steady, applying the pressure that had kept his blood and his life inside his body. So why had I nearly lost it now? Something was wrong, but I didn't have time to figure it out.

"Please..." he whispered, planting a palm on the pavement and trying to move. "They...they took my baby."

"Your baby?" I repeated like a fool before gathering my wits with a shake of my head. I dug in my pockets and found my personal computer. I found it annoyingly small, since I remembered when a personal computer was something that sat on your desk rather than in your hand. You couldn't make phone calls with it either—the march of progress. I unlocked the machine to open the phone line and found my attempt blocked by an automated warning: *Imminent Sunrise.* "Look, I can't wait with you, but let me call an ambulance—"

"No!" His hand snapped around my wrist with shocking speed and strength, enough that I took another sniff to make sure he was mortal. He bled like one, so adrenaline must have been lending him this power. "No hospitals!"

I pulled against his grip, testing, and found it unyielding.

"You're gravely injured, and I don't have time to argue—"

"Then don't," he snapped, tugging my arm closer to him. "Just take me somewhere safe."

I should have left him, dumped him there and abandoned him and his demands. But I felt bad about the strange blood lust; I'd almost eaten him and that wasn't something I could just brush aside. "Fine," I grunted, tossing my computer to my other hand and shoving it into my pocket. With my inhuman strength, I grabbed him and hauled him to his feet. "But if you die on me, I'm gonna sell your cadaver for science." I glanced down his body; none of his many cuts seemed deep or deadly, just numerous.

He was swaying, but he was on his feet. I felt his hands grab me, finding places to hold himself upright on my shoulder and hip. He was only as tall as me, and his dark eyes seemed all the more intense when viewed on the same level. "I'm not gonna die," he promised, and I believed him, just a little. "I have too much to do."

"Sure," I agreed, my tone the same used to briskly placate idiots. I grabbed one of his wrists, noting that he had a wiry, deceptive build. I could feel the long, lean cords of muscles in him as I doubled over, pressed my shoulder to his stomach and grabbed him behind his knee.

"What are you doing?" he gasped, sounding nervous.

I grinned with no small bit of spite despite the fact he couldn't see the expression. "Helping you," I explained just before I straightened and yanked him into place on my shoulder. He groaned and hissed painfully on the inhale, but he didn't argue. "Hang on," I said, glancing upward nervously. The sky was a shade I hadn't seen in years, and I could see the east-facing corner of a building blossom with golden light. I was fine, so long as I didn't get caught in that light.

I leapt off the edge of the building, taking the landing full-force with my legs, absorbing as much of the impact as I could with my knees. It wasn't enough; the guy gasped and went limp over my shoulders. He had passed out; probably just as well as this wouldn't be fun. I fared better; the shock of hitting the concrete from a thirty foot drop thudded dully in my legs, but there was almost no pain. That was good, because I had a long jog left if I was going to beat the sun. The guy's extra weight was no burden for me as I started to run. My only problem was keeping him in place and trying not to bounce him too much.

Gideon is a largely vertical town; the buildings that lined the streets shaded me from the early rays of the sun. But that couldn't last forever; some of the streets ran straight east-west, without anything to provide shelter. And Astbury was one such street. It had once had a row of lovely dogwoods which would have made it safer to cross, but they'd recently caught a disease and had died before the infection could be treated. Now, I faced an empty street already drenched in deadly, golden light.

With a soft groan, I huddled in the shadow of a building and considered my options. The problem was that I didn't have a lot of time to think. Every minute spent contemplating the sun was another minute that I risked being caught out here. One of my sires had always told me to get the bad stuff over quickly. The annoying thing was I could call for a rescue. Gideon's Vampire Management Agency had a crew who would come out with a light-tight box to pick up stranded vampires, but that wasn't an option with my tagalong. Grumbling, I shifted my companion. It was awkward, but I managed to get him onto my other shoulder. In his new position, he was protecting my head and much of my front and back. It was the best I could do right now. Drawing a deep and unneeded breath, I started to run.

The sun hammered my unprotected skin the second I crossed into the light; an itching tingle was my first warning, followed by a spreading numbness. I ground my teeth against the sensation, glad I was wearing pants so that my legs were protected. If my legs failed at this moment it would be disastrous.

It was a short run that seemed to take forever. But all things end and I was back in the shade, safe enough for now. I didn't stop to check the extent of the sun damage; I needed shelter. Besides, I knew exactly what I would see—a mass of melted skin, running and dripping down my arm and side. I could feel the liquefied flesh soaking through my clothes. If I got them washed soon, I could save them from staining.

The rest of the trip was accomplished without major incident. The last obstacle to safety was my own security door, and that was only because I had to unlock the door, open it, and get my passenger inside without dropping him or smacking him into something. I was mostly successful; he did slide off my shoulder, and I had to bump him back into place while my foot held the door open.

"I see someone had a fun night." The voice came from the shadowy manager's office, and I knew without looking that it was Drake, the super of the building.

Drake had the honor—assuming one wished to call it that— of being the only known dwarf vampire. He was properly pro- portioned, which was good for him, but he still came in at four feet. For all that, he was handsome, in his own way; thick, pale brown hair brushed his collar in back and hung past his ears in front. His skin was tinted enough to hint at a mixed heritage, a clue corroborated by eyes dark brown enough to match darker hair than he had. He was often smiling, usually a sardonic grin that suggested he knew the joke and you didn't. His mouth was small and his lips thin yet soft-looking, with a nose that fit his face. His biggest flaw was his forehead; it was too tall for the haircut he favored and overwhelmed the rest of his features. Still, it couldn't completely kill his attractiveness; his height did that all on its own. I think his creators must have had a really sick sense of humor, or maybe he was part of a circus. I don't know, and I've never asked. It doesn't seem like the type of thing that he'd like to talk about, really. Plus, he'd been my mentor when I got here thirty years ago, teaching me the realities of life in the open, living in harmony with the humans. Poking into his past seemed a poor way to thank him for taking me under his wing.

"Not nearly as exciting as it seems," I grunted, turning to look at him. The guy still hung limp over me, and Drake stepped forward, peering at him.

"Didn't know you liked Asian food, Misty. Though...hmm, he smells good," Drake said, smiling. There was a dark look in his eye, and it reminded me of my own bloodlust earlier today. "Got enough for two?"

I took a quick step back. Drake stopped smiling.

"He's not food. That's illegal. And I need to get to my room. Now." I kept my voice low and firm. Silently, I wondered about Drake's reaction; he rarely was this serious about anything, least of all what appeared to be a vampire with her illicit dinner.

Drake's small dark eyes watched me, his hand rising to

stroke his chin. It felt like he was sizing me up, and the hair on my neck started to crawl. I wasn't old enough to take him on in any capacity. My superior height would mean nothing when he was easily at least eight times stronger than me. I was starting to squirm and wonder whether I'd need to fight him when he spoke. "Yeah. Yeah, you take him up to your room." He took a step away from us. "And get him out of here as soon as you can, Misty. Before dark would be best."

My eyes narrowed. "Why?"

"Just...do it," was his cryptic reply, and I didn't have the desire to argue. Instead, I hurried to the stairs and ran up them two at a time.

Safe in my room at last, I leaned against the wall and shifted my load into my arms. It gave me more control over him when I put him in my bed. Or, if you wanted to get literal, on my futon. There wasn't much room in my apartment, so a couple of things had to serve double duty, like the television stand also serving as a bookcase. My limited belongings, all of them things that I had picked up here in Gideon, were scattered around the room. I had a bathroom, but aside from that, it was just the single room. I didn't need a kitchen; a mini-fridge was all I was allotted by Gideon. And while it was all I *needed,* it sometimes ate at me that it was all that I got, compared to the humans.

My guest was still bleeding a little, and there was a corresponding stain on the shoulder of my shirt. Thankfully, this wasn't a favorite top. But I needed to get his wounds sealed or I was going to have to worry about another body soon.

I kept a first-aid kit in my room; while it might seem weird for a vampire, we do like to repair injuries just like everyone else. The difference between humans and vampires is that the wounds or infection can't kill us.

I spent twenty minutes spraying aerosol antiseptic into his cuts and gluing them shut. I'd never used the antiseptic, so I applied it liberally, unsure if I was doing it right. Most of the wounds weren't bad; none were particularly deep, save a blade wound that had gone through the muscles on his left arm. I was worried about that one, honestly. Thoughts of calling Emergency Services crossed my mind, but it was a bit late. I was in too deep to extract myself easily. Plus, he didn't want me to call anyone.

The second I realized that, I stopped, wondering why I *cared*. I meet a stranger and nearly sink into blood lust; then I risk becoming an accessory to whatever he's involved in, which is probably illegal, given the bleeding. You don't get messed up like that over a mugging. Which reminded me I needed to do a bit of mugging of my own. I had already rolled him around to get to his wounds; now I eased him to one side to look for a wallet in his pants. I didn't find one in the back pocket, but a cargo pocket on the side of the right leg had a familiar bulge, and I dug a leather wallet out along with a phone.

His phone's ID file said his name was Li Chin, which could easily be an alias. I had no way to know, though my gut reaction to his name was telling.

It is a rule of the universe that when you have something in front of you that invades someone's privacy, and they are unable to stop you, you'll gleefully and guiltily invade that privacy. Vampires, or at least this vampire, are not immune to this syndrome. So I dug into the wallet with a nagging conscience, looking for more clues.

"Hmm," I muttered, going through the information, piece by piece. "You live in ChinaTile, which is very stereotypical of you, Li. 'Course, I live in the FangTile, so I guess I have no room to talk. And you're a service industry food specialist, which means you flip burgers at one of the Gideon cafeterias, for sure. And... you're broke. I'm guessing cooks don't make much cash, right?"

My shirt dragged drily across my skin as I moved, making me grimace. Melted skin feels gross; it's the result of the sun breaking down the chemical bonds in our flesh, so I'm not surprised that it feels disgusting. I'd forgotten about my wounds in my haste to care for Li. Placing his wallet next to the phone on my coffee table, I moved to the bathroom to see the damage.

The mirror showed me the same face it always does. One boyfriend had called it heart-shaped, though I didn't see that. I saw round cheeks and a small chin, with a nose that ruined my more delicate features by being too wide. My hair was dark, almost black. It curled tightly, making it an unmanageable mess without effort and product. Most of the time, like tonight, I didn't bother trying, so it hung in tight curls, already dried after my post-work shower. My skin was tinged with color, a mixture from my lighter and darker ancestors, recalling the hot, sensual nights of New Orleans. My eyes were grey, and were my best feature; they contrasted strongly with my dark complexion.

My hair was now dry and brittle where the sun had caught it. Some of the strands had already snapped off; I could feel where the sun had touched them and where it hadn't just by its changed texture. They'd replace themselves over time, but it was still annoying. My face was untouched, which was a relief; it would have been the hardest to hide. I peeled my shirt off, studying the blood and skin stains. "That's a lost cause," I mumbled to myself and shoved it into my trashcan. The bra had been black, and would be fine; it only had some blood stains, which couldn't be seen. My jeans had some skin stains at the waist, and I hurriedly ran cold water and began to soak the waistband in the sink. Same with the underwear; it wasn't as bad as the jeans, but they still needed attention.

With my clothes taken care of, I turned to my arm. Molten epidermis ran in dribbles down my skin; some had already hardened, and I had to scrape the globs away. Some of the burned skin was partially melted but still in place on my arm; with a grimace, I took my fingernails to it and pulled off anything that wasn't bound to muscle. The muscle itself also had some damage, which was more concerning than the skin. I needed that stuff to move; losing mobility was a concern. "What a pain," I growled to myself, clawing the loose, half-melted muscle away. When it was partly liquefied like this, it didn't heal as well as when straight out replacing the lost tissue. I don't know why, but that's the way it works.

When I was done, I had a long, wide swatch of exposed muscle in the top of my arm and the back of my hand. The underside, the part that had been pressed against Li, was fine, as was my upper arm because the shirt had covered it. Sighing from the aggravation, I started to wind gauze around my arm.

"You went through my wallet." Li's voice came from behind me; I jumped and spun before he'd finished speaking. He slumped against the door, looking awful; he was pale, and he had blue streaks from the wound adhesive covering large areas of his torso. His lack of vigor didn't extend to facial expressions; his eyes widened as his eyebrows rose. "You're hurt. And, just as a point of interest, naked."

"That's because I was bandaging my arm and you woke up too early," I snorted, turning back to my task. "There was no intention to be naked when you woke up."

"Here," he said, stepping forward and taking my arm. Pain throbbed dully as he touched exposed muscle; wincing, he drew back and looked nauseated. That passed as he set his jaw and said, "Tell me what to do."

"I can get it," I said, winding another circuit of gauze around my arm.

"I can get it better, since I can use both hands," he insisted, taking it from me. "Do I just wind it?"

"Yeah. Don't worry about it being sanitary. I just want it covered because it's gross and squicks people out."

"'Squicks' them, huh?" A hint of a smile curved his mouth for a second before it snapped away. It was a small smile, and unable to stand against the pain I saw in Li's eyes. A frown took its place as Li started to wind the bandage around my arm. "What's your name?"

"Misty Sauval."

"Thanks, Misty Sauval. I owe you big time," he said softly, his focus on the bandages. "I'm Li."

"I know. Wallet, remember?"

He made a face at me but didn't answer. "Is this going to heal?"

"Yeah," I answered, wishing that I had Malcolm's gift for making other people laugh. It might have helped him to be able to smile about something for a moment.

"I thought you guys burned," Li said absently, his gaze intensely focused on my arm and the bandages he was manipulating.

I sighed and considered whether to be helpful or obfuscate the truth, then decided it didn't matter. The scientists of Gideon regularly released their research on vampires to the public; it would be a simple matter for him to learn anyway. "Our bones burn."

"And your skin...melts?" His dark eyes met my gray ones for a moment before flicking back to my arm.

"It liquefies," I corrected, "though it's flammable. So when the skin melts off the bones completely, they ignite, which sets off the liquefied skin." Li had stopped his work and was staring at me with a mixture of morbid fascination and disgust. Hiding my irritation at yet another human finding reason to think I'm gross, I added, "Hey, humans don't make pretty corpses, either. The bowels loosen." Death is never pretty.

That drew an uneasy chuckle out of him, and I upgraded my opinion of his appearance. He's the kind of guy who looks best when the full force of his personality is allowed to shine through. "Well, I think," he said, his tone turning business-like, "that if you can hold this, I can tape you up."

I used my fingers to hold the tail of the gauze in place while he tore off pieces of tape to hold it down. "Thanks," I said, moving the arm and finding that the white pseudo-cloth didn't hinder my movements.

"Sure," he said, stepping back into the living room and turning his eyes away. "In return, could you put on some clothes?"

"Right. I think I can manage that." I watched his embarrassment for a moment before stating, "This doesn't bother us."

"So I've heard," Li said, his eyes firmly fixed on my blank television. "But it does bother us, and specifically me, as I have a woman."

"Huh, 'woman,'" I rejoined, sliding the door shut enough that he couldn't see me but we could still talk, "that's a little misogynistic of you, isn't it?"

There was a moment of silence; I could almost feel his flinch. "Sorry...I hang with people like that a lot, and I've picked up the slang. I love my fiancée."

"I think she'll love you more if you lose the gross slang," I told him, slipping on a shirt. "How do you feel?"

"Weak," he admitted. It sounded as if the word had crawled its way up from deep inside of him, as if it hurt to confess weakness.

Aren't you a macho-macho-man? I mused to myself as I finished pulling on my clothes.

"You have some odd posters," I heard him say as I attacked my curls in a final, futile attempt to make them obey. Giving up, I added a moisturizer to help my sunburned hair.

"What?" The walls of my apartment have several framed

posters from my era, the '80s. I'd been a teenager for most of that decade and it was fixed in my psyche; even death hadn't changed that. I'd had more before Hunters had burned down my home in New Orleans. "Oh, those. Those are vintage posters, from around the time I became a vampire."

"Oh, yeah...some of these...are old," I heard him reply softly.

I shrugged and said, "So am I." The moisturizer was in, but I didn't think it was going to help my hair. Scowling, I pulled it up into a hair clip and fluffed it a bit; if you're going to have a riot of curls, you might as well go for broke. I grabbed my belt, a wide, white one that barely fit through the loops on my jeans. It was also a reproduction of a vintage style, making me feel a little older still. I was fastening my belt as I slid the pocket door open with a foot. "Say, do I need to try to find you—" My words cut themselves short as I saw he was slumped back on my couch. "Li? Hey, Li?"

There was no answer and I knelt next to him on the couch, feeling for a pulse. It was barely there, thumping against my fingers way too softly. "I'm a moron," I huffed to myself. Why had I thought I could care for a wounded man?

I reached for my phone, already aware that I was in deep trouble for not calling in the first place. "Idiot, idiot," I muttered as I started to dial. I had no idea who or what he was, or why he'd been up there, bleeding.

The picture cupped in his limp hand caught my attention before I'd completed kicking myself or dialing the number. It was him with a woman and a baby in what appeared to be a post-birth pride shot; the adults were smiling, while the infant was greasy looking and red-faced. But despite the weariness on the woman's face, I recognized her. Li was suddenly single; his fiancée had been the one at the bottom of the nets.

CHAPTER 5

I pounded on Drake's door as I crouched, putting my face low enough to be seen through the modified peep hole. I had an inkling of what was wrong with Li, but I needed some equipment. Drake would have it; I'd never known him not to have something.

His door opened, and Drake was already talking. "I suppose you want to know what's up with your unconscious guest." Behind him, the shelves and boxes and cabinets of stuff he hoarded stretched throughout his apartment. He had about the same space I did, but eight times the stuff. I seriously hoped that if he ever moved he wouldn't ask me to help. My help would be an offer to throw in gas and a match and burn it down.

"Actually," I said, stepping past him into the packed hallway, "I need an IV needle and line."

"Ah ha," he said, moving deeper into his organized mess. "He's missing a bit too much blood, yes?"

"Yeah, how'd..." I shook my head. "Not that hard to figure out, huh?"

"It's a reasonable guess, Misty," Drake grunted, grinning as he pulled a rolling ladder to a shelf and began to climb. I didn't offer to help; that was tantamount to slapping him across the face. I'd offered that exactly once and ended up with a pissed mentor. "Boy's unconscious and bleeding; you come looking for the stuff that'd put blood in him. It's not a hard leap of logic."

"Sure, when you put it that way," I answered easily, leaning against a cabinet. "But what did you think I was coming here for?"

Drake paused and looked back at me. A slow smile spread across his features. "No."

"What? No, what?" I recalled what I was here for, and shook

my head. "Never mind. Look, I need that line, stat. People can die quickly of too much blood loss."

He nodded and moved faster, digging into a plastic storage container for a moment before pulling out a sealed packet with a plastic hose and needle and tossing it at me. "I'll be looking for another favor from you for this," he said as I caught the package and nodded. It was par for the course. But the next statement surprised me. "But when you figure out what I thought you were asking about, come see me."

"Yeah, when I'm not worried about bodies on my couch," I muttered, shaking my head. It seemed a paltry thing to worry about, whatever Drake was ruminating over, though I was sure it could come back to bite me. Drake was the oldest vampire I knew still existing; he was on the cusp of becoming an elder. Had Gideon's scientists not exposed vampires to the world, in a hundred years, Drake would be old enough to carve out his own fiefdom, to amass a mob of unwitting human allies and even create a family. Whether that would happen now was anyone's guess. This would have been his grooming time, when he would be amassing power. He'd started, in his own way, with his hoarding. It wasn't just supplies; he was also hoarding information. And that meant that he was beginning to play the higher games, a diversion of puzzles and enigmas and power.

"Go save your pet, Misty, while you can," Drake said. I would have argued with him, but that would have taken minutes I wasn't comfortable spending. I made a note to ask him later, but for now, he was right; I didn't have the time.

The elevator didn't work and hadn't for a while. The Housing Authority used to stay on the landlord to keep it working, but it was one more thing allowed to fall by the wayside over time. The landlord, Crofton Housing, didn't see why vampires needed working lifts; it wasn't like we could hurt ourselves climbing. The fact that they were right didn't help our feeling that yet again we were treated differently than the humans. It wasn't so bad for me. My concrete box was only on the third floor, and I'd long since mastered the best way to bound up the steps without missing a beat. All that practice served me in good stead as I dashed upward for the second time this morning.

The hallways were starting to fill up with vampires; we

didn't have to sleep during the day and many of us took the opportunity to get other things done. This was often the time that illicit deals were made. Lots of us were law-abiding citizens who worked and paid taxes by night, only to turn to the underworld for additional comforts during the day. There were known suppliers of weapons, drugs, and even willing bloodsticks; fixers rubbed elbows with forgers and con-artists in the hallways of our buildings.

I nodded to those I knew as I hurried past them. I wasn't worried about them mentioning me acting suspicious later; they would mind their own business, just as I turned a blind eye to anything I may have seen while in the hall. Plus, I was too worried about Li to fuss about what my neighbors were doing. I already owed Drake for the equipment; I didn't want to owe him for help removing a body. And there were other concerns, smaller concerns: there was a tiny infant who needed at least one parent alive. Though I still wasn't sure why I cared.

Li's eyelids were fluttering as I entered my apartment. "Oh, good," I muttered, breaking open the package. "You're a lucky man, Li, that I like O-Negative. Otherwise, I could be killing you right now." It only took me a few seconds to connect the blood bag with the IV line; getting a good vein was harder, especially given that Li was twitching.

"Suran," he murmured, and the muscles under my probing fingers jumped as he tensed suddenly. I growled to myself. This was hard enough without him flinching and jerking. Fortunately, the paranoia regarding over-feedings had made blood infusion a mandatory part of Gideon's first aid training, which I'd been required to take for my job. It probably was going to save Li's life, assuming I could get him to hold still. But he quieted after a moment and I didn't hesitate. I couldn't, not if I wanted to save him. My hands were steady, lacking the tremors of human flesh. I slid the needle in and Li moaned, "No." But he didn't fight; maybe he sensed I was helping him.

"I think I have a vein, otherwise, I apologize in advance for the bruise you're about to suffer," I grumbled as I released the tap, letting the red fluid flow. With my breakfast dribbling into his veins, I settled back on the couch and ignored my hollow middle. I could skip a meal or two. I'd done so for six years as a lonely hunter before the stability of Gideon's work programs. I'd survive; I just wouldn't enjoy life very much until I got another meal.

There was plenty of illegal blood to be had, if I wanted to deal with someone in the hall. But I avoided them; some blood-dealers watered down their stock with animal blood. They didn't have to meet regulations and it was very illegal, which made it hard to report them if you did get cheated. My grumbling stomach was hard to ignore, but vivid memories of the last purge of ingested animal blood stopped me. Plus, a fast would reduce the amount of fluid in my body and take a couple of inches off my waistline, which is a good thing for a girl. Or so I told myself as I waited for Li to finish my food.

Eventually, I got bored and turned on the television, sliding a folding chair next to the couch, near Li's reclined body. I had been drawn into the show that was on before a slow groan pulled my attention back to my guest. Li's eyes were fluttering; he licked his lips and grimaced as he lifted his head. "Can I have some water?"

"Sure," I said, hopping up and getting one of my bowls. I didn't have glasses, but I did have a set of bowls that I'd been given by Sarah as a well-intentioned house-warming gift. I filled one with water and carried it back to Li, who took it from me and drained it. He seemed stronger, more stable. "Feel better?"

"Ow," he said, glancing down at the IV still draining into his arm. The bag was almost empty, so he could come off it soon. "I remember sitting down. What happened?"

"If you'd let me take you to a hospital, a doctor would be able to tell you. But since you didn't, all I can do is guess that you passed out," I said wryly, hoping my irritation at the position he had me in was coming through clearly. Again, the thought passed through my mind to just call the police and be done with it, but again it was squelched. This time, I had the leisure to wonder why.

The answer was very simple. I didn't know. I just wanted to help him.

"Thanks," Li was saying, his dark eyes meeting mine. Gratitude filled his quiet voice with warmth. "I owe you, a lot."

"You can start repayment by telling me what's going on," I

replied, sitting down and leaning back in my chair until it rested against the arm of the couch.

"You don't want to be involved in this," he said, and all the warmth was gone.

"Newsflash, Li, if that's really your name. I'm already involved. I was involved the second I pulled you off the ledge instead of calling the police. I've put my neck—a neck that I've carefully protected for many years, mind you—on the line, and I think that I deserve to know what's going on."

Li sighed and looked away from me, his face thoughtful. "I know," he murmured after a moment, swinging his shaggy head back to look at me. "I just think that I need to keep you out of it as much as I can."

"That's a fine sentiment, but we're a little past keeping me uninvolved."

His dark eyes—I still couldn't decide if they were true black or brown—narrowed as he studied me. "Why do you say that with such certainty? So far, all you've done is aid me. That's hardly a deep level of involvement. I could walk out of here right now and never bother you again."

I didn't like that idea and quickly changed the subject. "Tell me something. How'd you get on that ledge?"

"I jumped," he said with a small grin.

"From the ground?"

"From a moving aero."

My eyes widened. The personal aircraft replaced the car in Gideon, though not everyone could afford to own or license one. But if he'd really jumped from one, especially a moving one, he was lucky to be alive. "All right. Why?"

"Because the guys inside it were trying to kill me."

"Good reason. So who is the woman in the picture? And who is Suran?"

A slightly goofy smile crossed his face at her name, a sure sign that he was head over heels for her. So I wasn't surprised when he said, "Both questions can be answered with this: she's my fiancée." He held up the picture. "This is her, and this is our baby, Masako."

Oh, boy. How was I going to tell him that Suran was dead? Was it even my place? I wrestled with it for a moment, trying to weigh my own sense of personal obligation with my comfort level about telling a stranger I'd discovered his fiancée's body. This wasn't something I'd ever planned on having to do, and I found myself staring at the floor nervously, trying to think.

I took too long. Li's hand only caught my arm for a second before I jerked it away, but it got me to look up at him anyway. "Say it," he said. "You know something bad. I can see it in your eyes. Just say it."

I thought about prevaricating and avoiding the subject. But there seemed no point to it. He was going to find out, and the only reason I didn't want to tell him was because I didn't want to deal with emotional fallout. I knew there was going to be some; vampires may not get every human reaction, but we do understand loss. It's all we do after we die: lose people and things. "Suran is dead." I met his eyes, unflinching. "They—I found her body in the bottom of a net, one of the ones that's used to protect the hydraulic fans. I don't know how she died. The police didn't tell me."

He stared at me, his face paling visibly. "What?" he finally asked; before I could answer, he jumped to his feet, his fists clenched. I prepared myself for an attack; I was the messenger, and I could become the target of his outrage. I would certainly not be happy about this news, either. Every muscle in his face bunched tightly, until he was nothing but hard planes and sharp angles. I had thought him attractive before, with his strong, sharp features; now he was a beautiful creature of rage. "They're dead," he growled, his clenched fists rising. "The ones who did this... they are *dead!*" The IV must have interfered or pulled his skin, because he reached over and yanked it out violently, throwing blood across the floor and television.

"Hey!" I yelped, grabbing at the valve and cutting the flow of blood off. With just one look he communicated that it was probably best if I addressed this grievance later. Too bad I didn't particularly fear humans; it was a fantastic glare. Unafraid of his dark expression, I took the needle and looped it up so that the remaining fluid in the tube wouldn't drain. Li moved past me, heading for the door. "Hey, where are you going?"

"I have to find Masako. I have to find Suran's body and prepare. I have to kill those who killed her," Li said, his voice deepened by the hate in his voice. He shook his head suddenly. "I have to be sure she was killed, even."

"True, let's not trust the vampire." The words were out of my mouth before I could stop them. "I'm sorry. That was a sucky thing to say."

"I have...I have to be sure." His body was taut with tension. "Thank you, Misty, for patching me up. I'll come back and repay you, somehow."

As he opened my door, I called, "Are you sure you'll come back in one piece?"

"I have to find her, in whatever condition she's in," he said, his back to me.

I could have stopped him from leaving, probably. I didn't, because he was right. He did need to know. "Good luck," I said as the door closed. I hoped he heard me.

CHAPTER 6

I spent the day waiting. I couldn't stop thinking about Li, wondering what he was doing; attempts to distract myself by watching television failed. Even Duran Duran, normally the best way to calm me down, failed to stop my irritating desire to pace. I finally admitted that I wasn't going to stop thinking about it. The time of day meant I couldn't leave, even if I wanted to find and help him. All I could do was plug into the 'net, and see if he landed in the news.

As I surfed in circles, I thought about what to do tonight. It was my night off, a thought that made me guiltily happy, since I wouldn't have to see Mal. I was at loose ends, with nothing planned. My brain immediately suggested I spend the night finding Li. I knew Li's address, and I could probably find him if I put some effort into the task. But should I? I'd put myself on the line already by helping him; I had committed criminal activities at a time when the police were already eyeing me for a murder. I told myself I was done with him, even as I scanned the news for mention about his arrest or death.

Coming on the heels of my decision, the knock on the door seemed to mock me. I turned off the television, and somehow, before I even got up to answer the door, I knew who would be there. Glancing through my peephole, I saw Li. I thought about not answering, but he was slumped on himself, one hand holding a new cut on his other arm. The surge of sympathy ran through me and left me no choice. I opened the door. "You're not getting my next meal."

"Can I come in?" he asked, his voice soft and shaky.

No, was what I wanted to say. "Yeah, come on," I said, stepping back and giving him room. As he passed me, I took a closer look at his arm. "I see you need more glue."

"What? Oh, yeah," he said, angling away from my couch and heading toward the bathroom.

I followed him in to find him sitting on my rarely-used toilet, staring at nothing. I sighed softly, wondering if this was shock or grief I was seeing. I had no way of knowing that without more observation, so I simply pulled my ruined shirt out of the garbage and pressed it to his arm. "Hold this against the cut. I'll get the kit."

I worked in silence, collecting all the tools I needed and setting to work on his arm. This cut was long but shallow, and had already stopped bleeding, which was good. Oddly, I was hungry, but I had no desire to eat him. It was turning into a very weird day.

I was in the middle of gluing the slender cut closed when he spoke. "You were right. I'm sorry I implied otherwise."

"I was right?" I asked, glancing up at him; I was down on one knee next to him, pinching skin with one hand and applying glue with the other. "About...oh, never mind," I finished in a soft voice. "I remember." I was still a bit embarrassed that I'd jumped immediately to the prejudice card.

"I can't find Masako." His voice broke on the final word. I watched helplessly as his face crumbled; he pressed his bloody hand to his eyes, but not fast enough to hide the way they welled with moisture. All too soon, his hand couldn't restrain the falling tears; they poured between his fingers, crept around the edge of his hand and spilled down his face, washing it with the tint of blood.

"Li," I whispered, forgetting about his arm for a moment. I touched his shoulder and he turned toward me, an instinctive response. His face pressed into the curve of my shoulder; with his face hidden, the first sob choked out of him. His arms curled around me and clung.

"They killed my fiancée and took my baby," he wept, the words forced out through a tight throat. Any further words were lost to the sobs that now racked his body.

I was shocked by his proximity; it took me a moment to react, and even then I was hesitant and unsure. I wasn't comfortable dealing with his grief, but with my shirt already wet, so to speak, I was dealing with it whether I liked it or not. I reached past him to cap the glue before curling my arms around his shoulders. It was awkward and not at all easy, but I managed. I even started a vague patting which may have been comforting.

Finally, his tears ran their course, and he pushed away from me. Silently, I finished gluing his wound shut. "Thank you," he said hoarsely, his voice thick with the aftershock of his tears.

"Yeah," I said, putting things away and pushing my hair out of my eyes. I studied him in the mirror; he seemed stronger now, more certain. Expressing his grief had strengthened him, or maybe all it had done was remove the crippling sorrow. "What are you going to do?"

"I have some people to kill," he said, rubbing at his face. "But I can't until I know where Masako is, and can get her back safely."

"Do you have any leads?" I shoved the last of my equipment into the plastic box and deposited the whole deal under my sink. Turning, I rested my hips on the counter and crossed my arms. "Where are you going to start?"

"I asked around. I found out some things about Suran I didn't know." The hands that had been rubbing his face migrated up into his hair, mussing it further. "Ugh," he muttered, looking at his hand; a knot of dried blood and black hair was trapped in the bend of his thumb. "I don't want to impose more, but..."

"Sure," I said, pushing off the counter. "While I'm thinking about it, have you eaten today?"

"I...uh...no," he answered after some thought.

"Okay, then." I moved into the living room and got a towel out of a basket. I tossed it back to him. "Here. Don't worry; it's clean. I hate to fold. You shower. I'll find some clothing and some food for you. I make no promises about the quality of either."

A hint of a smile played over his lips, but it wasn't able to penetrate the exhaustion that marred his features. "Anything you find is great," he told me before sliding the door to the bathroom shut.

I waited until I heard the shower running before mumbling, "You are so stupid, Misty." There was no good reply to that observation, so I snatched up some of my money and headed out into the hall.

The day-vendors were starting to pack it up for the night, but I caught Charlotte at her booth. Char looks like everyone's mom; she doesn't talk about it, but I suspect she had a big brood of children before her death. Given her age, I'm sure they're gone, and I haven't seen or heard anything about grandkids or family. I think that wherever they are, they're not in touch with her. Charlotte's the type of woman who'd hate that. It explains her general mothering to all. You could get some great deals from her if you sang a sob story. It wasn't really cheating her; she sold and traded things because she wanted to talk to people, not because she wanted money.

"Good evening, Misty," she said, pausing her knitting long enough to wave. Her large frame was wedged into a folding chair; she appeared to be at least two hundred pounds overweight, but it was deceptive. She was as fast as any vampire, and tough as nails. She was around a hundred years dead, but she'd only been here for about a year, and she still had that uneasy tension that all of Gideon's new arrivals possessed. "Can I help ya wit' something?"

"Yes, Charlotte, I think you can. I need some clothing for a guy. Smaller and thinner than me. Shirt and jeans, and a belt."

"I think I can do that," she said, standing and walking into her apartment with an easy, circular sway. That's another reason I like her; she makes me feel thin. We retain our body shapes at death, roughly; I had always run a little pudgy, and dying hadn't improved that. We can change our weights by consuming blood or fasting. So if I wanted to be hungry, I could be a size smaller. It wasn't really worth it, though I'd done it for a few months after my death—vanity, thy name is starvation. Alternatively, you could bloat yourself on blood, and go up a size or two. But nothing would ever make Char or me svelte.

She came back with a box, which she set on the table, light brown curls dancing around her face. "We've got the smalla sizes in here—do ya think you'll need a medium?"

I thought about Li's thin frame. "Uh, no. I'm sure not."

Charlotte watched me pick through the clothing; I could feel her scrutiny, like a pressure on the side of my head, but I ignored it. I couldn't ignore her next question. "Is dis for tha' shirtless boy visitin' ya?"

Ah, the rumor mill, fast at work. "Yeah," I admitted, keeping my tone casual. "He had some luggage issues."

Charlotte nodded as if she believed me, but her expression clearly wasn't buying it. "Get yaself out of this, Misty," she said softly. "Dis is trouble. He is trouble. I've heard things."

I glanced at her. "What have you heard?"

"Don't know 'em. Dey be lookin' for 'im."

I wanted to asked for names, but didn't. She probably wouldn't give them to me; if she passed on too much, she risked being cut out of the circle of gossip. A nagging voice in my head said I should listen to her, and I know it was right. But Li had come to me, and I remembered him crying on me: the feel of his grief vibrating through my skin, his choked weeping ringing in my ears. I couldn't walk away, not now. "I'll take this shirt, and these jeans," I replied, holding them up.

Her face flattened into irritated lines. "Girl, you don't listen to a licka sense, do ya?" Shaking her head, she exchanged the money for the clothing and stuffed them into a bag. "I tell you. Trouble. Deys are asking 'bout him, an' now some o' us hunt 'em."

"Do you know who?" I said, my irritation at her nosiness pushing me to ask, finally.

"No, neva' seen 'em before, but they around and they *trouble.*" She practically threw the bag at me, waving me away from her table. "Go on, get. I gotta get ready fo' work." She was starting to pack up, even as I was still standing there. I wanted to know more, but didn't dawdle; the other vendors would be closing, and I still needed some food.

Unlike with Charlotte, my transaction with Numeer went quickly. Numeer owned a convenience "store" of sorts; human foods and necessaries were available. Despite the fact that this was FangTile, there were humans who lived here, and there were humans who were hiding here. So there was a need for human supplies, even in the heart of the dead lands. Numeer's table contained a wide variety of chips and granola, and I grabbed several types of each. He offered me no warnings as he took my money.

I hurried back to my apartment, aware that the sun was getting close to setting and that soon I could join the hunt with Li. As I kicked my door shut, I called out, "Li, I'm back." I kept my eyes general and unfocused, just in case.

"Hey," he said from my couch, and I hazarded a peek. He had the towel around his waist while he rubbed at his hair with a dishtowel. I hoped he'd gotten it from my clean pile.

"Chips and granola," I announced and dropped the bag on the kneeling table I used as both a dining room table and a coffee table. "Clothes," I added and tossed him that bag.

"Thank you, Misty," Li said, peering in the bag of clothes. His hair was still a mess, but it had a clean, artfully mussed look to it, and I suspected that he styled it like that. He still looked tired; there were dark rings under his eyes and his face was slack with exhaustion. Despite looking completely sacked, he looked better than he had a half an hour ago.

Then I realized he was giving me a look, waiting for me to turn around, and I smiled sheepishly. "Sorry," I said, putting my back to him.

I heard him struggle into the clothes, muttering about the fit of them. When he spoke, his voice cut through those sounds and my thoughts like a discharged gun, making me flinch a bit. "I know what I'm going to do."

I frowned, and it could be heard in my voice. "What's that?"

"I found out that Suran owed the New-kuza money." There was a hard note in his voice, a bitter anger that would be there for a long time. I'd be angry too; the New-kuza was the mean little brother of the Yakuza; all of the violence with none of the charm. It's what happened when those who couldn't cut it in the Yakuza got a chance to build a new underworld in a city that had never been touched by the Yakuza, or the Mafia, or anyone. "I didn't know. Had I known, I might have been able to do something. Anyway, someone came to collect. I don't know who, but I'm going to find out."

I heard him ripping into the food. "How are you going to do that?" I asked, turning around enough to see he was dressed.

"Yeah, you can turn around, sorry," he muttered, eating voraciously. As I took my seat, he said, "I don't know." The frustration in his voice was thick enough to choke on, and he spat again, "I just don't know!"

"Well," I replied, thinking, "how did you find out about the money?"

Li crumpled his empty bag and ripped open another. "I have some...friends on the periphery of the New-kuza, someone who owed me a favor he was eager to pay back. But it wasn't enough to get a name of someone to go after."

"Hmm," I hummed, pursing my lips. "I might be able to find more information though my channels. For example, I was just warned to stay away from you because you're trouble."

Li bounced his knuckles on my desk in a nervous, frustrated gesture with one hand, stuffing food into his mouth with the other. "And they're right," he assured me between bites.

"I know," I said, shrugging. "But I'll still help you."

He frowned, looking suspicious. "Why?" His eyes narrowed. "Are you expecting a payment in blood or something?"

"Tempting, but no. Honestly, I want to help you." I didn't really want to explain myself, because I was sure that whatever I said would sound asinine. "And you need it."

"I can't take it if you're going to call in certain favors later."

I realized how seriously he was taking my offer. "I just want to help." And it was the complete truth. I didn't like the thought of him suffering on alone.

Li's dark eyes studied me intently. "All right then," he finally said. No doubt he was realizing that he couldn't do this alone. "So where are you going to find information?"

"We're going to *Veritas*." As he opened his mouth, I said, "I'll explain on the way. The sun should be down, so we need to get going."

CHAPTER 7

I'm no spy or covert agent, trained in the arts of secrecy. I'm something better—a reborn hunter. I was aware that we were being followed within a few blocks of my building. "Ah, crap," I sighed once I'd confirmed it.

"What?" Li's glance was dark and uneasy but he must have had an inkling or urge as well, because he was glancing over his shoulder in the next heartbeat. Or perhaps he was naturally paranoid.

"We're being followed." I started to tell Li not to look, but he didn't.

"Where are they?"

"Behind us. The four Asian guys, in the Harlequin jackets." For reasons I can't understand, bright and clashing colors were all the fashion rage right now—and not just in Gideon. Milan walkways seemed to be hosting clowns these days as designers tried to visually stun the audiences into approval. The people who were wearing the truly outlandish things were probably the rich ones—or ones who had access to resources outside of the norm.

"Plan?" Li asked, drawing his hands out of his pocket and beginning to flex them into fists.

"Confuse and confront."

"I like that last bit," Li said with a vicious grin. "Got any ideas where and how we can do the first part?"

"There's a building being worked on up ahead," I said, starting to angle in that direction. "There's a good spot for an ambush between some of the equipment. If they're after us, they'll take advantage of the isolation and jump us." Li gave me an uneasy glance. "I'm a vampire, dude. This is what we *do.*"

"I thought you worked for Gideon Water and Electric, but hey, learn something new every day."

"I was trained to be a hunter before I was a technician," I answered, feeling the wide grin on my face. It was too true. I may have given up hunting for Gideon's safety, but this encounter was reminding me that deep inside, I was still the hunter. I pulled open a hole in the safety fence, large enough to admit us and be an obvious clue for those following. We quickly surveyed the area, picking our way into the lower levels of the gutted building, where the supplies were housed. The room was dark, out of sight of the main streets and full of crap to use as improvised weaponry. Not that I intended to give them the chance to use it, nor did I believe they'd be unarmed. "Here, right in between these pallets."

Piles of supplies were stacked in rows, reaching ten or more feet in height. I selected a stack of drywall as the place for the ambush. Li may have only been human, but he proved he was a fit human. When I boosted him up, he pulled himself up on top of the pallets. I got up there by jumping and pulling myself up; then we were lying side by side, waiting. I closed my eyes, letting my ears locate them. They weren't bad at their jobs; they were just not as good as a vampire. The four guys eased themselves along, wary since they didn't see us. I could smell them too, even over the dust of the drywall: the warm scent of nervous prey.

When I judged them to be below us, I peeked over the edge. They were just about in the right spot—another three feet would be perfect. I don't know if I made noise, or if one of them got lucky, but as I was peeking, one of them looked up. Our eyes met in the dim light. He shouted a profanity-laced warning, and I burst into action.

I scrambled to the edge and dropped over the side, my arms spread to catch two of them. I only caught one; the other guy was fast on his feet. I wrapped the first guy in a bear hug and kicked at the one who got away. I missed, since he wisely didn't stop moving until he was well away from me. That was the smart one.

So I had one, all was well and good, but there were three more. One of them pulled a gun, then paused as he realized that getting a good angle on me would be hard. The other one, the second-smartest of the bunch, found a length of wood and hammered it over my back.

Fun thing about vampires is that hitting us with blunt objects doesn't do much. We can take someone punching us all day long; we don't even feel pain from it. So I just grinned and, without letting go of my prisoner/human shield, spun into a kick. I dragged him along with me, the guy squealing at the sudden motion. Kicks are usually too slow to work in a fight, but when you're as fast as a vampire, even a young one, you can use them. The club-user caught my foot in the chest and went sprawling with a pained grunt. Gun-boy didn't have a chance to fire before the human shield was back in place. Three quick dragging steps and I was over Club-boy. Without hesitation, I stomped on his chest, feeling and hearing ribs crack. Three on one.

Out of the corner of my eye, I saw Li land on Running-boy, taking advantage of the noise I was making to drop on him from above. I counted that as two on one, because I was sure that the human could keep him occupied. I glanced at Gun-boy. "The odds aren't too good for you. Why are you following us?"

Gun-boy hesitated and I squeezed my captive a bit. "Tell her, tell her!" my prisoner rasped, his head dropping as he hunched in pain.

"We were paid to!" I waited a moment, but that seemed all Gun-boy had to offer.

"By?" I asked leadingly.

"Some guy, said he knew we were looking for work, told us to follow that guy!" He pointed more or less at Li. My human partner was straightening up, dusting off his hands; his opponent lay still at his feet.

"Describe this 'some guy,'" I ordered.

"Asian guy, about my age, taller than me, dressed in a suit. I don't know his name, he gave us a hundred each and told us to call if we found something." He held up a phone. "Gave us this temp phone."

I snorted as Li took it, recognizing the model. They were cheap, one-shot phones. Generally, they only called one number. They were great for situations exactly like this. "Was it worth a hundred?" I asked as Li tucked the phone away.

Gun-boy looked scared and angry. "He didn't tell us there was a vampire involved!"

"He didn't know," I said thoughtfully. "Are you guys done with this job?"

"Yeah!" Gun-boy barked. "We don't deal with vampires!"

"Smart," I observed, releasing my captive. "Now, get out of here."

❉ ❉ ❉

Veritas is a bookstore on the Inner Ring, the kind that carries real books, a rarity on Gideon. With Li in tow, I walked into the store, bypassing the foyer of computer banks offering ebook downloads and the single display offering readers. Inside, the walls were lined with physical books, some new, most old. Most stuff doesn't even get printed anymore and almost no one realizes that *Veritas* actually sells "real" books. Only three types seek the actual books: print-heads, collectors and vampires, especially older ones. Julia was one of the older ones and this was known as the place to find her.

When I'd arrived at Gideon, I wanted word of my sires. I thought they might be dead, but I had to know. I'd been pointed to Julia by several vampires. She was an information broker who retained ties to the world outside of Gideon, as well as within. There were a multitude of rumors running around about her, including that she could leave Gideon because her powerful human allies would protect her when she was outside. She would have information, and she owed me. Or rather, she owed my family and as the sole known member, I could leverage her debt to them on my behalf. When I'd first arrived, I'd tried to use that debt to get information on my sires. She'd come up with nothing new and still owed me. I wasn't sure if I wanted to use my favor on this, but I couldn't think of another way to get the information Li needed.

The foyer of *Veritas* was all sleek brushed steel and neon lights. Inside, it was a different story. The large room was decorated in wood and tile in an elegant style that reminded me of Old World manor houses. The unmistakable scent of books surrounded me: books and vampires. Most of us were technophobes, and the two smells were almost synonymous for me. I could understand the feeling. I'd been born before cell phones, DVDs and portable computers. It had taken me five years to learn to play music on my cell phone, which could do a million other things and was far smaller than anything I'd called a phone while alive. I didn't have the patience to learn about electronic readers, which was somewhat embarrassing in certain social situations. My sires had more to be embarrassed about; they'd struggled with most electronics, both of them being pre-Industrial Revolution.

I steered through the shelves, nodding at the one vampire I recognized browsing near the front. There was a cashier manning the register; the female human looked really bored, twirling her blonde hair around her fingers and appearing near-comatose. Slow night in a normally slow business.

The back corner of the store was blocked by conveniently placed shelves, creating another room without the expense of walls and doors. That was an intentional design, allowing the circle of armchairs to hide in the nook formed by the shelves and walls. I stepped into this nook, then paused as I heard Li behind me. "Wait here," I murmured, pointing toward a shelf outside the alcove. The last thing we needed was for someone to get the urge to bite Li again. I really needed to figure out what that was all about, but later. Rescue the baby first, then learn what was wrong with Li.

I stepped just inside the alcove and softly inhaled. I was searching for the distinctive scent of vampire. I don't know how to describe what a vampire smells like. The way members of your family smell would be the closest; the smell of a rival would also work. We were predators, and we knew each other by scent, just as we knew our prey by scent. If I could smell a vampire, he could never act alive enough to fool me, no matter how many centuries he had to practice the vibrant, near-constant movement of a living body.

I scented everyone in there, picked out who was living and who wasn't, and who had been dead the longest. The longest-dead was the elegant woman in the far corner. She was lovely, slim and carefully dressed in a skirt suit with professional-looking heels. I looked even worse than normal in comparison thanks to my blue jeans and artfully ripped t-shirt, and everyone in the room was dressed similarly to her. I stuck out like a red-headed step-child. The cluster of chairs closest to her were turned toward her, as if they were about to commence with a book club meeting. But no one was talking; they were all reading. The second cluster of chairs fanned out in front of the woman and her attendants, but the occupants had their backs to her: guards, not companions. There was no conversation in this area, and the shelves and books provided a natural sound insulation. It was too quiet after the bustle of the ebooks storefront.

I was being checked out, too; nostrils flared around the room. I stopped and waited. I'd be called on soon, and moving forward before I was supposed to would not earn me any favor for my request. "Misty," Julia called after a moment, when everyone had had a chance to get a sense of me and my age. Her clipped, British voice held a touch of warmth as she spoke to me. "It's good to see you again. Please, sit down." She waved to a chair near herself; the silver-haired vampire next to her vacated his seat without complaint.

I stepped deeper into the alcove and sat down awkwardly, not enjoying the sensation of being an underdressed cub in a den of Armani-clad lions. But I was Julia's guest and probably safe. Probably. "Good evening, Julia," I replied, mindful to be on my best behavior. Though she owed me, I was coming hat in hand.

"How have you been, darling?" she asked, gracefully tucking a curl of brown hair behind an ivory ear.

"I'm doing well, well, mostly well," I answered politely, smiling without showing teeth, just to be safe. "Yourself?"

Her oval, British face slipped into a smile that was just as careful as my own. "I'm very well, dear. Now, with the pleasantries aside, what can I do for you?"

"I need a bit of help," I said, leaning close to her. She leaned over as well, and I murmured, "A woman—a human woman—was killed yesterday, and I'm looking for leads to her killers." Julia looked a little startled; it was an odd request for a vampire. I added casually, "She was dumped in my work area, and the police *may* decide to try to finger me for it. I want to be able to point them at someone else, should they formally charge me." Some of the speculation fled her face at my reasoning. Keeping myself out of prison was a really good reason and not entirely a lie. That Benoit fellow wanted to nail me—and not in the fun way.

"Darling, give me thirty minutes, and let me see if I can help," Julia said, rising and smoothing the wrinkles out of her skirt. That last statement was mostly *pro forma;* Julia could find anything on Gideon. I sat back, secure that I'd soon have Li's answer.

But I was wrong. Julia returned to the alcove after several moments, discreetly slipping a phone into her pocket. Her face was still set in a gracious smile, but I could see an edge to it. My sense of pending accomplishment slipped away as Julia said, "I am sorry, but I have no information for you, Misty. It...*grieves* me to have that answer for you, but that is how it is."

I narrowed my eyes at her. "Why is that?"

Julia met my eyes boldly. I knew that failure was a blow to her pride, but she didn't look away. "Other parties, to whom I owe more, will not release that information to me."

"Great," I said, drumming my nails on the arm of the chair. "So what am I supposed to do now?"

Julia licked her lips nervously. It was one of the few human habits she retained. "I'm very sorry, Misty," she said, and I heard the regret in her voice. "In compensation, I am a little more in debt to you, yes?"

"Forget that," I hissed, leaning as close as I dared. The guard tensed, but Julia remained cool and calm. "Just tell me who has the bigger tab on you."

She locked eyes with me and I wondered if she'd deny me. Suddenly, she put her cold lips to my ear and murmured, "Go talk to Father Vasyl. I can tell you no more than that."

I pulled back and frowned at her. Father Vasyl was well-known to us. He was a major human supplier of blood-bags on legs, and as such, imagined that he enjoyed a kind of vampire who isn't a vampire status. He was a hardcore wannabe. Talking to him was an unpleasant prospect, and I knew it could be messy should he get caught. That was a concern; I'd been to him once before when the lack of fresh blood was getting intolerable, before I'd learned to deal. His prices were outrageous and I had to leave dissatisfied. But more than that bad experience, I just didn't like Father Vasyl. He just gave me the creepy hanger-on vibe, like he wanted to be one of us and if he tried hard enough, we might give it to him. He'd never be one; he'd be dead before any of us would be old enough to be his sire, assuming anyone wanted to father a toady. "Father Vasyl?" I repeated. I looked at her, studying her gray eyes. "Thanks, Julia."

"I'm sorry, Misty," she said again, offering me a cool hand. I accepted it and shook it, mindful to remain in her good graces.

"Me, too. But hey, thanks for trying."

We left *Veritas* quickly. Father Vasyl's church was on the Inner Ring, but was a quarter turn from where we were. Li and I walked to the nearest Tunnel connection and waited ten minutes for a train. Like New York subways, the trains ran all around the Ring but unlike the Big Apple's underground transit system, it was usually on time. I'd been told they were like Tokyo's system, but I'd never seen that so had only comparisons to New York. It would have been hours to walk but was only fifteen minutes by subway.

"What are we looking for?" Li asked as we bounded up the steps from the arrival station.

"Mother of Mercy, which is on the sixth floor of the Gideon Christian Coalition Building." There wasn't room for churches in the minds of Gideon's leaders, so it was utterly unsurprising that they had a hard time getting permits to build centers of worship. Most of them shared buildings with other faiths, all comingling together to reduce the footprint they made and increase their chances of getting a building permit. Not even Rome could buy the space in Gideon for one of their churches to have its own building.

The Gideon Christian Coalition Building was a pretty structure, I'd give them that. It was mostly made of bone-white concrete, with prominent crosses in the design. It had a fairly bland façade as well, which was due in part to the fact that many different Christian faiths called it home. But I found the stark white lines pleasing; it was reminiscent of '80s architecture. Inside, it was decorated in "hotel lobby," meant to be pleasing and inoffensive, as well as uninteresting. I bypassed the desk and headed for the elevator, Li right with me. We escaped the chipper yet efficient looking woman sitting at the desk, but were cornered by a greeter.

"Welcome to the home of God in Gideon," the man said, stepping forward and offering his hand. He was older, with mostly white hair and a practiced smile. "I'm John, and I'm here to help you find the faith you're seeking."

"Mother of Mercy," I told him, ignoring the hand. Li shook,

mostly automatically, I suspected.

"They're on the sixth floor," he said, his smile remaining the same. I wondered if he were a parishioner with Mother of Mercy, or if he didn't care so long as we were seeking God. I rather hoped the latter; it implied something more pleasant than the former.

"Yeah, thanks," I said, brushing by John. "Knew that."

"Thank you," I heard Li say more pleasantly before he caught up with me. "You didn't seem to like him."

I shrugged. "He's religious. I'm a vampire. I don't bother playing nice with them because there isn't a faith out there that doesn't see us as a danger or demons."

"He might not be like that."

I punched the call button. "In my experiences, he's exactly like that. Let's just save some time and assume."

Li shrugged then stepped forward as the elevator's door opened. "Okay," he said, sounding disinterested. We rode the rest of the way in silence, getting off at the sixth floor.

Now it felt like I was in a Catholic church, albeit one with an elevator in the middle of their entrance foyer. The chapel itself was before us, with pews making a double line up the middle. The ceilings were high and vaulted, emulating a traditional interior. The windows were stained glass, though they were darkened and shadowed now. Together, we walked forward, heading past the basin of holy water. "Father?" I called. "Hello?"

A clatter of noise whipped my head around. A form rose from the back corner, up behind the pulpit. It was clothed in black, with a hood drawn over its head. We only had a second to stare before the form turned and dashed toward the back of the room, toward a door.

I jumped into motion. Part of it was instinctive; something was running from me. But that's not why I gave into the instinct. It was the furtive motion of the form that jarred me into action. Someone was up to no good. As I dashed up the center aisle, I heard Li yell something. I didn't care; I was deep in the hunt. Even the body sprawled behind the pulpit didn't slow me. I was intent on the chase; it was only after I'd passed through that I realized who I'd seen sprawled there: Father Vasyl.

CHAPTER 8

I ran through the door, hard enough that it slammed into its stop with a loud pop. I didn't pause to see if I'd broken anything. The person I was chasing was ducking into a hallway and I dashed after them. I could now see that they were wearing a blue Gideon University hoodie and black jeans; nothing that would draw any attention once they hit the streets. But they'd have to get past me before they could disappear into a crowd. They had just killed Father Vasyl, who was supposed to have information for me. I was betting that this person had information that I wanted or needed. And I *was* going to get it from them.

I already knew something about my quarry; they moved fast, faster than me. Were it not for the interior limiting them, I would already have fallen well behind. I hadn't caught a scent yet; they tended to disperse quickly. But I needed it before I could be sure of their age.

The hallway was lined with classrooms, designated by the grades of the kids. The form ignored them and raced up a set of stairs at the end of the hallway. It wasn't fire stairs; it was internal architecture. They were wide and appeared to be made of some dark, hand-carved wood, which meant they probably were. Had it been any church other than Catholic, I would have said plastic. But while the Vatican couldn't buy space in Gideon, they could import the materials needed to make what they did have impressive.

This level held the offices of the priests serving here. We both turned left, following the bend of the wood-paneled hallway. One would have been Father Vasyl's. Another belonged to some guy who heard us and stepped out of his office. "Here, what is goin—"

My quarry pushed him, so fast I almost didn't see it. The priest was thrown back into the office violently; I saw him slumped against his desk as I ran past.

I caught a scent as I passed that office. I already knew that I was chasing a vampire but now I knew that I was chasing someone who was several centuries old. I should have stopped. I was chasing an older vampire, alone. But I wanted to at least see the person and try to learn who was doing this, and why. I was sure they'd killed the Father to stop me from finding out anything about Li's daughter.

The prey darted to the right, taking another hallway. When I rounded the corner, I scowled. This ended in a door with a fire escape warning on it. The other vampire was already slamming that door open, turning right as they did. I followed them and saw the fire stairs. Unlike the internal ones, these were metal and concrete—exactly the kind of stairs you see in all buildings of this height.

The Gideon Christian Coalition Building has thirty floors. I counted each one of them as we ran, getting ever higher. Each of the levels was marked with the particular flavor of Christianity that was housed on that floor, which might have been an interesting read, at another time. For now, I was too concerned with the vampire that was staying about a floor ahead of me.

I almost caught up with the vampire at the exit to the roof; the few seconds it took them to force open the locked door was enough time for me to almost catch them. I was only steps behind as we came out on the roof, which was a mistake.

She turned on me, snake quick. The hood kept me from seeing most of her face, but I saw the finely pointed chin, ivory skin and full, feminine lips. Her hands caught my jacket and she twisted, sending me flying through the air. For a second, the edge of the building loomed in my vision; then I landed on the roof and rolled to the edge. Gasping, I tried to pull back, only to scuttle into hard, strong legs. Those lips curved into a smile again and she bent down, picking me up by the throat. "Who are you?" She had a faint accent; I couldn't tell what, but that confirmed she was probably pretty old—at least as old as Drake.

I wheezed and grabbed her arms, so that she'd have to peel me off her before she could drop me. Thirty stories wouldn't kill me; I'd just wish it had as I slowly mended shattered bones. "Who are *you?*" I managed to get out.

She smiled and I wasn't reassured. But to my surprise, all she said was, "Bridgette."

"Misty," I answered. "Why'd you kill Father Vasyl?" Hey, maybe if she was in a giving mood, I could get all the information I needed.

"He delivered his lambs unto the wolves. How many has he fed to you, like a dog seeking treats? How many of his humans have you taken from?"

"Since coming here?" I rasped. "None. I'm on the Work for Blood program."

Those lips twitched. "Then why were you here?"

"I was told he had information I need. I'm trying to help a friend find his kidnapped daughter."

The arm relaxed a bit and I felt my toes touch the roof again. I didn't release my grip on her arms; I still didn't trust her not to push me off. "A human. Why are you helping one of those?" She sounded confused, which worked for me. The longer she gave me to explain, the better chance I had not to fall to a sharp, painful stop.

"Because..." I wasn't sure how to put it into words, but I tried. "He needs help. I *almost* fed from him. I felt bad."

"You felt...*bad?* Remorseful?"

The conversation was becoming surreal. I'd never had a vampire ask me that before. We all dealt with becoming parasites in our own way. It wasn't something I'd talked about in a long time. I'd talked with my sires, but they acted like it was a very uncomfortable topic, and I'd never tried to bring it up again. What they had made clear was that I would have to find my own way to manage my guilt. "Yeah," I said uncertainly. "I did."

"How intriguing," she murmured and my heels were on the edge of the roof now. "Too bad that—"

The door to the roof slammed open and Li staggered out, panting. I was impressed that he'd made the run up, winded or not. "Li," I gasped, "get out of here!" She wouldn't kill me that easily, but she could accidentally rip his head off with a poorly-aimed blow.

"Put...her...down..." the human wheezed, managing to

push himself upright.

The vampire laughed. "Of all the people here, you are the most likely to find himself dead by the end of our discussion," she said to Li, her voice harsh with cruel merriment. I'd heard vampires sound like that before, usually right before someone died.

"Leave him alone," I snarled, setting my heels and trying to decide if there was anything I could do to save us from this mess.

She shook me, like a terrier shaking a rat. "You are not in cha—" She cut off as Li coiled an arm around her neck and pulled backwards. I had to admit, he was fast and he was good. He'd done this before. A human would have been dragged backwards, gagging. Even some vampires would have found themselves on their butts, wondering what happened. This vampire didn't move. "Interesting," she said, her voice sounding strained from the pressure he was putting on her throat. I had seconds to do something before she killed him. The problem was I wasn't sure what I could do to stop her.

I had to try. With a grunt, I drove the heel of my palm into her face. I knew it hardly mattered to her, but Li saw my movement and he did something too. To my shock, she collapsed, half-falling on top of Li and sending me tumbling to the concrete next to her. Her grip on my neck didn't loosen, but I rolled over her arm, trapping her as much as she had trapped me. I managed to get a leg around her arm.

This worked for about half a second until she rolled onto her back, taking me with her. She smashed Li under her and slammed me into the concrete on the other side of him. I groaned but kept hold of her arm. I wasn't sure what I was going to do with the arm, but it was what I had.

Sudden light flooded us, followed by a tinny command, "Cease and desist your activities. We are landing to detain you. Please separate and wait for the officers to disembark." The Gideon police, here to save the day.

The vampire threw me away—just tossed me like I was a kitten. I hit the roof and rolled several times before I came to my feet, turning to see what had happened to Li. He was springing to his feet, his gaze on the vampire. She'd wasted no time; she was halfway across the roof, running for the far edge. Two officers zipped down lines to land on the roof, already turning toward us as the air-car turned to follow her.

"Come on!" Li shouted, grabbing my arm and pulling me toward the access door. I heard the cops follow us with an angry curse. I didn't look back as we raced for the door. I got there first and found it had locked behind us; stupid security feature. I ripped it open with a grunt and held it for Li. The cops were still pulling clear of their rappelling gear and I turned away before they could see my face. I'd already been tied to a corpse; I didn't need more trouble.

Which led me again to the question: why was I helping Li? I still didn't have anything close to a good answer to that, which annoyed me. But it wasn't enough annoyance to make me stop helping him.

It was enough irritation to have me cursing at myself under my breath, mostly about what a moron I was being. We were running down the stairs we'd just come up and I was having a much easier time of it, naturally. I didn't let Li fall behind me, though I could have, and perhaps I should have. I did stay half a stairway ahead of him, ready to run interference if someone tried to stop him.

We were halfway down before Li stopped me. "Wait, wait..." he panted and I turned before trotting back up to him. "We can't... keep going...down," he wheezed.

"Why?"

"Because...the cops...can get down...faster than we... can," he gasped up at me, rolling up his dark eyes rather than straightening.

Enlightenment came and I scowled. "They'll be waiting. We'll be trapped."

Li nodded. "Didn't...you say...that priest...had blood-bags on legs...coming here?"

"Yeah..." I frowned, not sure where he was going with that.

"Would he have...them come in...the front?" He was finally able to lift his head and I slowly nodded as I caught up.

"No," I said, my voice musing as I thought. "There'd be another way...an entrance that wouldn't be obvious."

Li panted a little and waited expectantly before asking. "And that would be...?"

I shrugged. "I dunno. But given that they share this building, it's not likely a back entrance. I think…that really just leaves the Catacombs."

Li quirked an eyebrow, looking dubious. "The *Catacombs*. No offense, but that sounds like a scene in a horror movie."

I grinned. "Well, you're close. It's the nickname for the access tunnels under the city."

"Like the subway system?"

"These do connect to the subway tunnels, but remember, Gideon's built from the ground up. The concrete tiles are riddled with tunnels. It's how power and water get in and out of the buildings—all the pipes run under us. And they're run through tunnels rather than the concrete so that if there's a problem, they can be worked on pretty easily."

"Huh," Li muttered. "But you think there's a way to get into them from this building?"

"It makes sense," I said, shrugging a little. "Some buildings did have access points, and even if this one doesn't, it wouldn't be that hard to break through the concrete."

"Wouldn't someone notice that?"

"Sure. But there are ways to make sure those don't get reported. Come on." I turned and started down the stairs again. "It's our best hope for getting out of here without having to deal with the police."

My newfound acquaintance paused, but only for a moment. Looking grim, he followed me further down into the building.

Chapter 9

Li was lagging behind again quickly. I stopped to let him catch up, but I could tell that between the beatings he'd taken and the lack of sleep, he was flagging. "Come on," I ordered, turning my back to him. "Get on."

"What?" he asked, turning a little red. "You want me to ride on your back?"

"Yeah," I said, making a motion to get him to hurry up. "I can carry you and I won't get tired."

"No," he said, setting his jaw.

Great. Male ego rearing its ugly head. With an irritable growl, I turned to face him. "Look. Stow your pride and get on my back. We don't have the time for me to convince you that it doesn't make you less of a *man* to be outpaced by a *vampire.*" He flushed a brighter red and I snapped, "You can't find your daughter if you're in a cell for the rest of the evening."

That got me an angry glare. "That was a low blow," he said softly. His voice and tone might have scared me, had I been alive. He was really good at looking and sounding very dangerous; he had to have practiced it. It made me wonder where he'd had the chance to apply that kind of menace.

"Yeah, it was," I acknowledged. "It's still true."

He muttered something in Japanese; given his tone of voice, I was just as glad that I hadn't understood him. "All right," he said in a hushed voice. *"All right."* I turned away again and he put his hands on my shoulders. After confirming I was ready for him, he gave a little hop as he pushed with his hands. I caught him easily, his weight setting against me as if it were nothing. My arms curled around his legs; once I was sure he'd gotten his grip, I took off.

Running up the stairs with him on my back wouldn't have winded me; running down them was much easier. I mostly had to keep my feet under us while gravity did the hard work. I heard him gasp in fear as I built to some impressive speeds. I shouldn't mock him, but I felt a little grin on my face. How could I not? I was carrying a man who weighed about as much as I did, running full tilt down a massive flight of stairs. My strong legs held me up, pumping with ease as I bounded; my dense bones and tough tendons were solid where a human would have been in pain. Being a vampire could be inconvenient, but in this moment, I felt my own power. In fact, I was a little surprised by it. The last time I'd really felt what I could do was before coming to Gideon, more than thirty years ago. I'd gotten older *and* stronger.

We wound down and down; I slowed only when I saw a sign for the first floor. I didn't stop, not until we ran out of stairs at the foot of a door labeled *Basement*. "We're here," I said to Li, but he was already sliding off my back, pulling his clothes straight and trying to pretend he'd never been there in the first place. I somehow refrained from rolling my eyes as I opened the door and peered through.

The hallway beyond the door was dark and smelled damp. I scented more deeply, opening my mouth and inhaling like a smoker getting his last drag. There was a twinge of something— maybe the tell-tale remnants of a vampire. I suddenly wondered if that was how our assailant on the roof had gotten into the building. But there was no way for me to tell; I was a vampire, not a bloodhound. "Come on," I said to my mortal companion. "I think we're alone." Bad choice of words; Tiffany's version of the same song started playing through my head.

Li nodded, his sharp features indistinct in the gloom of the basement. "Which way?"

"Uh...good question." I hesitated, then went right. We had to pick a direction, and this was as good as any. I hoped.

The hallway turned around the corner and gave us three rooms before finishing in a dead end. "Go back?" Li whispered to me.

I wasn't sure why we were whispering, but it seemed right. "Check the rooms," I replied at a similar volume. "If they forced a way into the tunnels, they might've hid the entrance behind a door."

Li looked dubious but nodded. "I've got door number one," he murmured. I slipped past him and sidled up to the second door; I tried to twist the knob right as Li said, "Locked."

"Mine, too. Leave the third. Let's go left, and if we need to break into a room, we'll do it later."

"We're here," he said, quirking his eyebrow as he walked past me. "Do it now."

"It'll be locked," I said, shrugging. The others were; this one shouldn't be any different.

Li grasped the handle, turned it and pushed the door open. "You were saying?" He smirked at me.

I stared at the betraying door before looking at my smug companion. "Right," I muttered. "So what's in there, smartie?"

Li looked and the level of self-satisfied pleasure around him thickened. "It's got a hole in the floor."

I narrowed my eyes at him. "You're never letting me forget this, are you?"

He laughed, whispering forgotten. "Not a chance," he told me, grinning widely.

"All right, let's go," I said, unamused. I slipped past him and into the small room. Shelves lined the walls, holding boxes that were half-crumbling in the moist air. It was little wonder it was so humid; the damp smell from the hallway was much stronger here. I also caught the soft drip of a water leak coming from the hole before us. Little attempt had been made to hide the fact that someone had taken a sledge hammer to it. The edges were raw, broken concrete; a metal ladder stuck up out of the hole. I reached out and tested the ladder's sturdiness; it wasn't attached to anything, so I ignored it and dropped down into the tunnel below. I took a cautious look around; there was only the familiar standard utility tunnel, extending ahead and behind me. It was about five feet wide with an arched ceiling; a line of lights lit up the immediate area as soon as I stepped into it. The ceiling, walls and floor had been painted white to make leaking liquid easier to spot. Pipes, painted different colors according to their contents, ran along both walls. I didn't see, hear or smell anyone, so I waved for Li to join me.

"Wow," he murmured as he clambered down the ladder. It held him easily, but rattled around as he moved on it. "What's all of this?"

"Water, sewer, hydrogen and electric." I touched each pipe as I named it.

Li eyed the sewer pipe, painted a dark gray and as wide around as a folding table. "That's a big pipe, and a lot of sewage."

"Yeah," I said, smiling a little. "Whenever someone came down here, they were always surprised by how big some of the pipes are."

"Sounds like you know this system pretty well," the Asian man said, turning that dark, speculative gaze to me.

"It was my first job when I started in the Work for Blood program," I said, picking a bit of blue paint off the water line. It fluttered to the floor as I gave the rest of the area a wry smile. Just being here was a heady reminder of the first nights in Gideon: the uneasy fear of being hunted slowly melting into relief as no one came after me.

And then relief had become boredom and apathy. It wasn't that being in Gideon wasn't good; it was. It was a haven, and I would always feel grateful for that. But it also required me to leash and muzzle myself, to give up hunting and live like my prey. I understood why it had to be that way. But it was still so empty.

"Shouldn't we be moving?" Li asked.

His question jolted me out of my reverie. I glanced at him to find him watching with curious eyes, his fingers playing with a worn spot in the jeans. "Yeah. We should." I glanced around but didn't see any grid markers; the entire system was set up on a grid and they were supposed to be marked at regular intervals. But this section didn't seem to be in good repair and I wondered if they'd been removed or painted over. "Huh. Well, any direction that takes us away from here is a good direction, right?"

Li shrugged with one shoulder in a graceful and odd maneuver. "Hey, your guess was right last time. And we're going to find a way out sooner or later, right?"

"Sure, we'll find a way out," I said, frowning. "The question will be if we can use it."

"Why wouldn't we?" Li frowned at me.

"They lock these places up," I said, choosing left this time. "All access tunnels are secured with mechanical and electronic locks, since someone could really mess up Gideon if they got access to the utility system. We'll probably find ways out, but finding one that is unlocked and unguarded is not all that likely."

"Well, they would have to have a way to get the blood bags in and out, right?"

"Yeah, of course." I kept my eyes open for any indication of where we were on the grid. "The question is *where?* This place can be like a maze. Unless we find a sign, we're probably going to be looking around here for a while."

"Oh." There was a lot of emotion in that one word, and I glanced back at him. The seriousness of the situation showed in the unsettled look on his face. "What am I looking for?"

"Well, the city would paint black grid markers—every three hundred meters, there should be an alpha-numeric combination painted on the wall, about eye-level. What I'd really like to see is a sign not left by the city, an arrow or something—anything that might have been left for a blood bag to follow. But those could be anywhere; it'd make sense to put them half-concealed so they're not seen easily."

"Just not too hidden, right?"

"Right. Guideposts are no good if they can't be seen." We walked for a while, taking it easy, trying not to miss the marker. The hall terminated at a T-intersection. Li stopped to look closely behind pipes, on the ceiling and even the floor. "Whatcha thinking?" I asked when he straightened up, frowning.

"I'm thinking we went the wrong way this time," he said softly.

"Because...?"

"Because if they had left markers for others to follow, they'd be here, to tell people to turn here, and I don't see anything like that."

"Ugh, you're probably right," I sighed. "Unless they just gave people maps and told them not to get lost."

"There's a thought. Well, we can keep wandering, or we can go back and see if we can find the markers the other way."

I sighed. What had seemed like such a brilliant idea before was now looking like a major mistake. "Yeah, let's go, but if we don't find it another way, we should just go wait until we're sure the police are gone and then go back up through the church."

"Think they're going to let us leave so easily?"

"Um, we'll deal with that if we have to." I was aware that my answer was lame but I wasn't sure what else to say. I didn't have any other ideas so I was hoping that we'd find something going the other way. We were quiet as we hurried back, lost in our individual thoughts. By the time we'd reached the next T-intersection, I was pretty sure I was completely insane. That was the only way to explain why I was doing this.

I joined him in the hunt for symbols or markers. Within a minute, Li said, "Misty!" and I turned to see him pointing under a pipe. I knelt to peer at what he'd found, grinning when I saw the stylized drop of blood. The tip of the drop pointed up the hall we'd just traveled, and the rounded end pointed down the left-hand tunnel.

"Let's go!" I said, almost giddy with delight.

"I knew I was right," Li boasted; I ignored him as I led the way out of there. Two more painted drops led us to another ladder; without asking, I scaled it first. We had no idea where this went and I was going first in case it was someone who wouldn't like to see strangers coming out of their hole.

Unlike the entrance to the church's basement, this had a cover and had been constructed with more care. The lid was a light-weight metal painted white to match the tunnel and the room above. Benches lined the walls except where a small fridge had been built into them. There was a woman in bright clothing sprawled on one of the benches, but she was asleep. I paused to listen, look and smell. Distant pulsing music said I was at some sort of club while the acrid smell of drugs confirmed that assessment. A second look at the woman told me she was unconscious, not asleep. I climbed out and went to the door, leaving Li to pull himself up.

I opened the door a crack and peered out; through the gap came a flood of music. It was loud enough to make me flinch back and had so much bass I felt it in my chest. A dazzling mass of lights and gyrating bodies covered with unholy amounts of glowing jewelry, sticks and clothing created a visual cacophony that gave me vertigo. The smell of drugs, both smoky and bitter, immediately deadened my nose. I quickly shut the door, but I already knew where we were: a drug club.

Along with loosening morality laws of all kinds, Gideon was also reviled for lifting the prohibition of many recreational drugs. There were some that you could use without any supervision, but most required you to come to a club where you could be monitored by trained staff. Not unlike the opium dens at the turn of the nineteenth century, people could get high in the comfort of a place designed exclusively for their tastes. Some people turned on in dark opulent rooms on over-stuffed couches, while others chose to party through their highs. We were in one of the latter venues, which meant slipping out would probably be easy. Most of the people in there wouldn't even see us; those that did probably wouldn't remember us. Or so I hoped.

The door opened as I murmured to Li, "We're in a drug den." We both turned to see a woman in a nurse's uniform as designed by a producer for a porn film. The skirt was too short and the bodice dropped way too low, her heels were ridiculously high and I couldn't tell if the bite marks above her clavicle were real or fake. Despite her appearance, the look she gave us was cool and professional. She was probably a nurse on-staff at the club. "Did you come from the church?" she asked, looking from one to the other of us.

Li quickly said, "Sure. We're just passing through."

The woman didn't move from the door. "The Father didn't say anyone was coming through today," she said suspiciously.

"Didn't say he sent us," I growled, stepping forward and drawing my lips back. Like most humans, her eyes dropped to watch my facial expression, only to fixate on my fangs. "Said we're just passing through."

"Okay," she whispered, stumbling away from the door. Her fingers rose to brush her marks and I bet they were real. She was probably a blood chew given the way she seemed both excited and frightened by my fangs.

I looked away first. Blood chews make me uncomfortable. Who in the world gets high on the thought that they're being eaten alive by a predator? She was still shivering in a mix of hope and fear when we left.

CHAPTER 10

We were barely outside before Li pointed out the obvious. "So we have no leads and no ideas where Masako is," he growled, looking frustrated. He glared at me. "Got any more ideas? Any helpful ones, maybe?"

I wasn't going to take his anger personally. I'd been pretty upset when I'd been hunting for my sires and had no news or leads; the memory of that terrible time allowed me to shrug this off now. "Give me a moment," I said, sticking my hands in my pockets and heading for the nearest rail station. We were still on the Inner Ring, not far from the Gideon Christian Center. We had a temporary cell phone, which could get us information, if I knew someone with the right skills, which I didn't. "Gotta think."

My fingers closed around a slim form in my pocket. I pulled it out and stared at it, frowning as I remembered the phone jacker Basil had given me last night. "If you need me, just use this." *Man, was I really considering doing this?* "Li, how much do you want to...no, let me ask this. Li, are you willing to owe some *really* unpleasant people a favor for this?"

"Yes!" There was no hesitation and I nodded, expecting nothing less.

"Okay, then get ready to owe the Russian Mafia." Li winced but didn't say anything as I opened the USB5 port on my phone and inserted the jacker. The phone's screen went blue before a pattern of white dots started across it. A moment later, I heard the line open and dial, followed by ringing. I put the phone to my ear and waited for someone to pick up.

"*Da?*" The voice was Russian but not Basil's; it wasn't even male.

"Basil, please," I asked nicely, wondering if my jacker had

been jacked up.

"And you are?"

Pleased and disappointed that I wasn't being informed I had the wrong number, I said, "Misty. We talked yesterday."

There was a muffled conversation, then Basil's voice burst onto the line, thick as syrup and bright as the sun. "Misty! I had not hoped to hear from you so soon."

"Yeah, well, life can do that kind of thing to you," I answered, pulling my thoughts together.

Basil may have looked like the poster child for vodka drinkers around the world, but he wasn't dumb. "What do you need, my friend?"

Ugh. *My friend.* I really didn't need friends like this. Except right now, I *did.* This *sucked.* "I need information. A friend of mine needs it, more specifically."

"Where can you meet?"

"Can't we do this over the phone? Time is of the essence."

"Hmm, very well. Tell me what you seek, and then we can meet to give it."

I swallowed an angry retort, reminding myself that Li and I were beggars and didn't have a lot of say in how Basil chose to inform us—assuming he could at all. "A woman named Suran Assawaroj was killed and her year-old daughter is missing. We need to find the baby."

"Why is a bitty child so important to you, vampire?"

"She owes me fifty bucks," I replied flippantly. I was pretty sure that telling him that the baby was incredibly important to Li was a bad idea; let him think us coy rather than desperate.

"And I thought I was ruthless!" Basil laughed. "You know of the Lithuanian café in Tile Sixty-One? You will come there, and I will tell you what I have found."

"Done." We exchanged farewells and hung up.

"What's this going to cost us?" Li asked.

"Dunno," I said, shrugging as I pulled the jacker off my phone and shoved both back into my pocket. Together, we resumed course for the rail station. Tile Sixty-One was a good hike by foot and we didn't have time for the walk. "It'll probably be a favor that's way out of proportion to the actual benefit we gain."

"If we find Masako because of this, there is no price too great," Li answered, his voice hard. I nodded as I grimaced; it'd been dumb to say that. I remained silent, not sure what else to say. Li had kinda said it all, at least for him. I was still undecided on whether the prize would be worth the cost.

The Lithuanian café was called A Taste of Home and was decorated in folk something. The small, square tables were covered in green and white checkered cloths; the chairs were carved wood with worn cushions. A counter along the back wall displayed some desserts and the cash register. The kitchen was only briefly visible when the apron-clad waitress swung open the door, but what I saw was well-worn and well-cleaned. The large windows at the front of the store assured that my ilk would never be here in the daytime. I'm sure that the kitsch objects and home-style décor gave it a homely and comforting look in the warm sunlight, but under the hard glow of the LEDs, they looked tired and grimy. It was a slow night, or A Taste of Home wasn't that popular. Maybe it was a lunch place.

We let the waitress bring Li a coffee and me a water. The young brunette didn't blink at a biracial woman and an Asian man sitting together at the Lithuanian restaurant, though I kept trying to think of jokes that started with that description. Li sat anxiously next to me, bouncing the foot crossed over his knee and jerking his eyes to the door any time it opened. "Calm down," I murmured, putting a hand on his calf.

His foot stopped as he muttered, "Sorry."

"We don't want to give away how much you want this information," I told him *sotto voce* and he nodded.

"I know that," he sighed, dropping his head into his hands and dragging his fingers through his hair. "I just...I'm..."

I could have picked words for him. Desperate. Hopeful. Anxious. Terrified. I'd felt them all, for months. Only instead of being a father without his child, I'd been a child denied my parents. I didn't know how to say that I understood what he was saying. I could have just said I'd lived through it, but if we didn't find his daughter, I didn't know that it would be helpful.

The door opened and I sat up straighter as Basil entered. Next to me, Li stiffened, even as I touched his hand to let him know that our Russian had arrived. The waitress came out of the kitchen again, but this time she was all smiles, making her Slavic features look pretty instead of severe. She and Basil started talking in what I assumed was Russian, their tone friendly and almost teasing. I looked at Li to see if he could understand; he shook his head. My eyes darted back to Basil as he gestured to us. The waitress' easy demeanor faded a touch, along with her smile, and she nodded. She spun fast enough to make her apron flare in front of her as Basil turned to us.

"Misty!" he called, as if he was greeting an old friend. He even held his arms out, as if he was waiting for a hug. He was not getting one no matter how big his smile.

"Hey, Basil," I answered, giving him a wave. His smile didn't falter at my casual greeting and he eased himself into an empty chair at our table. "So what have you—"

The Russian's fingers rose in a gesture calling for silence and I obliged, feeling my jaw tighten as I did. I didn't like taking orders from him, particularly hand signals. It made me feel like a trained dog. *Sit, Misty! Speak, Misty! D'awww, who's a niiiice wampire, huh? Who-woo?* But I had to concede his point when the waitress returned immediately with a shot glass and a bottle of pomegranate-flavored vodka. As I wrinkled my nose at both the smell of the liquor and the mere concept of anything flavored with pomegranate, Basil poured himself a glass. "I would offer," he said in his thick accent, "but Misty cannot and you have drink." He paused and pointed the neck of the bottle at Li. "Unless you want flavored coffee, yes?"

"No, thank you," Li said, putting his hand over the top of his mug.

"Misty, who is your friend, who is needing my help?" Basil's voice was tinged with something sharp and unpleasant at the question; I realized he probably thought it was rude that I hadn't properly introduced them.

"Right, sorry," I said, feeling like a heel because it *was* rude. But it wasn't intentional—I just hadn't thought. Clearing my throat, I said, "This is Li, Basil. Basil, Li."

"Ah, the *rebenka's* papa." As Li and I both tensed, Basil smirked. "You ask me to find woman and child, and think I not find more, not find who she is? Misty, I am surprised at you."

"Yeah, well, that's one word for what I am at me," I muttered, angry that I had been so dumb. I should have known that Basil would learn things I didn't want him to know.

"What did you find out?" Li was leaning forward, resting heavily on his elbows. I'd told him to play it cool even as I realized that really wasn't possible. He practically radiated his eagerness like a wave of energy, his black eyes locked on Basil's blue.

"Price first," I said firmly. I was going to have to be the responsible adult here and make sure that Basil didn't screw Li over.

"No price. Nothing. Free," Basil said, jabbing a thick finger into the table.

"What?" I blurted as Li blinked.

"Nothing. I charge nothing to a man looking for his child," Basil grunted, reaching into his coat. He drew out a flat wallet and flipped it open, turning it to show us a picture of three children. The two girls and the boy all had Basil's thick cheeks and sandy hair. "Dese are mine," he said, tapping the picture. "So I not charge another father for his children."

I stared at Basil, feeling both shocked and ashamed. I'd always thought he was just another thug, just an amoral greedy mobster looking to make a buck off the little guys. I knew that he still was a criminal who'd break the law. But he had some principles and I felt oddly guilty for thinking the worse of him. "Thank you," Li said, smiling. "This is...I won't forget it."

I hid a wince, wondering if Basil was playing some long, obscure game for Li's loyalty. But the Russian just smiled. "All the thank-you I want is to know you find little girl. One father to another."

"One father to another," Li agreed. "What do you have?"

"I hear that Uchida Junichi has been short on money and so he calls in loans," Basil started, his voice almost conversational.

I stopped him. "Who is that?"

"Blond Johnny." Li's voice was hard. "New-kuza lieutenant."

I frowned. The New-kuza had been one of the first to break into the Gideon underworld. They'd gotten a foothold before anyone else and had lodged themselves in, rather like a tick.

"When Blond Johnny gets a loan who can't repay, he make an example of that one," Basil continued. "In this case, he pick Thai girl who borrow twenty gee's from him. She can't pay, he kill her and dump her body and take her baby."

"Twenty thousand?" Li said, his eyes widening. "Wait, are you saying Suran borrowed that much money from him?" Before Basil could answer, Li dropped his head into his hands. "Oh, no...no, no."

I put my hand on his shoulder as he sagged forward, pressing his hands into the table. "Li?"

"She told me not to worry about the money," he groaned, lifting his head. He was pale and looked sick, or like he was on the verge of tears. "She told me she'd borrowed it but that it was fine."

"What did she borrow money for?" Basil asked, arching a hairy eyebrow.

"Me," Li whispered, running his hands through his hair. "It was for my paperwork and visa to Gideon. Suran is dead because of me."

Chapter 11

After Basil had wished us luck and parted ways, we headed back to my apartment. There wasn't anywhere else to go. "Plan?" I asked as we left the sandwich shop.

"Plan is," he said, his voice tight with repressed emotions, "I need to go find Blond Johnny and make him tell me where my daughter is."

I nodded. "And you know where to find him?"

He paused for a second, and his dark eyes flickered up to me. "Yeah, he should be at the Tiger Club. Word is that he's having an affair with one of their regular singers. He's there most nights."

"Never heard of it," I said, moving around a pack of teenagers shoving and daring each other to do something that I missed.

"It's in the Zephyr Tile," Li said. "It's swanky." He said the last word with a silly accent, and the grin he flashed me was crooked. I answered it with my own grin, but his faded quickly. I wondered if it would linger longer when he was not mourning.

"Zephyr is a swanky tile," I agreed, crossing my arms.

"Yeah." Once again, his pace slowed. This time, when he looked at me, I saw him gather his resolve. "Misty, I don't want to ask this, but I have nowhere else to turn. Johnny's men beat me once; I can't fight him alone. And it will be a fight—me against a bunch of other guys. A vampire would even the odds."

I frowned. "You're asking me to go to a club and start a fight? I'm a vampire—the courts are less than friendly to us."

"There won't be an arrest or trial, Misty, not with these guys," he said, shaking his head. "They won't involve the police if they can avoid it. They'll handle it themselves."

"So you just want me to mess with guys that will drag me

out into the sun?"

"The New-kuza have an agreement with King Connor. They aren't going to kill you, and they'll have to go through Connor to punish you. And he won't let them do anything too bad to you."

I rolled my eyes at the mention of the red-headed mountain that claimed to be Viking. Not a real Viking, but one in spirit; he wasn't old enough to allege to be a real one. He also claimed to be our king, at least to the powers of the underworld who would exploit us if they could. Too many vampires found themselves falling into a criminal lifestyle whether they wished it or not; not all of us could handle the Work for Blood program. Connor was another option for them. Most vampires let him claim the title; if he wanted to put himself forward as a target, more power to him. Sadly, some vampires believed his hype and he had a small but potent army. It did allow him to bargain with various groups, but also gave him a seriously swollen ego. I gave him this much: he really protected us. Every vampire knew that if they were in serious trouble, Connor had their back. Maybe I shouldn't roll my eyes quite so hard. "Li, this is serious. I could get in big trouble."

"I wouldn't ask if I weren't in so much trouble, if it weren't for my baby," Li replied quietly. His dark eyes were distressed. "I don't know anyone else who can help me."

I was confused. Every rational part of me was telling me that it was the worst kind of foolishness to help him, that I was going to get involved in the very thing I'd avoided for decades: trouble. And this wasn't a casual trouble either; this was a bad kind of trouble. This could get me killed. And despite that, I nodded. "Yeah, Li. I'll help you."

I'm an idiot.

Back in my room, I made Li eat something and sleep for a while. The singer Li had mentioned, Angela Kangara, had her first set at 11:00. We had time, and he needed to sleep since he'd been up all day. It wouldn't be enough, but it would help. He insisted that he couldn't sleep, but he passed out when he hit the pillow.

I did some research. The Tiger Club appeared to be the hot spot for certain groups. Its status as a trendy spot was assured by its placement on the Inner Core, but the reviews and news stories I read indicated that it went beyond that. It was rumored to be *the* party place for the New-kuza, which meant that the staff would not be neutral; they'd be openly hostile to Li and me. This was looking better and *better* all the time.

Still, this was our lead. While that might have been the sad truth, I had other resources. Flipping open my phone, I dialed Drake's number. This seemed to be the day for running up my bill.

"Misty," he said when he answered.

"Drake. Do you have a moment for some questions?"

"Naturally." I could hear his shark's smile. "We'll add them to your tab."

"Naturally." I was pleased to hear that I echoed him exactly. "What do you know about the Tiger Club?"

"I know that it's a nest for Japanese snakes. I know that the owners never intended for it to become that. And I know that the bartenders take breaks on the roof at two in the morning."

"Yeah, I was hoping more for information about one of its regular attendees," I said, bemused that he was showing off while hoping that he wasn't going to charge me for the information I didn't need.

"Well, Misty, you have to ask for what you want." Drake's voice was chiding, but not in a cruel way.

"Yeah, fine," I grumbled, keeping my tone down. "What do you know about some dude named Blond Johnny?"

"You really need to lose some of that eighties slang," he shot back. "The word 'dude' is dead."

"Blond Johnny, Drake," I said as patiently as I could.

He sighed softly. It was unnecessary for us to draw in and release air like that, but we did it anyway. It was an expression that some of us carried on after death. Strange what we left behind and what we carried over. "He's New-kuza, and since you're asking, I can only assume your young human has pulled you into some trouble."

"Something like that," I admitted uneasily. "I know he's a lieutenant for them."

"*Lieutenant* is a good English word for it. Mr. Johnny is a *fuku-honbucho,* a second man to the second man." I could almost see Drake's smug "lecture face." "He supervises several gangs, so he has lots of boys he can call on. Don't mess with him——he's vicious. I've heard ugly stories."

"Heard anything about killing a mother and stealing her baby?"

"Wouldn't surprise me—the slave trade is alive and well, even here," he remarked, his voice level. "And even with my love of personalized vengeance, I'm telling you to stay out of this."

"Assuming I'm not going to stay out of this," I drawled speculatively, "would going to the Tiger Club be the best way to find him?"

Drake laughed, and this time, he made no attempt to repress the mocking chuckle. "Misty, you'll never get into the Tiger Club. You're a sweet blood sucker, but you're completely in the wrong class. Social class."

I sighed in frustration. "I have a nice dress."

"Ha. Did it cost more than five hundred?"

"Dollars?" I almost shrieked, lowering my voice at the last moment. Li still mumbled and stirred, and I dropped my voice further. "Drake, I'm a GWE maintenance tech. I'm not made of mo—Oh. I think I see your point." And if I was going to have that problem, Li would, too. "Do you know where I can borrow a dress like that?"

Drake laughed for a full minute. "No, Misty," he finally said. He was quiet for a moment before heaving a sigh that must have come from his toes. "Are you serious about this?"

Was I? I glanced at Li, deep in sleep, and closed my eyes in defeat. "Yeah, I'm serious."

"Then call Connor. He can get you into anywhere in Gideon."

"God, that blowhard?" I groaned softly, mindful of Li sleeping.

"He has the connections you need. Short of you stealing a dress or someone else's identity, he's the only way you're getting in that door."

"You don't need to sound so gleeful about it," I muttered, picking up a penny off my carpet and rolling it listlessly over my fingers. The repetition was vaguely soothing, but only if I didn't think about Connor at all. He really got on my nerves.

"He's a resource, Misty."

"An annoying one."

"And as long as you think like that, you're missing out on a valuable connection."

It was not an unreasonable remark, but it didn't make me feel any better. "You swear he can do this for us?"

"You, yes. I'm not so sure about your interesting friend. But Connor has this weird honor system, and he'll help you out, if you can convince him it's good for a vampire."

"If you're sure he can help, I'll call him," I said, scowling as the penny slipped through my fingers.

"Oh, he can. He might even do it. Good luck. You'll need it."

"Thanks," I muttered to the dial tone. I closed and opened the line again, dialing a number I had memorized, but hoped I'd never need. Despite my reluctance, King Connor's promise to help any vampire in need seemed sincere, and I wouldn't pass up possible aid right now. If I went into this without help, I might end up in a bind. Hopefully, Connor would accept requests for preventive aid as well as corrective.

"King Connor." The voice on the phone was deep and authoritative, and was what you'd expect from someone with the self-title of King.

"Hi, I'm Misty Sauval. We've never met, but I'm a vampire here in Gideon."

"And you need help." I could hear the smile in his voice, not something condescending, but simply pleasurable. You could hear that he enjoyed helping others. It made me a little more comfortable with calling, but also a little unsure. What kind of vampire was so giving to other predators?

"Well," I said, hearing the half-truthful tone in my voice as I spoke, "I do, but you may not agree."

"Tell me, my dear, and we'll see."

And with two words, he lost any good will he'd built up. We didn't know each other well enough for him to use an endearment. But I couldn't think of a way to point that out without pissing off the guy who I was asking for aid. "I need to get into the Tiger Club tonight. I and a friend."

"I...I confess to confusion," Connor said, his deep voice going deeper, as if talking lower would help him think.

"Yeah, I'm aware that it's weird, My friend needs to talk to someone there. Neither of us has the resources to get in on our own."

He was quiet for a moment. Finally, he asked, "Who else would I be helping? Who does your friend want to talk to? And why are you asking?"

Great, three questions that would sink or swim the whole thing. "My friend is named Li Chin. He's not a vampire." No point in lying; he'd find out soon enough. I went on talking, hoping to get the words out before Connor could refuse. "I know that you wouldn't help a human, not without a hell of a good reason. Blond Johnny took his daughter, and we need to find her. I'm going to help him, and it will probably land me in a heap of trouble, so maybe you could look at this as a preventive measure to keep me out of trouble?"

Connor was quiet for a long moment. "If I don't help you into the club, then you'll not be in trouble, correct?"

Damn it. He didn't seem inclined to help. "Then we'll jump him in the parking lot. Blond Johnny kidnapped a baby and killed her mother. Li is the only family she has left. Who knows what will happen to the child if she's left at Blond Johnny's mercy. And you may not care about them, but..." I trailed away, at a loss for words.

"But you do care," Connor replied, his voice soft. "Why?"

"I don't know," I admitted. I didn't care about humans, not like this. But Li was different. He'd done in hours—no, in minutes—what it had taken Malcolm years to do. "But I do. He's...my friend."

"What do you need from me?"

I sagged with relief at those words. "I need some clothes and some money—basically, just enough to get inside."

"Then you'll probably need ID as well. Give me some time. I'll call you back later."

"Connor, thank you," I said, my gratitude clear in my voice. I didn't add that I took back most of the bad things I'd said about him. It didn't seem to be a prudent way to say thank you.

"Well, let me see what I can do, first."

After he got our clothing sizes and general descriptions, we hung up. Then I had nothing to do but sit back, worry and wonder just what was going on in my stupid, stupid head.

The phone rang at 9:30, and it jerked Li awake. As my human companion blinked and slowly stretched, I answered the familiar number. "Connor?"

"Actually, one of his knights, Sir Gregor," a crisp voice answered me.

I blinked. "Am I getting passed down the chain?" I asked with a forced laugh. I wasn't sure I liked being handed off to a minion.

"King Connor often assigns requests for assistance to a knight," Gregor told me. I'd already dropped the title from his name. "He asked me to handle this. Where can we meet for the exchange of resources?"

"Umm... how about the Four Winds Park on Zephyr? Or, do we need somewhere more private?"

"Were you planning on changing clothes in the middle of the park?" Gregor's haughty tone set my teeth on edge.

"You said exchange," I said, my voice tight with irritation. I hadn't met the guy and I didn't like him already. It helped that he was an obnoxious prick.

"As you want it. I will be at the Four Winds in half an hour." The phone went dead in my ear.

"What's the word?" Li asked groggily.

"We have help that will get us into the Tiger Club. I've also been strongly advised not to get involved, at all. Are you sure you want to do this?"

Li glanced up at me, his face fierce as he pulled on sneakers. "I don't have a choice," he growled. "I have to get my daughter back." His expression and tone softened together. "But...you have a choice. You don't have to go. I know I asked, but I had no right."

I quirked an eyebrow at him and gave him what I hoped was a brave smile. "You say that *after* you begged and I put a call into King Connor," I said, keeping my tone light. "I'm not sure I can back out now."

"King Connor?" He frowned, pulling his shirt back on.

"Yeah, the vampire who acts like he's our keeper," I sighed, moving to the door and holding it open. Drake's words rang in my mind. "He might be a tool, but he's a useful one. Or rather, Gregor is."

Li frowned as he exited the room. "Who's Gregor?"

"I'll explain on the way," I said as I locked the door and led him down the stairs. It would give us something to do on the ride over to the Core.

CHAPTER 12

F our Winds Park is a wind chime park. It's one of Zephyr's premiere attractions, though I'm not sure if that's because it's the tile's name, or the tile was named for it. Either way, it's an impressive sight: a large green space, always a rarity in Gideon, intersected by trees and elegant metal frames. Both the trees and the frames hold chimes of every shape and tone; their music could be heard with the slightest breeze. They'd placed it on the edge of the Core, where the wind would come off the Inner Sea and its music would spread outside of the park to the surrounding areas. The park stops at a thirty-foot retaining wall, but the chimes were still audible from the path at the top of that wall. I could hear them as we were walking along the path, heading for the stairs down to the park.

Li had been quiet since I explained the exact nature of Gregor's help. I wasn't sure if he was upset or just thoughtful. I was content to remain silent myself, as I tried not to think about this mess. I let myself focus on the feel of the steps under my feet, the smell of the flowers that grew in pots along the stair way. It was too cold for the poor things; they'd been dragged out of a safe, warm greenhouse and thrust into a harsh environment.

I knew how they felt.

At the bottom of the stairs, the grass was soft and spongy under my feet. I'd been in Gideon long enough that the feel of grass was a novelty. I smiled to myself wistfully, remembering the days when it wasn't a big deal to walk on plants and dirt. It's amazing how quickly we can forget where we came from, when we surround ourselves with concrete and steel.

Li didn't seem to be as introspective as I was at the moment. "So where is he?" he asked, glancing around the park. Most of open space was visible, but some of the area was obscured by trees or chimes. Luckily, I didn't need to see. I closed my eyes and inhaled, seeking the scent that would tell me if another of my kind was here. Initially, all I could smell was Li. His scent was already becoming familiar—familiar enough that I felt myself relax a little more. It was an instinctive response to his nearness. I took a few steps away from him and tried again, and this time, I caught a whiff of vampire. "This way."

The source of the rival-smell was on the far side of the park's centerpiece, the Clockwork Chime. It was half-clock, half-chime, but its primary attraction was that visitors were able to alter the chimes. It had three wheels set in a single control panel; by twisting them, you could change the angle of the chimes, or turn them, or alter their height. It allowed you to personalize the music, if you got to the point that you could figure out how a given chime would interact with a given breeze. I wasn't quite that good; I'd only played with it for an hour or two here and there.

The vampire I was tracking was manipulating the chimes, but unlike most, he knew what he was doing. Most people would have been jerking the wheels back and forth, spastically trying to stumble on the right sound. This vampire was moving the wheels in careful, precise ways, seeking the desired tones through careful adjustments. His clothing also gave that impression of determined precision. A dark suit fit him so well that it had to have been tailored for him. He was average height, and extremely thin, but he didn't look frail. Glasses framed his face, hiding his eyes. The only thing about him that wasn't perfect was his long brown hair. It curled thickly, fighting to escape the clasp holding it against his neck. Calling it a pony tail sounded too feminine, but that was the word for it.

I stopped thirty feet away from him. Li started to stride past me, but I grabbed his arm. He glanced at me, and I shook my head, hoping he'd keep his mouth shut for just a moment. We were about to observe some etiquette.

Among vampires, you don't just wander up and say hi the first time you meet. Julia and I knew each other, and the strange vampires at *Veritas* had been her guests. I had gotten a free social pass from them even though I hadn't met any of them formally.

That meant something different in our culture than for humans, something a bit more than a handshake.

But I had no one securing my safety from Gregor and we'd never met before, so we had to do the formal song and dance. There's a long moment of assessing one another and determining relative ranking. Or as my sire Aibek had told me once, "The sweet stench of 'Who can defeat whom?'" By Gregor's smell, he had the upper hand; his pheromones gave him at least half a century on me, but probably not much more than that. It meant he'd be a little faster and tougher. I was used to being the underdog; there weren't many vampires younger than me. It wouldn't help me if he initiated a massive beat-down on me.

Gregor was downwind, but that may have not been why he wasn't acknowledging us. No, watching him play with the Clockwork Chime, I was pretty sure he was making us wait until he was done. It was another way of expressing dominance, especially since I had come to him for help. I waited tolerantly, while Li vibrated next to me, fairly dribbling impatience off of his body.

When Gregor did glance up at us, it was with a movement as precise as the rest of him. He studied us, watching as I grabbed Li again, who had started forward when Gregor looked at us. That hadn't been a gesture to greet him, but a sign that he had seen us. He and I competed for the same resource; it was instinctive to be adversarial. This wait and watch was all part of our social dance, so we wouldn't jump each other at the slightest provocation. Once we were comfortable, we would proceed. He probably wasn't going to attack, without some provocation; he'd have already jumped us if he were going to. It was a good way to start.

Once the chimes sang with a delicate beauty, Gregor stepped away from the controls, signaling that he was ready to talk to me. He turned to us, slipping his hands behind his back and rotating his body toward us. I stepped forward too, doing my own signaling of truce by thrusting my hands in my pockets. We met with the green grass cushioning our feet and the wind making the chimes sing. They made a nice backdrop for Gregor's precise voice. "He is not of the Blood."

"Is he saying what I think he's saying?" Li asked, his voice tense.

"He wants to exchange business cards," I said, reaching up to squeeze Li's shoulder. The gesture was partly for comfort, but it was largely a warning to let me do it my way. "Can you give us a moment?" I saw protest rise on the human's face. "The sooner we finish this, the sooner we can move on."

He recognized the truth, but he still gave Gregor a dirty look. And Drake thought I had no poker face. "Don't take long."

I resisted the urge to say "Or what?" but I knew it was a waste of time and would cause unnecessary anger. "It won't," I promised before watching him walk away. When he was out of hearing range, I turned back to Gregor, and found him watching Li, too. "Gregor. Gregor?"

"Yes," he said, returning his gaze to me. I could see now that his eyes were a deep, dark brown. They took what was an unremarkable face and turned it into something special. He must have been quite the looker when he was alive and vibrant with warmth. Now, he was dead and cold; his eyes were meant to be warm but they were like polished agate. Still lovely, but missing vital heat.

"I assume you want the full diatribe," I sighed, quirking an eyebrow up.

"Diatribe? The Recitation is not a diatribe," he said mildly enough, but I could tell I was irritating him. He irritated first, so I wasn't feeling too bad about it.

"It was the elders' thing," I pointed out. "We are a new generation."

"If you argue, it will just take longer," Gregor said, his face implacable as he echoed what I had just said to Li.

Translation: I'm not going to help you until you do it. I made a face, sighed and started. "I am Misty Sauval, born of flesh in the Big Easy. I am the third child of Daffyad, of the line of Pendragon of the Blessed Isle. I am the fourth child of Aibek, Son of the Line of Bab-ila-on. I am Oak and Fire, respectively." Just saying their names hurt; my dear blood-fathers, missing and most assuredly dead. They were largely helpless in modern society. Daffyad had never learned to drive; he'd had to be chauffeured everywhere. Aibek had loved to drive, but that was the limit of his abilities. I'd tried to show them how to use phones and all the other things that would have let them blend into society, but the elders had never been good at learning new things. It was the reason they were gone. I wouldn't have to worry about that. So long as I stayed in Gideon, I would be safe to fall behind the times.

"I am Gregor Richter, born of flesh in the Divided City," Gregor said, his words flowing off his tongue easily, unaware of my inner struggle. "I am the seventh child of Lady Isabella dela Léon, *Amarrar-asesino*. I am the first child of Heinrich Wolf, of the *Drei Wölfe*. I am Death and I am the Hunter."

How fancy. My fathers had never taught me any of their titles in a foreign tongue. Nor had their heralds been so dramatic; it made me think this haughty 'tude that Gregor was tossing around was inherited. Of course, his folks may have chosen him because of his own personal nastiness.

I wasn't being fair. But death and hunting as heralds? Heralds are supposed to be one or two words that sum up what you do or wanted to be known for. They're usually chosen when you become an elder; until then, you borrow your blood-parents' symbols. Daffyad had been a Druid in Britain, when that sort of thing was still popular. He'd chosen oak as his herald for some arcane reason associated with that. Aibek had been a surgeon, both alive and dead. Fire had been a tool when he'd been alive, and was one of the things most feared as a dead man. I personally found Gregor's family's choices a wee bit pompous but it wasn't my call to make.

I nodded to him. "Nice lineage. German and Spanish?"

He gave me one nod and said in turn, "Yours sounds strong and full of grace."

Full of grace? Who talks like this? "Can we bring Li back over?"

"Of course." Gregor looked at the human and waved him over.

"I didn't get to see the secret handshake," he snitted as soon as he was within range.

I sighed at him. "We did it faster than the human eye can follow," I lied, then had to fight a smile as his eyebrows raced for his hairline.

"If we're done playing, we should move," Gregor said. Pompous and humorless—lovely combination.

"Yes, let's go," Li agreed. He paused, tilted his head and

asked, "Where are you taking us? I thought we were getting some stuff from you."

"Yes," Gregor said, looking pissed, "but I left it in the aero. Come with me to get it."

Back up the stairs, Gregor led us to a parked aero, hidden just around the corner. As we got close, a driver bounced out of the seat in the front and opened the door; I caught a whiff of his dinner-like scent as he held the door for us. Li scrambled for the rear-facing seats, reaching for the bag there. I took the forward facing, waiting for him to be done with his digging. "The Tiger Club," I heard Gregor say, and then he ducked in, settling on the seat next to me. Every hair on my body stood up; I tried not to look at him. It was a little close to be sitting for two predators.

"You're giving us a ride?" Li asked as the aero's blades began to smoothly turn. "And in personal transport, no less."

I was impressed as well. Having even a small aero was a sign of status; Gregor probably was loaded, which seemed likely from the suit-car combo, or King Connor was. Now I was kinda curious about that. However, this didn't seem to be the time to ask.

"It gives you privacy to change, and saves time," Gregor said coolly. Without a lurch, our ride left the ground, swiveling smoothly onto its computer-aided path. "It will give us time to talk, as well."

"Talk?" I inquired as Li tossed something red at me from the duffel bag that had been in his seat. I unrolled it to find a small wrinkle-resistant dress. And by small, I mean, I thought parts were missing at first. Holding it against my front, I queried incredulously, "You're serious?"

"It's the current fashion, according to my assistant," Gregor replied, glancing at me. "You'll need it to enter the club. You are aware that Blond Johnny keeps roughly a dozen guards around him, at all times? You'll be outnumbered by at least six to one."

That was a sobering thought, even more so than the dress. It was starting to sink in what I was agreeing to do. I looked at Li and found him watching me. He was sitting stiff and resolute, waiting for me to refuse to go, and I knew I couldn't let him do this alone. "Then we'll be outnumbered," I said, reaching for the buttons on my shirt. Li favored me with a smile of pure relief; he'd been terrified that I'd back out. He should be scared, because I knew that I shouldn't be here. But I was, and I was going. I was also officially a moron. "Is there any hose in that bag?" I'd died with shaved legs, but I liked the way hose smoothed them out.

"No," Li said, pawing through the duffel. "No hose."

"Ech," Gregor snorted. "You don't wear hose with an Estellen." He frowned as I shed my shirt. "The bandages are going to look terrible with that dress."

I shrugged as I glanced down at the covered burns. "It's a fresh burn; trust me, they'll be glad they're covered. Also, I didn't realize you'd be putting my body on display, or I would have said something." I glanced at the tag and confirmed it was a dress from Gideon's premiere designer. Wow, these things cost a pretty bit of money. I was going to feel like Cinderella in it. "So we're definitely outnumbered," I picked up the conversation where it had been diverted. "What else can you tell us? Something positive would be a radical change."

"The club will be heavily monitored," Gregor answered, his tone becoming brisk. "Within an hour of revealing yourselves, you'll both be made. By tomorrow, they'll have all the information they need to wreck both of you."

"I don't care," Li said, pulling off his clothes, a red blush creeping up his cheeks as he struggled to change and be modest at the same time. It looked like he had a suit of some sort to wear.

"I wasn't worried about you," Gregor rebutted. Those cold eyes latched onto mine. "Misty will pay the worst price. Charges will not be pressed, but problems will occur with your data. Gideon's Central Administration will look into it, and they'll find that your documentation was false. You'll be deported back to China, Li, to live your life there. Misty will be deported too, but she'll land in the United States, in a pyre." I hid a shiver as I silently pulled on the dress.

The cold eyes were all for Li now as he pushed on. "That's what they do to us in America. They burn us. Misty's skin will melt, running down her flesh to be added as fuel for the fire. Her bones, once bared to the flame, will ignite. We don't feel much pain, but she will be in agony for the time it takes her to burn and die. Or the New-kuza do it here, in Gideon—kill both of you, and if you're lucky, your daughter will live. She'll grow up never hearing your name, raised to be a house slave by some fat New-kuza, who'll rape her wh—"

"Shut up!" Li snapped, his voice shaking. "So what, I'm supposed to leave her with them, hope they're nice to her because I rolled over?"

"No," Gregor said. "But you can prepare more."

"I'm all for that," Li said, yanking clothing on. He was very careful not to look at me pulling on the tiny dress, which was actually expandable and not as small as I'd first thought. "You didn't have to try to mess with my head to get me to agree. How?"

"First, you can take me, and I will make it clear that King Connor is weighing in on this issue, which will provide us something of a position of power to start from when we open the negotiations," Gregor replied, crossing his arms. "Second, I'm hoping that you have further information, something that we can use as blackmail?"

I said, "We have a temp phone we got from some thuglings of theirs." Then I saw Li's expression.

Li's reaction was interesting and telling; nothing crossed his face. He probably should have just mounted a sign over his head that said, *I know what you're talking about.* "I have no idea what you're talking about," he said, which only made his imaginary sign shine all the more brightly.

"Come now, Mr. Chin. Did you think I wouldn't do a check on you?" Gregor said as I fit the cups of the dress over my breasts. The damn thing bound my middle in what was probably a sexually appealing way but didn't so much contain my breasts as mount them on a red, cloth platter for display. Clearly, Estellen was designing with men and lesbians in mind. I was so perturbed that it took me a moment to integrate what Gregor had just implied.

"A check?" I asked. "What kind of check?"

Gregor glanced at me, then reached out and adjusted the bodice of my dress with a quick tug. A human might have been offended; my near-reaction was more defensive as Gregor said, "Yes, a background check. I'm always particularly interested in why someone chooses to come to Gideon in the first place."

"I'm here for a new life, and that's what I want," Li snapped, dropping to his knees on the floor of the aero so that he could tuck in his shirt.

"Aren't we all? But that doesn't negate the fact that you have a very special reason to be here—you are running from the real Yakuza, so you come here, where the Underworld is run by New-kuza who didn't like being bottom dogs, and who don't communicate with the gentlemen in charge back home. That means that they wouldn't hear about whatever you did."

"All I did was leave," Li said, his dark eyes angry as he looked up at Gregor. "Suran was pregnant; I couldn't imagine raising a baby in that world. So I went to the one place where I could escape."

"Well, if you have nothing, what can you make up?" Gregor asked.

Li frowned and swallowed. "That's dangerous," he said softly.

Gregor snorted, a short, mocking noise. "And what you're planning to do isn't?"

"I have to," Li said, turning up his collar so that he could tie the blue tie, which was odd with the purple suit. But even I knew that this was the latest thing—mismatching suit and tie purposefully. "I have to rescue my daughter."

"Then look at it that way," Gregor replied softly. "You're going to do what you need to do for your daughter's health. That includes an assault on Blond Johnny, so why would lying be so much worse?" Li's face was tight and reluctant, but he nodded. "And I'll take that phone," Gregor said, holding out a hand. Li slapped it into his hand and it disappeared into Gregor's jacket. "Thank you," Gregor said, glancing out the window. "We're here."

CHAPTER 13

The gaudy light blazed out over the night, white and orange in three-foot-tall letters. A painted tiger, done Eastern style, stretched beneath the lights. My mind sought a distraction and immediately decided the poor animal must be hot. I shook that errant thought off and concentrated on my human companion.

Li was escorting me with a hand on my arm; his grip was tense on my skin as we glided toward the club. Gregor sauntered behind us, both arrogant and smug. Which wasn't a surprise; he seemed to embrace both attitudes with vigor. Ahead of us, a line stretched to our right, down the side of the building—eager patrons, trying to get in and party at the hottest of hot spots. Or they liked the thrill of knowing they were brushing elbows with rumored criminals. It was likely that the real New-kuza had a VIP room all to themselves but the thought allowed the eager partiers a safe thrill.

I almost felt sexy in this expensive, tummy-tucking dress and high heels. I wanted a bit more coverage over my cleavage, but I wasn't exactly getting a choice in the matter. No bandages would have been nice. And my hair was probably a fly-away mess; Gregor had given me a comb to slip in, on the left side. I hadn't been sure why it had to be left, but Gregor insisted. As we approached the head of the line, where a weary-looking bouncer waited patiently, I became suddenly aware of how much I resembled a target, with the bright color and specific hair-placement. Well, I did until I glanced at the girls in line and realized that each of them had ornate combs sticking out of their hair, on the left.

Stupid fashion.

At the door, the bouncer was still waiting, like a patient Aryan poster child: tall, blond, Scandinavian but built like a flesh wall. He put his hand on the latch for the velvet rope, but didn't do anything as useful as unhook it or let us through. Instead he just watched us, his blue eyes bored—no, not bored. Jaded. He had seen it all, and nothing was interesting anymore.

"Good evening, Mr. Nielsen," Gregor said genially behind us, smiling. "I trust you're having a good evening?"

The Scandinavian mountain shrugged. "Close enough," he said in a voice that was accented with the tone of Sweden. What do you know—I guessed right. "How are you?" he asked as he waved Li and me aside.

"Good, good," Gregor said, then reached forward and grabbed the back of my neck. It was surprising, but I let it go with a flinch; he must have done the same thing to Li, because he jumped out of his skin. Only my grip on his warm arm kept him in place as Gregor said, "These are mine, if you don't mind."

"Of course not, sir," Mountain Nielsen grinned, moving the rope aside. "The boy needs some more work."

"Oh, I know," Gregor said, smiling broadly as he released us and passed several bills to Mountain Nielsen. "But I haven't even tasted either one, so some jumpiness is understood."

My eyes widened as we moved forward; did Gregor just imply that he fed off humans? Maybe it was a show for the doorman. I just didn't know enough about him to know the truth. Was it my business? I glanced at the pale, anxious Li and decided: only if he made it my business. Then we'd find out if fifty years advantage was enough to prevent me from kicking his ass.

Inside was the usual riot of noise, color and smell that was always found at the blood buffets known as nightclubs. My stomach twisted instantly and insistently; I'd hunted in places like this almost exclusively when I'd lived in America, or I had until they had started checking pulses along with IDs at the door. It was mostly black inside, though a few lights were strategically placed. A little more illumination came from the strobes flashing on the various tiger-themed decor. The dance floor of the club was sunken, lower than the rest of room by about three feet. Wide steps angled down into it with inset lights to help high-light the stairs; it still looked like a lawsuit waiting to happen. The dance floor was flanked on three sides by the rest of the main room, while the final edge of the square was at the foot of a stage. This place actually had waitresses, who circled the tables like sharks in mini-skirts and almost-shirts, taking orders and bringing drinks to those too lazy to walk twenty feet to the bar.

I ignored my Pavlovian response to find dinner and allowed Li to steer me to a table in the corner, which our group claimed. We had a pretty good view of the door and the floor. "Now what?" I asked, raising my voice to be heard over the pounding bass line.

"We wait for Blond Johnny to arrive," Li shouted back over the music.

"Great," I muttered, pulling out my phone and connecting to Gid-Net; maybe I could find an online crossword puzzle to do. The Tiger Club had other ideas; they blocked external access, so all I could do online was order a drink—and blood wasn't on the menu—or I could request a specific song from a playlist. A quick scan of the list told me I was musically out of luck; I wasn't a huge fan of J-tech, or any of the other J's. Like all Japanese-based music, they were too erratic, high-pitched and sung by people with crazy chipmunk voices. Give me Depeche Mode or Duran Duran, thanks.

"We won't have to wait long." Gregor didn't appear to be yelling, yet I could hear his voice clearly. Showoff. "This is about the time he makes an appearance."

I tucked my useless phone back into my dress and contented myself with people-watching. It was kind of relaxing; like pulling on a worn pair of jeans you found in the bottom of your drawer. Only I was feeling comfortable remembering what it was like to assess people: who would fight, who would not, who could give me the most blood. It was a bad, old habit I shouldn't indulge but it was second nature even after years of being on the government blood-train. I scanned the room again; I saw a familiar blond man and all the comfort fell away.

Benoit was here, looking attractive in a nice suit, much nicer than he'd worn at the crime scene. It was even fashionable—the fabric was a pale sea-green while the tie was black or midnight blue, hard to tell in the club's lighting. I glanced down the lines of the outfit, slowly realizing that it was a *really good* suit; it accented his butt perfectly. But that didn't alleviate my current issue.

"Gregor, Li," I said, tapping on one shoulder then another

to get their attention. "Remember how we were worried about the New-kuza recognizing me and making my life hell?" They both nodded, though Li was distracted as he continued to watch the room like a hawk. "Well, a cop who knows me is here. Specifically, the one trying to tie me to Suran's death."

Gregor cursed softly; the police was an area where Connor had little influence, unsurprisingly. "There is a VIP Room, upstairs. We'll have to wait until Blond Johnny goes up there, and gain entrance." He didn't have to say that doing that would be a lot harder.

"Or remove the cop," Li said. At our startled looks, he said, "Not like *that!* Convince him to leave, trick him...something!"

"Got any ideas?" I asked, gazing at him. "Cause I'm getting nothing."

"We can work around him." Gregor looked annoyed that Li had come up with another idea. I bet Gregor wasn't the kind of person who liked his plans being ignored or trumped. "He won't be able to go in the VIP Room, so we'll hit Johnny there."

I narrowed my eyes at him. "I thought we were avoiding engaging him in a room with his buddies. Something about being outnumbered six to one?"

Gregor nodded. "Our options are limited by the cop. Unless you can get him to leave, or one of us could convince him to leave, things are harder."

"Fine," I sighed, rising to my feet. "I'll do what I can. I may only raise his suspicions, but maybe I can pull a miracle out of my butt."

"Such a pretty *derrière* is sure to contain a surprise or two," Gregor said, giving me a hint of a smirk. I blinked, feeling like I should blush, but I didn't do that anymore, so I probably just looked puzzled. And I was; that statement had come from nowhere.

Giving up, I turned my mind back to what I was doing. "Wish me luck."

"You won't need it," Gregor said, nodding with a confidence I didn't feel. I snuck a glance at Li; he was single-mindedly watching the room. Sighing softly, upset for no reason I could place, I gave Gregor a parting glance, and found him smiling as if I'd done something funny. That just ruined my mood further and rather than giving Gregor more fodder, I headed toward the cop.

Benoit was leaning against the bar, contemplating the amber liquid in his glass. I leaned against it next to him, but facing the other way, a move that I'd always found sexy when Don Johnson had done it. It probably dated me, but I wasn't exactly trying to score here. Kinda the opposite in fact.

I had a moment to see the stern handsomeness of his face, before he recognized me and bunched his forehead into a scowl. "You," he snarled. "Didn't get enough from the Thai girl?"

"Well, I was hoping to have cop next, though not in the way you were thinking." I was trying not to throw up at my own clumsy insinuation. "It still involves sucking, though."

His mouth crinkled into a moue of disgust. "I'd rather get a blow job from a light socket," he snapped, angrily downing his drink in one easy maneuver. Quite the practiced flip; made me wonder how much he put away, and how often.

"Too bad," I sighed, reaching out to touch his arm. He recoiled from my hand and so I slid my body closer to him.

"You can't take no, can you?" Benoit growled, turning to face me and propping an elbow on the polished wood of the bar. "You have to push and push, until you get what you want. Is that what happened? Was Suran Assawaroj something you wanted, and you had to kill her to get her?"

"Why would I do that?" I asked dryly. "I couldn't play anymore, if I broke her. I'm not into necrophilia." I eased away from him, letting him get a more comfortable distance from me. I probably should have continued to play the flirt, but I was running out of the desire to even pretend.

"What an irony," Benoit snorted, the disgust easing a bit. "The dead doesn't fancy the truly dead."

"Irony often makes life interesting."

"Is that what you're supposed to be to me?" he asked, leaning into my personal space a little. There was a glint in his blue eyes that hadn't been there before. Or had I just not seen it? "Interesting?"

This was something new. There was a spark there, and I suddenly wondered if Benoit was a closet blood-chew. It wouldn't be the first time that a man had pretended to be more-virtuous-than-thou while seeking out a roll in the coffin. But there are usually signs of that, more than a sudden change in attitude in a second meeting. I'd seen nothing to make me think that he was anything other than a cop until this little flare of desire. "I'm not supposed to be anything, Detective Benoit," I remarked carefully. "If you find me interesting, that is hardly my doing."

He took another step forward. "Oh, I find you interesting, Sauval," he said, leaning forward so he could whisper in my ear. The fact that this left me within striking distance didn't seem to bother him; all I had to do was twist to the right and dive for his neck. I could make it. He was that close, and I was that fast. I could feel my jaw ache with desire, and I ran my tongue over my canines, a bad habit from my early nights of death. "I find your continued involvement in this case...all the ways you keep turning up, so very interesting," Benoit continued, oblivious to what was going on in my head. "One could even say I'm getting a fixation, with all the times I see you coming up."

I couldn't protest my innocence, not in a way that he'd believe. I struggled for a response, but I was saved by something even more interesting than me. Benoit had eased back a little, looking at me; when he glanced past me, I saw him stiffen. A casual look to my left allowed me to see the group that had just come in the door.

Tall, thick men and beautiful women swarmed around a short, slightly overweight Japanese man. He was dressed at the height of current fashion: a deep purple shirt framed a white tie, and his suit was the color of eggshells. He didn't have the looks to justify that kind of retinue, so he had to have something else that caused people to fawn over him like he was some kind of weird rock star. He was also, I noticed belatedly, a blond.

"Johnny!" Li's shout somehow carried over the music, drawing attention to him and the man at whom he was screaming. Everyone was looking, including Benoit.

Well, crap.

CHAPTER 14

I had expected the plan to have some hitches, but I hadn't counted on Li losing his cool. Gregor was nowhere near him, making it appear that Li was alone. Blond Johnny froze, looking in the direction that the shout had come from; he wasn't concerned or worried, although he did stop moving forward. In other words, Li's shout hadn't bothered him.

It had riled his guards, though. Several of them had jumped to attention at the shout, eyes searching for the source and presumably the danger. Benoit had pushed away from the bar, taking in the tableau immediately. I stood there, unsure what to do and feeling stupid, my eyes moving to Li. He was standing on a table; just as I spotted him, he hopped down and began to walk toward Johnny. Also disturbingly, Benoit's glance at Li was one of recognition. He knew Li, somehow. As Suran's fiancé? I really hoped so.

The drama on the floor continued as I was watching Benoit. Li's intent was clear, and the first bodyguard moved to intercept him. With a sudden, fluid motion Li stepped to the side, catching a grasping hand and twisting it. The bodyguard's arm snapped into a stiff position and he stumbled to his knees, yelping as Li joint-locked him.

In a second, the atmosphere of the room changed. The party mood quickly shifted to hostility; amazing how quickly dancing and sexual tension can turn to violence. Yes, some of the people definitely were scrambling out of the way, recognizing a fight being spawned amongst them. But others had come here spoiling for this very thing.

One person stood up and punched one of the men surrounding Blond Johnny; the guard didn't even flinch. Instead, he just smiled, a wide, lazy grin of amused pity. When the guard returned the punch, he did it with such force and speed that I knew what he was: he was just like me. I'd have to get closer and smell him to know his age but he was certainly dead.

Gregor was suddenly at Johnny's side, reaching for his arm. I think he said something to the human, but my line of sight was blocked as the crowd moved like a gigantic beast. Instantly, Gregor and Johnny were invisible to me, and I took a step, intent on rejoining Li.

A form appeared before me, blocking my path. The tall man was thick and built like a wall; he smiled down at me, the scent of his humanity and his preferred alcohol filling my nose. "Hi. I've been looking for company all night. And you're about right."

What kind of guy thinks that the middle of a fight is the time to pick women up? Oh, wait. He may not be talking about a date. I glanced down at his hands, and sure enough, I saw the glint of something that was probably a needle or skin infuser. The moment he saw me look down, he lunged for me.

I wasn't in any danger, but I did hesitate, trying to figure out how to stop this guy without killing him. It was a matter of necessary force, probably, but I didn't often fight people unless I wanted to kill them. Despite this guy oozing "rapist perv" I wanted to avoid murdering him with a cop in the room. I took a step backwards, and found my back tight against the bar, which probably wasn't the right idea.

Benoit stepped in front of me, his body in a classic shooter's stance. I couldn't see if he actually had a gun, but the guy reacted as if he did. Spinning around, the perv pushed his way into the surging crowd, and was swallowed by the living creature the mass had become. Benoit turned to me, and I saw him tucking a snub-nosed pistol into his pocket as he took me by the arm. "I saw you trying not to hurt him," he shouted down at me, and the look on his face was really weird, like he was sorry about that. Before I could figure out what was going on behind those blue eyes, he'd turned me toward the exit. "Get out of here, before you have to hurt someone."

I nodded, having no intention of leaving, not without Li, anyway. But it seemed to satisfy Benoit, who gave me a little push to propel me toward the door. Agreeably, I headed that way, glancing back to see him shove into the crowd himself, his blond hair glowing in the ambient light. It looked like he was chasing after the creepy man. As a cop, maybe he felt the need to protect and serve, even now.

I had my own urge, and as soon as Benoit was out of sight, I lowered my shoulder and forced my way into the crowd. The stream of people was pushing toward the exit with panicked determination, and it was like walking sideways through a raging river—if a river had shoving arms, kicking legs and a high-pitched wail.

One woman was pushed hard into me and our legs tangled. I stayed on my feet through sheer strength and toughened body; she didn't have such advantages and I felt her leg give around mine. She shrieked and was thrown down; in a second, she was kicked under my feet. I wouldn't normally have any problem staying up, but she threw my shoes sideways and the surging crowd did the rest. With an undignified yelp, I went down too. I lost sight of the woman; I literally couldn't see anything but legs and feet. People were stepping on me and falling over me as I tried to get out of there. I crawled blindly, turning myself perpendicular to the stream. I was tripping people left and right, but I couldn't get up. Drinks rained down around me; I sloshed through a watercourse of spilled booze, sliding ice and plastic cups. The smell of alcohol, blood and fear was suffocating.

I emerged from the river of people in a tumbling sprawl, falling when the pressure of the stampeding humans was no longer holding me up. Glancing up, I saw Li go tumbling from a vicious uppercut delivered by an Asian fighter who was bouncing around like Bruce Lee. Gregor was briefly invisible, then he heaved upward against the people puppy-piling him, like Atlas shrugging. As men and women pooled around Gregor's legs, still grasping at him, I saw the big vampire guarding Johnny well away from the action. The flood of people was starting to dwindle, and I saw Johnny turn and push through the few left, flanked by his dead man. The stairway to the VIP area was right behind them, and I knew that I had to stop Johnny or he'd get into the VIP section and out through another exit.

I scrambled to my feet, ignoring the spectacle I was creating of myself as I surged toward Johnny. The floor was slick, covered with alcohol and worse, but I had lost my shoes and my toes gripped the floor with ease. I managed to dodge around the vampire only because he hadn't seen me until I was nearly past him, and slammed into Johnny. He shrieked as we tumbled to the ground. I had betrayed my nature with my speed, and he knew he was in danger. I wrapped my arms and a leg around him, my face seeking his neck and my fangs bared. I hadn't consciously signaled my lips to pull back or my jaw to distend slightly, giving me room to bite. It was purely instinctive: to take down, grapple and go for the throat, and the comprehension that I wasn't completely in control made me hesitate.

In that moment of self-realization, Johnny's pet vampire grabbed me, his fingers closing on my neck like a vise. His scent rolled over my nostrils, igniting my instincts again as I recognized him as an enemy and about my own age. I released Johnny and twisted my body around, ignoring the discomfort from the clamping hand rolling and pinching my skin. Snarling, I used my left arm as a club to force his elbow to bend while catching his jacket and jerking his body forward with my right hand. I saw his expression register surprise—he wasn't used to fighting someone with his strength and power, or he was just over-thinking everything—just before I bit him.

It was a hell of a bite; all four canines sank into his face. The elation of *biting* something was warring with the voice screaming that I was throwing my safe life away. I didn't have to worry about feeding off of another vampire; we can't subsist on each other, so there was no worry about silly things like feeding laws. I would have to deal with, at most, an assault charge. But I can look really innocent when required; against a vampire who worked for the New-kuza, I was going to look like an angel. That was assuming this got anywhere near the cops, which was unlikely with the New-kuza. In an instant, I had decided: it was a free-for-all, baby, and I was gonna have some fun.

He had reached the same conclusion, or maybe he'd decided not to be a law-abiding vampire a long time ago. With a roar, he tore me off of him, nearly dislocating every finger in my right hand when I refused to release him. I came away with a chunk of dead flesh in my teeth, which was his nose and part of a cheek. I spit the solid hunk back into his face as I slammed my left elbow down on his shoulder, trying to shatter his collar bone. He still had the hand around my neck; it was an easy place to hold, even if it had no effect on my fighting ability. Now his other hand dug into my crotch, tearing through my clothing and bruising skin. With his two-handed grip, he tossed me into the mirror behind the bar.

It was a good move; had I not been luckier than I deserved, he might have sliced a muscle I needed. While I could fight with most types of injuries, rendering one or more muscles useless would screw me. I had a few cuts when the glass stopped falling, but nothing too deep or disabling. But if he felt free to use glass, I'd return the favor.

I stood up behind the bar and grabbed a bottle by its neck. I drew back to put my entire body into the throw, sending the bottle end over end at incredible velocity. It smashed into his chest, showering him with glass and alcohol, but sadly, his jacket and shirt took the worst of it. Growling, he bounded toward me, and I had time to hurl two more bottles, aiming both at his head. The first he ducked, but he stood up into the second, and was graced with a few new cuts in addition to the gaping hole I'd left in his flesh.

As he leapt onto the bar, I smashed the base of the last bottle, giving it a jagged edge. I slammed that edge up into his body before he'd even caught his balance. I cut into his pelvis right between the legs but missed anything important. A human would be out for the count, but nothing vital passed through that region for a vampire, since we don't bleed out. I was still cursing when he caught his balance and smashed his foot into my chest, knocking me off my feet onto the floor. Sneering, he dropped over the edge of the bar onto my body. I heard ribs crack, the bones slashing my internal organs as he landed. I didn't need ribs, but the fact that he was fumbling for a piece of glass was a problem.

The bottle was still in my hand, though shortened from the impact with the floor. I shoved it at him, slashing in a quick double-slice, aiming for his arms. I clipped his left arm enough to make it start to fail. Rearing back, he tested the arm and was able to straighten but not bend it.

His balance was off, and I curled my knees up, shoving them into his butt. Cursing, he tumbled forward, catching himself on his right arm—the arm which I slammed the bottle into with all my strength. The glass sliced, shattered and sliced again, before stopping its progress with a strange squeal. He screamed and jerked backwards, taking the bottle with him. The glass container appeared to be stuck, and his right arm now couldn't curl up to grab it either. He hissed, a sibilant, hair-raising noise and I watched him give himself to the rage. That makes it sound really dramatic, but humans do it too—they become so angry they go a little crazy. That can be bad, but given how much stronger we can be, it gets a lot worse when a vampire gets enraged.

The vampire leapt off of me, coming straight up off his knees. I didn't hesitate; I kicked backwards into a roll, jerking my legs over my head. I got to my feet as he came back down, landing where I had just been. Snarling, he kicked at me, his feet as fast as his fists. Man, if we were reduced to kicking and punching, this would be a long fight.

I had a thought, a way to take him out fast. Normally, the best thing to do against a vampire was to break them down—destroy their ability to move. The slow way was to take out a limb at a time, by severing or destroying muscles. The fast way was to remove them all in one bold move. The problem is that bold moves don't always work well in real life, or don't work at all.

I blocked his leg and stepped inside his kicking-range, twisting and putting my back to him. It looked freaky, like I'd decided to stop fighting and start dancing. His left arm, a touch more functional than his right, tried to wrap around me; I felt more than saw his head drop, moving to bite the shoulder I was offering him. He sunk his teeth in as I wound my arms around his neck and set my feet. I felt him ravage my shoulder as I doubled over and rolled him over my body, ripping his teeth loose. He bit again, his mouth drawing in whatever flesh he could as his now-falling body gained the necessary momentum. When he was most of the way over I reversed my crouch, rising straight up and tightening my grip on his head.

He kicked his feet, trying to catch himself and stop what was happening, but he didn't manage it. Instead, what I was aiming for happened: the energy from the change in direction climaxed in his neck. I felt it snap cleanly; with a grunt of disgust, I dropped my opponent to the floor. He flopped for a moment as he tried to move, but his brain was no longer telling his muscles anything. It was temporary for vampires, but temporary was all I needed.

I took quick stock of myself: crushed ribs that slid and stabbed me internally with each movement; fingers that wiggled with the loose suggestiveness of near-dislocation; and a line of bites that started on the top of my right shoulder and ended at the middle of my upper stomach. Nothing that was going to slow me down, and I turned to assess my companions.

Standing in a small circle of downed bodies, Gregor was flinging one man off of his right arm while a woman clung to his back and a man was trying to shoot him without hitting a companion. I vaulted the bar and body slammed the shooter, knocking the shot wide. A few seconds of tussling and I had the gun; I quickly brought the tail of the grip down on his head, knocking him out.

Gregor was watching me, bemused. The man who'd just been tossed was lying on the floor, holding his back and groaning. The woman was slumped on the ground, unmoving. "Where's Li?" I asked—or rasped. I was shocked by how raw my voice sounded.

"Hhh...here," I heard him pant behind the curve of the bar. Gregor and I followed his voice around the corner to find him pinning our blond target, panting and sweating. Li's scent swirled thickly in the air, elevated by sweat and exertion. I heard Gregor inhale sharply, surprised by something. But there was no time to worry about him; we were in the Core, and the cops would be responding soon.

"Li, we need—"

"I know!" he said, his voice thick, tired and filled with rage. There was a knife in his hand and he pressed it to Johnny's neck. "Now, my daughter! Where is she?"

I guess the interrogation had already begun.

CHAPTER 15

I don't know what you're talking about!" Johnny yelped, trying to crawl into the wall Li had shoved him against.

"Wrong answer!" Li snapped, impressing me with his scary gravelly voice. I wouldn't have been intimidated, but for a human, it was impressive. He was not done making an impression; without missing a beat, he moved the knife, slicing into the curve of Johnny's ear.

The New-kuza man cursed loudly, one hand clapping to his ear. "Stop! You have no idea who you're fuc—"

"I know who you are," Li snarled, leaning into the arm he had over Johnny's throat. "You're Uchida Junichi, Blond Johnny, a *fuku-honbucho* to Terada Hiroharu. But none of that is important because what matters here is *who and what I am*. What you don't know about me is that I'm a father. My baby, my Masako, is just over a year old. You killed her mother, Sunan Assawaroj, because she owed you money. For *that alone* I should kill you! But I'll let you walk if you give me my daughter back. Masako was with her mother when she disappeared. I want to know where my child is!" The last was said in a scream, his arms so tense that they shook.

Johnny said something in Japanese. From Li's expression, it was rude and unhelpful, and Gregor glanced at me. "Misty, you might be of some service here," he said softly.

"Sure, I can break fingers," I answered, stepping forward.

"Something faster," Gregor said, tilting his head. His dark eyes caught mine in a meaningful glance.

I sighed. A lot of people were unnerved by a vampire feeding on them, and the experience varied based largely on the subject's personal preferences: someone who liked pain would enjoy being fed on more, as an example. There were a lot of dominance and submission issues that feeding could trigger as well. There were people who enjoyed the sensation, but they were in the minority. Gregor was asking me to test Johnny and find out. If he was one who didn't like being fed on, I could break him faster.

"No, I've got him," Li proclaimed. He lifted the knife so that it was level with Johnny's face. "The next one takes your eye."

"Just threaten his balls," Gregor said, looking bored. "Humans prize those."

"I do know how to torture someone," Li snapped, sounding almost offended that Gregor was offering advice. The knife crept closer to the New-kuza's eye. "Just tell me where my daughter is, or they'll be calling you *One-eyed* Johnny."

"A plane!" Johnny barked, his eyes crossing as he tried to watch the blade threatening him.

"Where?" Li snarled; Johnny waited too long to answer, and Li made a quick slash that struck just over his right eye. Screaming, Johnny clapped a hand to his face. Gregor nodded with grudging approval as Li hissed, "Tell me!

"An American couple! They bought her! Their plane leaves tonight!" Johnny cried, shaking. He was sweating copiously and seconds away from needing a new pair of pants. I was unimpressed. The New-kuza just couldn't match the Yakuza for verve and balls. That's what happens when you recruit spineless bullies.

"Names and flight numbers, please," Gregor said, his voice calm and even.

"Their name was Sanya! Lap Sanya! His wife was white, with an American accent—a red head! He never said her name!" Johnny babbled, bloody tears pouring from under his hand. "I didn't ask anymore than that!"

"He's telling the truth," Gregor said.

"You sure?" Li asked.

"As sure as I can be without several hours in which to work. Honesty has a special ring when utilized by the desperate."

Li nodded and releasing the sobbing man, allowing him to sink to the floor. "We need to get to the airport," Li said, pushing past us. He had that determined look on his face again, the steel-hard look of absolute action.

Gregor nodded and followed; I paused and glanced down at the man trembling and sobbing on the floor. He'd rebuild himself. He'd rationalize that no one had seen him like that but us, and he'd order us killed. When we were dead, he'd tell himself that it hadn't really been like that; that he hadn't broken quite so bad. And without us around to remind him, it'd be the truth in time. It's what his kind always did. I should kill him.

But I didn't. It wasn't mercy or pity or any of those virtues that stopped me; it was the simple knowledge that I didn't want his blood on me, that killing him would cross a legal line that I wasn't willing to cross—yet. A pitched fight, where I'd wrestled with someone trying to kill me, was one thing to a court; slaughtering a sobbing man in cold blood because I was afraid of what he would do was another. And if the court didn't get me, the New-kuza would have to; Johnny alone might be able to rouse some arms against me, but he could gain more soldiers dead than alive. I'd be either arrested, deported and killed, or just killed. I might have gotten away with it, but I wasn't sure I could.

The aero was idling quietly in front of the club, waiting for us. None of us wasted any time scrambling through the choppy air to climb into the back; the shrill call of the police sirens was already shredding the night. The second Gregor's foot cleared the ground the aero rose into the air. None of us enjoyed the ride; we all turned to peer out the back window, watching to see if the cops would spot us. The first police aero was nosing around the curve of the block as we went into our turn. Another couple of minutes of tense watching passed before we sank into our seats, sagging with relief.

"The airport," Gregor said; I hadn't seen him press a button which allowed him to speak to the driver, but I did see him release it before settling back in his seat. Despite being the last one in the car, he had the rear-facing seat all to himself; Li and I were sharing the longer seat. Honestly, though, I didn't want to touch anything or anyone. I was covered in blood and beer. I really wanted a shower even as I knew there was no time for that. At least I could change back into my clothing, instead of the rags to which my dress had been reduced. I thanked my lucky stars that I hadn't paid for it.

"Not to annoy," I started as I grabbed my previously

discarded clothing, "but are we sure we can get the baby from the people who have her?"

"She was sold illegally," Li pointed out quietly. As I tugged the dress off, he turned and looked out the window. "If they give us a problem, I'll remind them of that."

"You may still have problems," Gregor pointed out evenly. He didn't appear to have just come from a fight; while Li and I had both ruined our clothing, he was just sitting there without a wrinkle, stain or mark. I hated him for a second. "I'm sure they have some proof that the baby is theirs, or something that seems legal. Otherwise, they couldn't fly out. And while the police may hold them, there will be a lot of questions about what you have been doing."

"They won't know about that." Li sighed at the answering look that Gregor gave him. "You think they'll find out?"

"I think that I'll be shocked if airport security doesn't have our descriptions by the time we arrive."

Li slumped, elbows resting on his knees. Despite his distraction, he remembered to not look up at me as I changed. "Okay," he said after a long, quiet moment filled only with the sound of me stripping out of the remnants of clothing. "Your suggestions were great last time, Gregor. What do we do now?"

He was quiet; I pulled on my bra, wincing at the sticky feeling on my skin. "Anything that I have thought of would take too much time to set up," Gregor finally answered, crossing one slim leg over another. "I think that the two of you should just walk in." He held up a hand to stave off our protests. "They'll be looking for three well-dressed people. Two who have changed their clothing—and changed so rapidly—will be harder for them to note."

"Why not three?" The panic in my voice was just noticeable; so what? I didn't want to go into this without Gregor; we'd never have made it out of the Tiger Club without him, and we might need him again.

Gregor was quiet, and his expression was somber, even more so than usual. "They will be looking for three," he said, his voice broadcasting his reluctance with the idea. "Two will be better. Li must go. And this is your affair, Misty, not mine. So you two should go without me. I can spare this." He pulled a device out of a pocket next to the seat; it looked like an over-sized pager, something I hadn't seen in a *long* time. "This is a security jammer. It interferes with the signals on a digital security camera. They won't be able to capture your images when you use this. It also messes with other security and wireless devices, so be careful about where you activate it." With quick fingers, he showed me how to turn it on and off.

"So me, a human, and a camera jammer," I stated, feeling the dread in my stomach. It didn't seem like enough, to be honest.

"Sounds crazy," Li said with a sardonic laugh. "I'm in." In a sudden motion, he grabbed the sleeves of his jacket and pulled his arms loose. Or he started to; he hissed suddenly and froze, his face twisting with pain.

"Are you hurt?" I asked, turning to him as I got my shirt down over my head.

Li nodded, his face tight. "Just some bruising. Jacket took the worst of it." Taking a deep breath, he finished shedding the jacket.

I saw a new cut, under his arm; it was still seeping a little. "Not just bruising," I said. Glancing at Gregor, I asked, "I don't suppose you have a first aid kit."

He reached under his seat and slid out a box. "Just gauze and tape, I'm afraid."

"I remember when this was the stuff everyone used," I muttered, taking the plastic box.

"I remember when that was the new thing," Gregor replied, his smile mocking and crooked. Yeah, he seemed to be the kind who liked one-up games, so long as he was the one up.

"If there's any left, I'll redo your arm," Li offered as he carefully pulled off his dress shirt in a quick movement that left him gritting his teeth tightly.

I glanced at the bandage covering the sunburn, only to find it was gone. It had come off during the fight and I hadn't even noticed. "I'm sure getting soaked in beer didn't help it," I said, shrugging. "I wore it because open wounds freak humans out, not because it was at risk of infection."

"What about those bites I saw?" Li asked as I positioned his arm to take another look at the cut. His lean torso was bruised with yellow and purple blemishes and criss-crossed with blue skin glue from the first time I'd patched his wounds. Unwinding the gauze, I leaned closer, wishing I had a first aid kit for humans. Gauze wouldn't numb the area, or disinfect it, but maybe that would be for the best. Maybe it'd slow Li down, keep him from getting hurt worse. He was in great shape, but the human body can only take so much.

It was dark in the aero but that wasn't as big of a problem for me as a human. I still had to get my eyes within inches of his skin before I got my first real look at the wound. That look chilled me as I saw it wasn't a cut; it was a graze from a bullet. I swallowed hard as I realized just how much danger my new human was in, and then again when I realized that my thoughts toward Li were proprietary. That was disconcerting.

"The same," Gregor answered for me, as I was too distracted to reply. "She won't catch anything, though bandaging will shield them from more damage. It's much more imperative to stop you from losing...blood."

The emphasis he'd put on the last word startled me; I shot a look at Gregor, trying to decide what it meant, if anything. He looked the same; calm, collected, utterly in control. "My bites are fine," I said, not sure what else to do but turn back to Li's side and continue working. I carefully taped over the bullet wound as I added, "I would like to get some bandages for my ribs, though. They keep moving around."

Li stared at me speechless; Gregor picked up the shredded dress and said, "If we remove the skirt and...breast-part, it will constrict your ribs nicely."

"The cups?" I asked, partly relieved to find something he didn't already master. I ran my hands over Li's skin lightly, looking for other open cuts. I could feel that the skin glue from earlier was holding firm, so far; I might have to replace it later if a bruise swelled enough to rupture the glue's seal.

"Yes. The fabric acts as a pseudo-corset," Gregor said. "If you turn it into a tube, it will suffice for now." A real grin played over his lips. "Wouldn't Estellen be mortified?"

I chuckled as I leaned away from Li, satisfied that I had done a decent patch job. "Probably," I agreed, taking the dress from him and starting to rip it apart. Beside me, Li was struggling out of his pants, cursing softly. I smelled fresh blood and glanced at him; he had a scrape on his leg that oozed blood. Without me asking, he turned so that I could reach the wound. I worked quietly, feeling him watching me. When I was done bandaging, I locked eyes with him and asked, "What?"

He was startled by my directness. To his credit, he could have fumbled and bumbled, trying to work around the truth; instead, he answered, "I'm just...I wish I could have your ability to ignore damage."

I shrugged. "It has its downsides," I reminded him, tapping my half-melted skin. "Sure, being a vampire can be cool, but it was a lot cooler before we were outed." I tucked my shirt into my jeans.

"I bet," Li said, smiling faintly. The aero landed with a soft bump and the smile disappeared as he grimaced with pain.

"Sir?" The intercom made me jump. "We're at the airport station."

I glanced out the window, peering through the tinted glass to see the elevated cable car that would carry us all the way out to the airport, which rested on the Outer Ring. It wouldn't take long; this car would be an express, no stops until we got there.

"We ready?" Gregor asked, quirking an eyebrow. I put my hand on the latch, ready to open the door.

"Once I have my pants on, please," Li quickly said, a note of panic in his voice.

Gregor and I just exchanged looks. *Humans,* it said, *what a bunch of prudes.*

CHAPTER 16

Li didn't say anything as we walked side-by-side through the blue-and-chrome airport. We didn't need to say much; we'd whispered out a quick plan on our walk. Our options were slim. The police might or might not assist us; like all criminal organizations, the New-kuza had bought off some of the cops. Li was unwilling to take the chance that calling them for help might not be helpful at all. So no cops, no Gregor, no backup—just him and me and a magic pager. If I could sweat, I'd be dripping right now. Li appeared to be sweating for both of us.

I had the camera-blocker off as we passed through the first round of security. I wasn't sure if it would affect metal detectors, as Gregor hadn't said. I was taking no chances as we waited our turn to be scanned. The woman ahead of us was squat and blonde, her voice loud as she chattered on her phone to her friend. She was talking about her cousin's venereal disease as if it were the newest Robert Gorman movie. She managed to describe in exquisite detail the exact symptoms her cousin had complained of before security made her turn off her phone. Li looked about ready to vomit as he tapped an impatient foot. Then it was our turn.

"Turn off all cell phones, remove all metal from your pockets," the guard intoned, holding out a plastic basket for our items. Li turned out his pockets. I had one moment to wonder if Gregor's magic pager was going to draw attention before I dumped it into the basket with the coins from my pocket and my phone. The guard didn't even look at it; he put the basket on the shelf on the other side of the metal detector and waved me through. I felt tight muscles relax as I cleared the machine without incident.

"Hard part's done," Li said, looking around at the shops

lining the hallway.

"First hard part," I muttered back, tugging at my hastily-braided pigtails and trying not to look as conspicuous as I felt.

He tapped my arm and motioned to a store. I followed him into a coffee shop and watched as he selected a Gideon Atoms hat. After paying for it, he tugged onto his head. I saw why immediately: it changed the profile of his head, hid all his wild hair and would hopefully help disguise him. All I had were my pigtails.

"There're only three flights to America in the next two hours," Li said, pointing at a Departure Board. "We can check all of those before they leave." He didn't add that the couple's flight may have already left. I wasn't sure what he'd do if that was the case, if his daughter had already been stolen across the sea. But more terrifying was the fact that I couldn't answer what should have been a simple question: would I go to America to help him? I should have been able to just say no. America was full of people who knew how to spot me and would enjoy killing me—a lot. It was a horrible idea for me to go there, and yet I couldn't tell myself that I wouldn't, not if Li asked for my help. Screwed, screwed, I was so screwed and I had no clue why.

Thrusting those unpleasant thoughts aside was an effort but I needed to focus. The airport was a long, straight building with few branching hallways; one side of the central corridor was lined with kiosks while along the other side ran the boarding areas. The boarding areas were separated from the hallway by a clear barrier that rose about twelve feet, with three boarding areas per division. The runways outside the floor-length windows that formed the far wall of the boarding area ran parallel over the rest of the tile, stretching right and left. Beyond the last runway, the sea foamed and frothed, a black mass untouched by the stars above.

I got the feeling it should have been bustling, alive with people and traffic. Instead, it was nearly dead. It was pretty late now, and that was probably the reason, but it still made me nervous. Crowds would make it easier to hide and lose pursuers; without their cover, I felt naked. I wasn't worried about witnesses, to be honest; people make terrible eyewitnesses, generally.

There was a cluster of men and women in the hallway, dressed in jeans and casual shirts. They were mostly Asian, with a white girl and two black men thrown into the mix. If they weren't somehow related to the New-kuza, I was going to feel bad about racial profiling. At first glance, they appeared to be just a group of friends, chilling in the airport, waiting for a flight to arrive. But they all had hard faces, with pinched eyes and permanent scowls. All they needed were the neon lights over their heads pointing and saying, *BADASSES*.

We walked past them, moving briskly. Look, just a couple of people hurrying to meet a plane, nothing to see, move along. I subtly scented the air while watching to see if one of them did the same. But if someone else inhuman was sniffing for smells, I failed to see them. I could feel some of them studying me; did one just point at us? My fangs began to ache, anticipating my need for them; I fought it back. There was no reason to get hot-in-the-tooth over what might be nothing.

"They just flashed a gang sign," Li said, turning to look at me with a little smile. His statement and his expression didn't match at all, and I had a moment of confusion before I realized that he was trying to pretend we were talking about something else. All they'd seen was the back of my head, or else I would have given us away.

"What kind?" I asked, schooling my face from something pissed or afraid to something more casual.

Li shrugged, still giving me that soft smile. "I don't know. It could be New-kuza; it has a certain similarity to a Yakuza sign."

I gave him a look that was part curious and part skeptical. "How do you know Yakuza hand signs?"

Li shrugged. "We all were someone before coming to Gideon."

I probably should have kept my mouth shut. "Were you a *Yakuza* someone before Gideon?" He had told Gregor he was running, that he'd left them. I thought he'd meant he'd left Japan but was it the Yakuza he'd really run from?

He shrugged again, his expression becoming strained. "Can we talk about this later? Around ten till never?"

I paused to stare at a shirt for sale in a kiosk; it was pink baby doll shirt with a neon green test tube on it; black letters said, "100% Certified Sexy by Gideon's Government Labs." Cute. I might have worn something like that, in another life.

Turning as if to look at the next item in the store display

window, I snuck a peek back at the crowd of hard-faced youth. They were still watching, milling, like sharks who knew that the chum bucket was coming. Most were watching the entrance; one was watching us openly. Great.

"Done shopping?" Li asked, and I glanced at him. He was angry, and I realized how it must have looked: he'd refused to answer my question, so I'd deliberately ignored him.

Rolling my eyes, I stepped away from the window and took his arm, leading him further away from the watching sharks. He stiffened, so that his arm pressed my hand into his side. "Li, I was checking to see if that group of people had noticed us, using the reflection," I told him, smiling at him with as much fake sweetness as I could manage. It couldn't be much. "The window shopping was a ruse."

"Right," he said, looking abashed. "That's the second time I've doubted you. I gotta stop doing that."

Acknowledgement that he was wrong; almost as good as an apology. Almost. "Yes, you do. We're just getting to know one another, but here's a clue. I don't lie well, so I try not to. Also, I'm not going to forget why we're here. Not when it's this important." I glanced into the first boarding area as we drew even with it, looking for a woman with red hair.

"Hey." His voice was soft and strange; it pulled my attention back to him. Li smiled at me; it was a real smile this time. "Okay, I'll remember that," he answered, putting his warm hand over mine. "I won't forget what you've done."

"I know, and I won't forget that you were in the wrong—"

The scream came from ahead of us, the shrill cry of an angry child. Li jerked upright, like a hound going on scent, his ears catching something as ethereal as a vampire catching a whiff of blood. I stood on my tiptoes, peering down the corridor, and I just saw a red head bobbing ahead of us, stepping out of a bathroom. "Hey!" Li shouted, but she was too far away. Cursing, he broke into a run.

"Li!" I shouted before engaging in some cursing of my own and dashing after him. This was *not* the way to avoid detection. Reminded of our toy, I flipped the switch as I ran, praying it worked as advertised.

Without any crowds to bar our way, we ran unimpeded,

gaining on her. But she didn't have far to go; we saw her turn—and there was a child in her arms—as she walked into a boarding area.

Li didn't slow as he approached the barrier—and a barrier it was, a Plexiglas door, set in the Plexiglas wall. The guard saw a man running toward him, yelling, and he did the sensible thing. He leaned into the door and threw the bolt, locking us out. "Hey!" Li shouted, pounding on the door. "Hey, let me in! That's my daughter!"

I looked past him; the woman was standing with a Thai man. She hadn't seen us; he had, and the look on his face made it clear that he had immediately deduced the situation. He stood and put an arm around his wife, leading her toward the boarding gate. Li saw them and redoubled his efforts; he must have looked like a madman.

We were running out of time. I jumped into the air, catching the top of the barrier. People started, then recoiled as they reconciled my easy movements with my species. Li jumped next to me, but he wasn't able to get any height, and it only magnified what I was able to do. While he used the closed door as a rough ladder, I pulled myself over the barrier, clearing the eight-foot gap between the top of the semi-wall and the ceiling in a powerful rush.

Grinning, I tumbled over, flipping so that I landed on both feet. Both of my targets were aware of me now; she was running toward the gate, as if the plane was home in a strange game of tag. Mistake. I'm a predator, and a running person equals dinner getting away on an instinctual level. There was no hesitation as I darted after her.

A row of interlocked chairs blocked my path, but that was nothing. I ran to them and leapt on the back of the chairs with perfect balance, feeling power and strength that I hadn't allowed myself to experience since coming to Gideon. I'd been afraid—afraid to unleash myself, afraid to act, afraid to *be*. And now, free from cameras, free from restrictions, I flew.

Not literally of course. But I'd bet money that some witness would later claim that I had done just that. I leapt quite far, naturally, but it was just a leap. I landed on top of the stewardess' console, causing one wide-eyed woman to shriek and cower behind the desk. I barely noticed her; my eyes were on the prize, the woman with red hair. I'd reached the console just ahead of her and the Thai man.

My fangs were showing again, but I didn't falter. I could control myself, I would control myse—

I slipped when I stepped on the computer monitor and it tilted. I was falling before I could stop, and then I didn't want to stop, because I was going to make it work for me. I fell between the Thai man and the woman, shoving him to the ground and wrapping my arm around her and Masako, clinging to both. She didn't fall immediately, but my weight was too much. Vampires are denser than humans and she really didn't have a chance, especially when I kicked against the console as I fell past, pushing my weight against her with more force. With a sobbing scream, she tumbled backwards; I pinned Masako to her chest and hoped.

As we fell, I caught scent of the child, and I found myself suddenly emboldened, like I had been when I'd met Li. It was a giddy, reckless feeling, like a high. It was mingled with the spike of fear from the woman, which didn't help my determination not to eat her.

I was first to land, as planned, using myself as a cushion, though the consideration was all for Masako, not the woman. The red-headed American landed on top of me, and I felt my ribs crack and break further. It didn't hurt, not really, but it would take that much longer to heal. Masako landed last; both of us were holding her tight. It didn't slow her screaming at all.

The man, Lap, rose over me, shouting with rage. I think he said something, but it was incoherent. The savage kick to the side of my head was clear, however.

I twisted, rolling his wife to the side, keeping my arm stiff around Masako. It meant I had my left arm pinned, but I didn't care; I twisted back, putting my hips into it and kicking high with my left foot. I caught him in the stomach and knocked him backwards, giving me some breathing room.

I rolled over the woman, keeping my arms locked so that I didn't crush either of the two humans. One brave man, a stranger, rushed forward, reaching for us, but I hissed at him. My fangs were prominently displayed and he backpedaled madly, yelping,

"Vampire!" That triggered a chain reaction in the crowd; even though they'd known, seeing my fangs made it more frightening.

The woman whimpered and clutched Masako; this must have been a nightmare for her. But I didn't care; she wasn't Li and so she wasn't important. I heard a familiar tempo of running feet; his scent swirled around me as he knelt at my side, reaching for his daughter. The second she saw him, there was no doubt this was his child. She reached for him, even though she was still screaming. Good, we didn't assault the wrong red-head with an adopted baby.

"My baby!" the woman cried, clutching her; I grabbed her wrists and pulled her arms open. Li scooped his daughter up into his arms, cradling her to his chest, his eyes fluttering shut as he murmured, "Shhh, shh, Masa...Daddy's here. It's ok."

I rolled up and knelt next to the woman, holding her as she tried to grab for Masako again. Quickly, I glanced around the room, assessing the situation. People stood around uncertainly, but soon they'd gather themselves and react.

Something slammed across my back, jarring me. I rose and spun around, shaking off the attack without effort. Lap dropped the cane he'd been holding and stumbled backwards as I hissed again. "She's not yours!" I shouted.

"She's mine," Li said, his voice thick. I glanced over my shoulder to see him talking to the woman, the would-be mother. "They killed her mother, and sold her to you, illegally. I never consented to the adoption."

"No," the woman said, but it was the heart-broken sound of someone losing a dream.

"You!" The cry brought both our heads up as the sharks filled the now-open doorway. "Get them!"

"Misty!" Li cried, and it was a plea of desperation. He couldn't fight, not with Masako in his arms; it was all on me. Time to improvise. I took two steps to the side and grabbed a length of interlocking chairs by their metal frame. With a grunt, I flung it at the doorway, forcing the goons to fall back. All of them made it save one, who was caught between the barrier and the chairs. He took it in the gut and slumped over the chairs, moaning.

I spun and grabbed the next row of chairs at the end and at the quarter-point mark on the frame. I swung it like a battering ram, aiming at the floor to ceiling window looking over the tarmac. The chairs slammed into it perfectly, fracturing the glass with a terrible crack. I swung again and released the chairs, and they soared through the window, opening a hole and crashing onto the ground below. The cold night air roared into the gap, and people screamed as some of the glass rebounded into the room, shattering on the floor. Outside, in the plane once bound for America but now not going anywhere, I could see the pilots peering dumbfounded at the chaos before them.

"Give me Masako!" I shouted to Li, and he only hesitated a second before he passed her to me. She cried and clung to him, but she wasn't near as strong as me. As I cradled her in my arms, I was hit again with that strange sense of fascination for her. There wasn't time to analyze the feeling; the sharks were approaching.

I leapt out the window, falling into the darkness below and hoping Li would follow.

CHAPTER 17

All the lights at the airport tilted up, with most of the other light blocked by the darkened plane, creating a spot of near blackness below the window. For a second, it was like I fell forever; then I saw the asphalt of the concourse, and I had just enough time to brace. *About twenty feet,* I decided, even as I landed, my body shuddering from the impact before I went limp and rolled. Normally, I would have rolled forward, dispersing the force of the fall into my arms, but there was Masako to worry about. So, instead, I rolled backwards, tumbling into a rough somersault, locking my arms around her. I would have been fine, except for the glass.

It cut up and into me, slicing through my back. I gasped as I finally felt pain, finally had real damage being done to me. I continued through the roll, landing on my knees, shudders passing through my body. Masako screamed and wiggled against me, fighting to get away from me. I held her as gently as I could, afraid to put her on the glass-covered ground.

Li landed in front of us, falling forward into his own roll, tumbling twice before coming to rest on his back. I heard him grunt as he landed, and for a long moment after he stopped rolling, he lay still. Then I heard him say, "Masako," and he stumbled to his feet to tend to his crying daughter. As he took her from me, he glanced at me with concern. "Are you okay?"

I stood slowly, feeling wobbly. Fighting would be iffy now, because I couldn't move my torso easily anymore. The glass had severed something important. "Maybe."

Above us, we heard voices: "Are they there?" "Can you see them?"

"We need to go," Li said, and for once he was the strong

one, pulling at my arm while holding Masako with his other arm. Nodding, I turned to follow, and pain lanced up my back. Humans get adrenaline and shock to make stuff like this better. I had no such advantages; my dead body didn't produce nerve-numbing hormones. "What's wrong?"

"Glass," I gasped, not sure how I was standing upright. "It cut something. I think it was something I need."

He stepped behind me. "Oh, fu...fudge. It's still there."

"Yank it," I gasped. "Can't let it cut anything else."

"What if I break it off in you?"

"Don't." I felt his hand fumble at my back; then there was a blaze of pain and a tugging sensation. I gasped and dropped to my knees, proud that I hadn't screamed.

"I think I got it in one piece," I heard him say before he flung the glass away. "You okay?" I nodded and glanced up at him. "Can you run?" Li looked concerned.

I pulled my arm away from him and took a step, and another. It hurt unless I tensed up my back and moved with a stiff gait. Despite that, I nodded. "Yeah. I'm good. Let's go." He looked at me with doubt in his eyes but things were too dire to argue about this.

I let him run first. I didn't want him to see me faltering. I'd been the strong one until now. I jerked into a rough, shambling run behind him. Walking had hurt; running was constant pain. But I persisted because I knew it wouldn't kill me.

Li ran down the tarmac, rushing toward an opening in the side of the building. I wondered if he knew where he was going, or if he was just running. I didn't care. I just wanted to get the running done so that we could rest.

The opening in the building led to the baggage area; a luggage carrier zipped past us onto the tarmac, making Li jump to the side. I staggered to a stop next to him, resisting the urge to lean against him. "Where to?"

Li looked into the bright area, at the busy workers loading and sorting suitcases and bags. "Hey!" Li and I glanced toward the voice. A man with nice slacks and a dress shirt was walking toward us. "You can't be down here!"

"How do we get out?" Li asked, speaking loudly enough to be heard over his crying daughter.

"Take those stairs up to the concourse—"

I cut him off with a shake of my head. "Not. Happening." My voice was tightly clipped, and I made an effort to speak more smoothly. "Got a back way outta here?"

It was his turn to shake his head. "This is a restricted area. Leave or I'll call secur—"

I leapt, clearing a distance that I shouldn't have been able to manage, landing in front of him. The landing made my back flare with pain again, but was worth it for the guy's girly scream and pathetic attempt to flee. Grabbing him by the collar, I snarled, "I'm having a very, very bad day. I want to go home, have dinner and fall into a coma until it's no longer today. So tell me how to get out of here!" Shaking, the man silently pointed toward a hallway. I patted him on the cheek. "Thanks."

It was just a normal hallway, which turned to the right and tilted upward slightly. Even at this hour, people were coming and going, most of them wearing uniforms from various departments in the airport. Li and I sprinted down the hallway, ignoring the odd looks we were getting as we ran. The man had to have called security, and they'd be after us soon.

We took the right turn and came to stairs; groaning, I started to climb as Li paused to shift Masako. I was three steps ahead when security forces appeared at the top of the stairs.

"Freeze!"

I stepped to the right automatically, putting myself in front of Li and Masako. Anything that security would use in this situation wouldn't hurt me too much, not even the guns they were starting to brandish. "Put down the hostage, and face the wall," the lead guard ordered, his voice commanding and firm.

"She isn't a hostage!" I protested, scowling at him.

"She's my daughter!" Li snapped at the same time. I doubt we were very clear.

Pounding feet behind us made me turn and glance, quickly. I immediately cursed; the sharks had found us. Grabbing Li's arm, I pulled us over to the wall, pressing him to it and flattening myself over him.

"Stop where you are!" the guard ordered the New-kuza, but the leader of their group just smiled.

"I don't think so," he said, pointing at us. "They have

something of ours."

"She's not yours," I retorted. "She's a person. You can't own her." That's right. I was relentlessly painting them as the villains here. If I could have figured out a way to make it sound credible, I would have accused them of wanting her for their stewpot.

The leader rolled his eyes, putting his entire body into it, twisting and turning. Too late, I saw that the eye-roll had been a cover for him; he'd pulled a gun as part of the smooth motion, and he had it pointed at me. "Come on, Ebony," he coaxed. I saw one of his black gang-mates turning a glare on him. "Step away; we'll turn you over to Connor, and you'll walk with a slap on the wrist."

"Put the gun away!" the guard shouted. At least the guards' guns were all pointed at the sharks now. Yay for being unarmed.

Alpha Shark shot him. There was no warning, beyond the shift of his gun to the new target, no polite statement of intent. Just boom. And that was only the first shot.

Li and I didn't wait for the outcome. We had both gone into a crouch at the shot, him shielding Masako, me shielding him. As the gunfire roared around us, impossibly loud in the stairwell, we shuffled up the stairs. We must have looked ridiculous, like some kind of human crab who had found a vampire shell. I'm sure Masako was still screaming—she hadn't stopped since I'd seen her—but I couldn't hear anything.

A bullet hit me in the side, punching into my torso. I ignored it; a small caliber bullet would punch a hole in me, but it was unlikely to kill me. Well, one bullet by itself; several of them at once would probably screw me up. Regardless, it was better for a lot to hit me than a lot to hit Li.

At the top of the stairs, the guard closest to us spun and pointed her gun at us, telling us to freeze, I think. I still couldn't hear anything other than the howling explosion of firing guns. She was in our way, and I lunged at her, faster than she could follow. Grabbing her face shield, I yanked downward on it, sending her tumbling down the stairs. The gun fell at my feet, and Li snatched it up.

I had no idea what he planned, but he handled the gun well. Pointing it at the next guard who seemed to be taking an interest, he forced him back through sheer bravado. The guards stopped worrying about us at that precise moment, because the New-kuza jerk with the big gun had arrived. As Li and I cleared the top of the stairs, he kept a good bead on the guard. Then we were in the clear, running for the doors at the end of the hall, hoping that no one shot Li or Masako.

We staggered through the doors at roughly the same time, dropping to our knees. Li recovered and started to push the doors shut immediately; I tried to help, but was more leaning than pushing by the time the latches clicked. It was only when we were safe that I looked to see where we were.

It was outside the airport, at the cable car station; we must have found the employees' exit. The two women at the shelter were watching us with wide eyes, and I realized we looked awful. Both of us were bloody and sagging with pain. Li was sweating and panting; I was barely upright. Masako was reduced to silent, hiccupping sobs into her father's shirt, which had a noxious-looking white stain on it. "You have vomit on your shirt," I said.

"What?" Li shouted at me before pointing at his ear. "Can't hear you. They're ringing."

I pointed to his shirt. "VAH-MIT!" I shouted.

"Agh, she threw up," Li groaned, still too loudly. "Too much bouncing around. Here, please, for a moment. I *need* to get this shirt off before I throw up."

I took Masako, cradling her against my body. It was my first chance to take a good look at the tiny bit of flesh that had caused so much trouble. She was still crying, but she had lost her voice. She was cute, with a tiny round face that remained Asian without declaring any one heritage. Dark eyes squinted up at me and short, black hair stuck straight up, as messy as her father's. "Hi," I said, smiling hopefully. Masako just looked more freaked out at my greeting. She hiccupped, and I realized that my hearing was recovering.

Li was folding his shirt so that the vomit was on the inside when something tried to open the door. "Hold it!" he shouted needlessly; I was already shoving myself against the door.

"We need to brace it!" I shouted.

"How? I don't see anything! Wait, got it!" Spinning, Li quickly used the dirty shirt to tie the handles together. It wouldn't hold forever, but hopefully long enough.

"Come on, we can't wait for the car!" he shouted, taking Masako from me.

I nodded, even as I glanced up the rail, hoping to see it coming. To my shock, I could see the lights on the car as it sped down the rail. "Li!" I shouted as I caught his arm and pointed.

Li broke into a grin and laughed, "Someone loves us."

"And it's about time," I chuckled in return, falling into step next to him as we headed for the station. The two women already waiting shrank against the far wall; I ignored them as I dug out the fee. The silver, pill-shaped car slid into the station, coming to a smooth, hissing stop on its magnetic rails. After a moment, the doors opened, and several people climbed out, most dragging luggage and clutching tickets. Travelers, all bound for somewhere else. I envied them their freedom, for that moment before my life required my full attention again.

This car only served the airport, so it was empty as we climbed aboard. Li and I handed over our money as we stepped in, paying the bored operator, who didn't even blink at our appearance. But then, he hadn't seen as much as the women.

Speaking of whom, they were lingering on the platform, already making waving motions. "We'll wait for the next one," the shorter of the two said.

"Probably not safe for you to be here alone, right now," Li said. He shifted Masako in his arms. "I've got my kid with me, and my friend won't hurt you. But the people on the other side of the door...they might." The operator, finally interested in our appearance, glanced at us, then looked at the door, where someone was poking at the knotted shirt. He was wearing a guard's outfit, so hopefully, it would be his buddies on the other side and not the New-kuza. "Come on," Li said again. Slowly, the women got aboard, though they were clearly hanging back from us.

I didn't care. As the car took off again, zipping across the water to the Inner Ring, I sank into my seat. As I did, I felt something grate over one of my ribs. Oh, goodie. I had a bullet to remove later. I doubled over, pressing myself to my knees.

"You seem...Misty, what's wrong?" Li asked.

I sighed, trying not to get angry. I had already told him, and I hated repeating myself. It had been hectic. It had been crazy. He may have forgotten as he tried to get his daughter out of there.

"You know how bullets and beatings and cracked ribs haven't slowed me down?"

"Yeah," Li said, rubbing his daughter's back as he cradled her to him. She'd stopped crying and was sucking her thumb, sniffling occasionally.

"Well, slicing muscles so that they aren't connected anymore does slow me down," I explained. "And because it was real damage, it registers as pain. Lots of it. Along with a bullet that will need to be cut out unless I want to store it in my body long term."

"Do you...what can I do?"

I leaned close to him, trying not to freak out the women any more. "Get me some blood; let me rest," I whispered.

"Done," Li said, nodding. It probably wouldn't be that easy but I didn't have the heart to say so. I just remained curled over my knees, worn out and down.

CHAPTER 18

It was strange to buy blood from someone other than Brad. I had chosen the blood shop that was the closest to Li's place; Brad's was almost half-way around the Ring. Normally, I'd be pickier, but tonight I didn't really care that I didn't know the guy. I was tired and hungry and cut and sore, and all I wanted was dinner and bed. Optimally, that would have been dinner from Brad's, and my bed, but that wasn't going to happen. We'd agreed to stay together, and we didn't have time to get the things Li needed and get to my place. It was risky; they might come at us during the day, but Li assured me that we'd be secure until tonight. I didn't care, so long as it was safe. The healing sleep was pressing on me, and my body kept trying to shut down.

"We're going to my aunt's," he finally admitted, "after we get the baby stuff. Fang and Shu will let us stay there a night."

I raised my eyebrows as I waited for the guy to come back from the back fridge. They were out of O-neg in the front fridge, and I had argued until he'd agreed to go pull some from the back. That I wasn't budging on. "Even me?"

Li sighed and drummed the thumb of his free hand against the counter. "It'll be fine."

"You don't sound completely sure. I mean," I quickly added, seeing a hint of irritation cross his face, "there's going to be a problem if they try to make me leave at high noon."

Li nodded after a moment. "I get what you're saying. I won't let them throw you out; at worst, you may have to hide in the basement."

"I don't care," I said as the man returned with my two bags of dinner. I signed for them and took the plastic bag in which he had stowed them, tossing the handles over my arm. "So long as

137

I can sleep."

"I think we can arrange that," Li agreed.

Slowly, we limped onward. I found myself wishing for Gregor's aero so that I wouldn't have to walk any further. Finally, I could take it no longer. "Li, I have to eat," I said, pawing one of the bags out into my hand. "I'm sorry. I *have* to eat."

"Uh, sure," Li said, tilting his head, his dark eyes glazed with exhaustion. "Sure."

And there it was; even in eyes dim with fatigue, there was that glimmer of morbid curiosity. However, the show wasn't that interesting. I just pulled out the plug on the end of the built-in straw and started to suck it down. And then I didn't care that he was watching.

It was cold, but my stomach was cramping with hunger, and I didn't care that the taste was a bit off due to the lack of freshness. I didn't care that it was thicker than normal, slopping around inside the bag. When it hit my tongue, it was life. Blood's a funny thing. It tasted a little different every time, due to differences in each person. But more importantly, each time it reminded me of a different food. A lot of movies and angst-filled books had us bemoan having only blood, and missing food. I didn't miss food; I *had* food and it was good.

I felt better once I'd sucked the last drop out of the bag. Sighing with pleasure, I felt my stomach ease and untwist. I'd have the second bag later, once I had some privacy and less urgency. I glanced at Li and found him watching me. He didn't appear to be upset, like some people were; it made me wonder about which side of the like-the-bite vs. hate-the-bite fence he fell on. I wadded the empty bag and shoved it into the sack the other one was in, trying to break the mood. It didn't work. "And?" I asked, more to dissipate the weird atmosphere than anything.

"That was weird," he chuckled.

"But not freaky?"

Li shrugged. "It just was. Did you think that after all you've done for me, I'd flip out because you were a vampire and—*gasp*—drank blood in front of me?" He shook his head. "That'd be ungrateful. And I am grateful." He hugged the sleeping Masako a little closer. "Very grateful."

"Will you leave Gideon?" The question had popped out

before I really considered it.

"No," he said immediately. "My family is here. My job is here. I'm not going to be driven off. If they want the money Suran owed them, then I'll repay it. But I won't be harassed."

That's often the last grand statement someone makes before they have a tragic calamity that defies physics but the coroner clears as an accident anyway. But it's not my problem; this has never been my problem, and I need to extract myself. "Say, do you really think we need to stick together?"

The gut-wrenching fear that flashed through his eyes almost made me retract my question, but he was already shaking his head. "No, Misty, you've done enough. I've got it from here."

My head was telling me to take the out and flee, but my heart was shouting at me to stay. My hurt back broke the grid-lock and voted to leave. "You sure?"

He gave me a crooked grin that didn't quite reach his eyes. "Yeah. I'm sure."

"Okay," I said, even as a part of me said it wasn't okay. "Stay safe—do you want my number?"

"That'd be good," Li said, nodding. "I don't have my phone, though."

"You know my address—I'm listed." This was getting more and more awkward, and I had the definite sense that we were rocketing toward a train wreck. "Keep in touch, Li." That was said with the awkward unspoken question: *will you really call me?*

"Sure," he said, in the tone that meant *absolutely, as soon as I can, which we both know means no time soon.* It was just the way things happen; if you don't make an effort to keep someone in your life, they fade away. The question was whether Li and I would make the effort. At this point, I think we wanted to, but he had a kid and a price on him, and I was a vampire. Both tend to put a damper on one's ability to freely socialize. But he gave me a hug and murmured another thank you, and I hoped that we might talk again.

I walked to a tram and took the rail car home, trying to not think about my back or the worry now plaguing me. For a while, I managed to distract myself with the thought of having to go to work with a bad back tomorrow, but I could only muse about that so far before I gave up. And when I gave up on that topic, my brain moved to another. Like why I was so torn up about Li. Or why I'd helped him in the first place. And whether he was safe without me.

I sighed as I glanced out the window, careful not to move my back. It was dreadfully confusing. I didn't make friends like I did with Li. And I didn't risk my neck to save them; I wasn't sure that I would have done all of this for Mal. My choices didn't make any sense to me, but I had chosen them. And I couldn't say I wouldn't make them again, now, just sitting and rationally contemplating it on the seat of the rail car. Nothing of what I had done in the last two nights made any sense, and it was driving me nuts.

But I had no way of fixing it or changing it, and so I just went home, clutching the rest of my dinner. I was going to save it for tomorrow, because I wanted to have Drake check out my injuries and then get some sleep.

That was my plan, anyway. When I walked up to the building's exterior door, a familiar form stepped forward from under the awning. How a man in a business suit can hide so well in the shadows was beyond me. I'd never have managed. "Gregor Richter, Death and Hunter," I said, greeting him formally. He probably would prefer that to "Yo, dude."

"Misty Sauval, Oak and Fire," he replied with a nod.

"What can I do for you, Gregor?" I added a meaningful glance upward. "Will this take long enough that you will require hospitality?" Never put a fellow blood-sucker out in the sun. It was about as taboo as murdering a sibling is to a human.

"I hope not. We want to know about Li."

My eyes narrowed. "We? And know? Know what?"

"Come now, Misty. Are we playing so dumb? You can smell it. He's special. He could be turned."

A surge of protective rage rose in my chest. "I don't play. And you're not nearly old enough to be an elder, so I don't know what you're so excited about."

"My lord will attain the elder power soon," Gregor pointed out, smiling slightly. "And we should all play the games, Misty. The elders are gone. We may be the proverbial children, but those same elders would have suppressed us, held us back. We have an opportunity that no other vampires have had before us—a near-level playing field."

"So what do you want?" I sounded very tired and awfully grumpy. And hungry—don't forget incredibly hungry. I'd gotten two bags for a reason.

"I want a child. I want to continue my line. And I think that's why Mr. Chin smells the way he does—he'd be easier to turn than most humans. That has to be why I feel this drawn to him."

I fought to keep my face clear of surprise. Gregor felt it too? But then, so had Drake, almost certainly—his reaction to Li had been too strange for it to be anything else. The man had met four vampires, and we all felt a tug toward him. Something was up, and if I wasn't careful, I was going to end up with a dead friend. Or a dead me. Both would be very bad, to me at least. "What kind of draw?" Oh, crap, now I *was* playing dumb. It was really annoying, the way that Li could get me to completely change my standard way of doing things.

I was apparently bad at playing dumb, because Gregor shook his head. "Don't play me, Madame I-don't-play. I'm much better at it than you."

That alone made me want to punch him in the face. I restrained myself. "Okay. So you want to turn him?"

"I want to try. But not just yet. Because I'd like you to be the other sire, and you need to gain a bit of age before that. After all, it's only fair, since you saw him first." His smile became a bit dreamy. "Fire and Death—Oak and Hunting...which would be best to give to our child?"

My eyebrows shot upward, a clear tell to him that I was completely shocked. And I was; I couldn't have stopped that eyebrow rise if I'd thought to try. It wasn't the reaction I'm sure he was expecting; I'm sure he thought I'd be thrilled. Instead, I nodded calmly, hiding my panic. If he—or we—tried to turn Li, we'd kill him. "I'd have to gain a lot of age. About four hundred years worth. And you'd have some growing to do, too."

Gregor smiled. "I suspect that in a few short years we could successfully turn him. We have time to think about it."

Yeah. We had time to think about attacking my friend and draining him completely dry. Then Gregor crossed a line, probably one he hadn't known was there. "And if he dies before then, we can check his daughter for the same gift. Does she have the same draw?"

I saw her in a flash—her big, teary eyes and red face. Nuh-uh—there was *no* way I was going to calmly let Gregor do that to Masako. "We have time before we do anything."

"Yes, time," Gregor answered. Both of our phones buzzed a warning—cute, we both had sunrise alarms.

"You need to get going," I said. "You *sure* you have somewhere to go?"

"Yes, I'm staying at a friend's around the corner."

I tilted my head. "You didn't have to camp at my door to wait for me. You do have my number."

He just smiled, and his smile said it all: *I wanted to surprise you.* "Good night, Misty." He didn't wait for a response, but turned and marched away, his back straight and firm.

CHAPTER 19

Given my unease from Gregor's visit, I drank my second bag of blood immediately. In fact, I did it in Drake's room, while he *tsked* over me and prepared for surgery. "You are a *mess,*" he said critically. I'd taken off my shirt and pants, and the array of my injuries was clear.

"Thanks. You're pretty hot, too," I told him wryly.

"Now now," the dark-eyed dwarf chided, "a doctor cannot have that kind of relationship with his patient." He leaned closer to my side. "Hmm, I may have to cut this out."

"Fantastic!" I blurted, taking another long pull on my blood bag. "More to heal."

Drake merely smiled and fetched a scalpel. As I gripped the edge of my chair, he sliced carefully into my side, seeking the bullet. I cursed and snapped insults at him, but held myself still. It only took him ten minutes to find and pluck out the slug, but it seemed longer. "There," he said, straightening and offering me a bit of metal smaller than my pinky.

"So small, and yet it hurt so much," I sighed, taking it from him.

"That is true about a surprising number of things. Small and yet they matter." Drake set aside his tools and peered at me. "So what happened?"

I started to tell my story, only to stop. Drake's words from earlier floated through my mind. "I'll tell you, if you take the information as payment on what I owe."

"Done," he said, looking amused and pleased. "I'll make you an elder yet, child."

"Right," I grunted, and took another swig from the bag of blood. Between drinks, I told Drake what had passed since I last left the building. When I finished, he was quiet and thoughtful.

"Interesting." That was Drake's only comment. I thought of the vampire on top of the GCC and felt a shiver.

"That's it? No insights?" I asked.

"None. Get some rest."

❈ ❈ ❈

I didn't need to sleep, but when I lay down in my bed, I immediately passed out. The next day, I called in, taking advantage of the fact that despite not getting sick, vampires still get sick days. Sometimes, equality works for you. It helps that vamps still need unplanned days off, because if we get bad blood, we'll feel just as bad as a sick human.

I was deeply asleep when I heard someone at my door. I dragged myself out of my healing sleep and glanced at the clock. 4:30 a.m. Groggily and painfully, I rose and went to the peephole. When I saw Detectives Benoit and Criado outside, I groaned. The detectives had their timing down; I would just be getting home from work, were I working. Sighing, I swung my door open. "Morning, Detectives."

"Good morning, Ms. Sauval." Criado smiled at me. "We have some questions that we need you to clear up. May we come in?" Benoit hovered silently behind him, his expression bland and closed.

"Uh, I'm...sure. Yeah. Wait, let me call Rick first. My case manager."

"Of course. Do you want us to remain outside?" Criado was actually polite. I found myself wishing he weren't trying to pin a murder on me.

"Please. I'll be just a moment," I answered before shutting the door. Rick answered immediately when I called. "Rick, those detectives are here. Should I talk with them?"

"That depends. You need someone there? I'm not a lawyer, but I'd be happy to come and offer advice. Serve as a witness. It's your right to have me there."

"Can I make them wait while you come over?" My fingers tightened around the phone; I was still sore and I really didn't want to deal with this right now. Too bad I didn't have a choice.

"Yep." I heard a door close over the line. "I'll be there in thirty. The good officers can ask you whatever they want, but you

144

don't have to answer until I'm there."

We hung up and I opened the door a bit. "Detectives, my case worker is on his way. He'll be here in thirty minutes."

"We'll be back then," Criado said, nodding. Benoit mirrored his partner, still silent.

While I waited for everyone to come back, I cleaned up a little. I started to put clothing into the hamper but bending over was still painful, so I kicked what was left under the futon. The basket of clean clothing and my shoes were pushed into my closet with my feet. I felt too bad to tackle the bathroom; I just closed the door and hoped no one had to use the facilities. Folding my futon into an upright position was beyond my physical abilities; getting the clothing into the hamper had been excruciating. It would just have to remain a bed.

By the time I was done, Rick was at the door. I let him in and directed him to the futon. He glanced at me, his face speculative. "You're not okay," he observed.

"Hurt myself." My voice was rasp of pain. "Don't suppose you wouldn't mind helping me wrestle the stupid futon?"

"No problem," Rick said with a smile. His job didn't technically cover that, but Rick was a good guy.

By the time we'd wrestled the futon into its upright position, there was another knock at the door. I answered it as Rick settled into the futon. The two detectives were waiting just outside the door. Criado was smiling warmly; Benoit was smiling stiffly but politely. I invited them into the room and waited until they were settled. Criado took the futon; Benoit was out of seating options unless he wanted to sit hip to hip with his partner and my case worker. I didn't want to sit between them myself, so we were both standing.

"You have questions for Misty?" Rick was kind enough to start us off once pleasantries had been exchanged.

"Just a few," Criado replied, opening a notebook and preparing his pen.

"What's wrong with you?" Benoit's question caught me off-guard and I looked at him, blinking.

His sky-blue eyes were focused on me. My unease swiftly turned into anger. "What does *that* mean?"

"You're holding yourself oddly," Where my voice had been

heated, his was bland. That didn't placate me; he was being too well behaved. "I'm just wondering why."

I glanced at Rick; he nodded to me. "I hurt myself," I said. "Cut muscles in my back."

"The riot at the club," Benoit surmised and I didn't correct him. "Sorry to hear you were hurt."

I stared at him silently. He'd sounded sincere. "Thanks."

"We'll make this as painless as we can," Criado replied, his voice gentle. "Ms. Sauval, I know you don't normally deal with the nets. But did you notice anything odd before you started working?"

"Nothing." I was wondering when they'd get around to my motive and means. I guess I should just be grateful they hadn't brought out the bright lights yet.

"Any strangers, people who didn't look like they belonged?" Criado's voice was professional and brisk now.

"No." I shook my head.

"When you found the body, was there anything you saw that stood out as unusual?" Now Benoit was asking questions.

"You mean besides the body?" I probably shouldn't have answered like that but pain can make me grumpy

Neither one of them seemed amused at my humor; Rick restrained a smile. "Yes," Criado replied.

"She had a ribbon in her hand that didn't match her dress. It was caught around her fingers, small, slim and pink."

"Hmm. How about at the club? Did you know the Asian man who started the fight?" Benoit switched gears and I was left fumbling mentally behind him for a second.

"Club?"

"The riot at the Tiger," Criado jumped in without warning. "You were there, right?"

"Yeah," I replied. "Look, I was at the bar with Detective Benoit when that started. All I really saw at the start was the guy who threatened *me.*" It was almost true, so I was comfortable with that statement.

"You can press charges, if you'd like." Criado again. His offer seemed sincere.

"You collared the guy?" I asked, turning to peer at Benoit.

"We were there for him." Benoit smiled tightly, looking

quietly pleased.

"That's why you didn't try to stop things?" I asked, quirking an eyebrow.

"Criado saw a vampire, and we were not equipped for that," Benoit replied.

"Gotcha." Human cops can't go toe to toe with vampires without special equipment and maneuvers. Sometimes those don't help. But tactics, equipment and numbers go a long away. Normal cops were instructed to back off and let the Fang Squad handle the situation if a vampire was there. The detectives hadn't been prepared to fight a vampire, so they'd backed off. Sound reasoning.

"Do you want to press assault charges?" Criado asked.

"No." I didn't say it was because I didn't want to fight against an assault charge when the guy couldn't hurt me anyway. "Do you have more questions for me?" There were a lot of questions that they could ask but I tried not to think about that.

"Not at this time." Benoit snapped his phone shut. "We should let Ms. Sauval rest."

He was being way too nice, but it didn't seem prudent to start questioning his civility. "I appreciate that." I mustered a smile for them. I managed to get the two detectives out with a minimum of fuss. "That was easy," I muttered to Rick, leaning against the door jamb. I felt almost weak with relief.

"It was." Rick's eyebrows arched over his eyes in a thoughtful expression. "They weren't questioning you like a suspect. They were questioning you like a witness." He smiled at me. "It's a good sign."

"Yeah." It felt like a really good sign and I wasn't sure I could trust it.

❋ ❋ ❋

The glass must have cut deep, because I ended up taking the next two days as well. I slept through those days and nights, focusing on healing. We heal faster asleep than when we're awake, though we're not sleeping like humans do. We look dead: motionless and cold. And we relive memories; we climb into the past and walk through some aspect of our lives again. This is a mixed blessing, naturally. But for all the bad memories, I'm glad to have a way to hold onto the good, too. Maybe, when I get older, I'll change my mind. But I can't imagine ever regretting the chance to see my fathers again.

On the fourth afternoon after leaving Li to his life, I woke up without any pain in my back. The bite marks were long gone, too; it was as if that nightmare had never happened. I felt like myself again.

I needed to get back in touch with Li, but at the same time, when I wasn't around him, I knew he couldn't talk me into doing anything insane. And if I stayed away, maybe Gregor couldn't find him either.

But there was one thing to do first. I'd woken up with an idea, a thought that wouldn't leave my mind. Maybe I didn't need Li around to talk me into craziness.

It was 5:00 p.m. now, so I had a few hours to prepare. I had the night scheduled off, and I successfully fended off my boss when he called at six to see if I could come in anyway. "I have plans."

"Gosh darn it," Gabe growled. I heard a rasping noise, and I realized that he was rubbing his temple so hard that I could hear it over the receiver. "Misty, we've been short-handed for three nights now. I really need you."

"Sorry. I can't tonight. I'll be back tomorrow, promise." I hung up before he could argue, and checked SunWatch, the program in my phone that displayed the time of sunrise and sunset. I had fifteen minutes to go, and I impatiently waited, listening to Madonna's *Like a Virgin* album. As the first tones of "Material Girl" floated out of my phone, I saw that it was time. Plugging in my earphones, I be-bopped out of my apartment, excited to be on the hunt.

I'd just cleared my block when a hand lashed around my throat. The world blurred in my vision as I was savagely jerked into an alley between buildings and roughly pushed into a wall. The motion didn't hurt but I still felt the strain on my neck and spine. Any thoughts of pain fled when the smell of my attacker rolled over me; it was familiar and frightening. Bridgette lifted me off the wall and slammed my back against it again, her eyes blazing with rage. I would have preferred pain to the fear that gripped me.

"You filthy childling!" Bridgette's voice whipped through the air, trembling with rage. "Sniveling little race-traitor!"

"What!" That insult was enough to anger me and I struggled futilely against the older vampire's strong hand. "I've never betrayed a vampire for *any* reason!"

"Then your pet human did!" Bridgette had drawn her lips back in a snarl; her fangs were bigger than I remembered at this range. My struggles meant nothing to her. "He told the police my name—they have my description. He betrayed me!"

"Li?" I could have kicked myself the moment I said his name. "Why would he go to the police? What we were doing was just as illegal as what you were doing!"

Her dark eyes were shaped like Li's but had none of his warmth as she narrowed them at me. My words were being heard but she still looked unconvinced. Her voice became querulous as she asked, "If not you, then who?"

I snorted. "I have *no* idea who else knew you'd killed Vasyl." I wasn't sure this was wise but I wanted to know the truth. "What is your part in all of this? Are you working for the New-kuza?"

Her pretty lips twisted into a sneer. "I have nothing to do with food."

"You didn't have anything to do with Suran's death?" If she was talking then I was going to keep asking.

"Who is Suran?" Her confusion was unmistakable. The vampire had no clue.

"A human whose death I'm investigating."

The hard grip on my throat eased and she lowered me to push her face closer to mine. "My, but you are fond of your pets. Do you enjoy playing with your food?"

She was one of *those* vampires. They were the kind of vampires that the humans assumed we were as they grabbed pitchforks and torches. Stereotypes exist because there is a kernel of truth to them. "Li's a *friend.*"

"Food cannot be a friend." There was no room for doubt in her statement. It was the proclamation of a fanatic.

"Li's not food." I tried to keep my tone respectful but there was a growl in my voice as I added, "Regardless of his status, he is *mine.*" It was true.

Bridgette stared at me coldly. "I have no desire to contest your claim." I didn't have time to be relieved before she continued.

"But I remain unconvinced."

I sighed in annoyance. "Fine. What do you need to be convinced?"

"Hunt with me." Now her tone verged on the sexual. Had I not been experiencing a remembrance of being a vampire, I might have been disgusted. Instead, I sympathized.

Regardless of my recent experiences, I wasn't keen to break the law just to prove my loyalty to a vampire who opened dialogues with attacks and threats. However, I was currently planning something just as illegal so I wasn't sure I had moral standing. I knew she wanted something to hold over me. Perhaps she'd allow me to tell her about something incriminating I'd already done. "I don't suppose you'd take a confession." At her sneer I added, "My word on my lineage, maybe?"

I didn't expect that to work. Swearing on your lineage was considered in inviolate oath but how inviolate depended on each vampire. Those old enough to remember a time when your word was your bond treated it as an unbreakable pledge. Some vampires were just pretentious; Bridgette was on the cusp where she was just old enough that she might remember those times or just might be full of herself. Whatever the cause, she released my neck. "I will accept your word, on your lineage." Brown eyes glared at me, coupling with her tone in a clear threat. "If you have played me false, or if your pet has, I will return to make you sorry."

"I'll ask him about it, but if he went to cops it'd raise some awkward questions about what we were doing at the church."

Her brown eyes grew curious. "What *were* you doing, childling?"

"What were *you* doing?" I left the various insults off my sentence. She was old enough to insult me without retaliation. It meant she was old enough to force me to tell her, if she made an issue of it but I wasn't going to volunteer the information.

She shocked me by answering. "I was killing Vasyl for giving us humans like he was feeding pets. For denying us the power of the Hunt. For making a *profit* off our people. Would that I could do it to all the humans."

You are insane. I didn't say it, of course. I had more common sense than that. "Right. Gotcha. Can I go now?"

"Swear. On your lineage. As you promised." What I had previously thought was a glint of anger in her black eyes was actually the disturbing shine of insanity.

I considered the words. They had to have some formality to them in order to make the other vampire happy. "I swear that I didn't betray you on my sire, Daffyad. I swear that I didn't go to the police and talk about you on my sire, Aibek. I swear on Oak and Fire."

"And your pet?"

I grimaced. "Him too." That didn't satisfy of course, so I had to elaborate. "I swear on my sires, on Oak and Fire, that he didn't say anything to the police about you. Happy?"

"Happy enough to leave you in peace." I wasn't comforted and her next words didn't help. "I know where you live."

"I'm aware." I hadn't been sure and I think Bridgette heard my annoyance in my tone. She said nothing and turned away from me, leaving me alone in the alley. I watched her go before turning to my own task.

A ride over the Rontgen Bridge put me on the Core, and I began to walk toward the Tiger Club. I didn't look like the girl who had been there three days ago; she had been suave and dangerous, dressed in an Estellen. I was wearing tight jeans, t-shirt, thin tennis shoes and a short denim jacket, straight from the '80s. I even had the big bow in my hair. I would claim that this was a disguise, but it was actually what I liked to wear.

Angela Kangara was performing again, but I was really early. The club hadn't opened yet, and that was the way I wanted it. I would have all night to watch.

I managed to scale the building across the alley and leap to the club's roof, and from there I was able to drop onto the overhang above the main doors. Among pigeon poop and dirty frames holding up the glowing sign, I settled in, waiting. I was shadowed by the blinding light of the marquee, ready to be the patient hunter.

It was hours sitting there, watching, waiting. I saw lots of people come and go: first the staff, nervous and tense about the first night open after the attack; then the guests, jumpy but anticipatory. They were secretly hoping for another fight. Too bad I wasn't interested in a show.

My target finally arrived around 11:00 p.m., in his aero. Blond Johnny looked a little tense as he got out of the vehicle and surrounded himself with his goons; sadly, his eye looked fine. I wondered if he was just going to stay for Kangara's performance. The thought that we might have made him nervous made me smile a little. The smile faded as he entered the building, and one of his thugs got into the aero, lifting back into the air. Let him get inside, have some *sake* and relax; we could talk a bit later.

He must have been worried; barely an hour later, I saw a goon step outside and look around before waving at someone back in the club. I pulled my scarf out of my pocket, wrapping it around my face. Johnny and some henchmen came out, and the aero dropped to the curb. The pilot hopped out and held the door for Johnny, who started to enter. In that moment, when everyone thought they were in the clear, I moved.

As Johnny started for the aero's door, I leapt, landing next to him and grabbing him. My left hand came down on his shoulder while I put the knife in my right hand in front of him. I wanted to actually cut him, but we weren't there yet, and I had the blade positioned over his crotch before his thugs could react. "No!" I shouted as someone went for his gun. "No one moves! Johnny and I are going for a drive."

The goons looked conflicted before glancing at Johnny. The *fuku-honbucho* was already shaking, and I dug my other hand into his shoulder until he cringed. "Tell them we want some alone time." I tightened my grip until he nodded.

"Stand down. Go away!" he shouted to his minions. I pulled backwards on his shoulder, drawing him into the aero. I crawled over the bucket seats and got into the passenger's, forcing him to take the driver's.

"Now go," I told him as everyone backed up.

"Where?" he asked nervously.

I whispered into his ear, "Get onto Watson-Crick Boulevard." It was a major airlane around Gideon, plus it went close enough to the Inner Sea for my purposes.

He nodded and put the aero in gear. Slowly, he took off, trembling harder as the protection of his goons fell further and further behind us. "What do you want?"

"Faster," I told him, and the aero sped up, the blades

overhead whirling harder. A few other aeros were in the lane with us, their lights blinding in the darkness. It was a privilege to drive, and I didn't see an aero that cost less than a hundred grand up here. The good news was that cops rarely patrolled the lanes either, so Johnny's speed wasn't going to get us in trouble. When I felt like we were going fast enough, I said, "I want the answers to two questions."

Johnny swallowed tightly. "Okay."

"First, who killed Suran?"

Johnny looked puzzled for a moment, shooting a quick glance at me. I pulled down my scarf and sneered at him. His eyes widened and he nearly drifted out of the lane. The computer informed him of this in a soft voice as he jerked the wheel back over. "Oh, god...it's you!"

"I want answers, not statements," I said coolly.

"My third, Seiji, killed the woman but it doesn't matter. Your walking slurpie already killed him."

"Good," I said, pressing on the knife until he rose out of his seat. The aero went faster as he put more weight on the throttle in response. "I hope he suffered."

"I'll give you a job," Johnny said, leaving me blinking in surprise. "That's what this is about, right? I get it, you're good at this. You want a job, I could use a pretty guard like you."

"Who raped Suran?" This was just a guess, but I knew what these guys were capable of, and I wanted to know if they had lived down to my expectations. For a moment, I thought I was going to have to fight him for the answer.

But his resolve crumbled and he gasped, "Please...whatever you want...it's yours. I can get you anything." I watched the sweat roll down his face, and it became clear.

"You," I hissed, rage burning through my blood at the thought of him stealing not once but twice from Li. I looked up for the first time, taking note of where we were going. The Newton Cross-station was approaching fast, a place where bridges from the Rings and the train met. It was on the outer edge of the Core, with only water behind it.

I grabbed the wheel with one hand, holding it straight. My knee nudged behind the throttle, pushing it to its maximum speed. Johnny began to scream as he realized that I wasn't stopping. He fought me, trying to get me off the wheel, or the throttle, but I brought the butt of the knife up and smashed it into his forehead. He collapsed, reeling from the blow as the aero sped through the air. When we were over water, I killed the engines.

The blades whined to a stop and we started to fall. We arced only a little further before plunging more down then forward. The aero hit with a splash that washed up over the windshield. Though the doors were closed, it was only seconds before the water started to work its way into the cabin. Johnny regained his senses when cold sea water began to coil around his legs. I just smiled as he tried to unbuckle his seat belt—a buckle I was now holding in place. He fought me, but it was just laughable. He was a human and I wasn't and he had no chance. Just before our heads went under the waves, I said, "There's no mercy for people like you, Johnny."

He didn't struggle long.

When he was dead, I swam away from the sinking aero, holding tightly to the air in my lungs. It countered my dense frame and I swam for the sewer access in the bottom of the Core.

Down under the Core, it was like being in another world. Each tile was a tall cylindrical slab of ferro-crete, bound above the water's surface by metal connectors and with the air trapped under them. The tethers that connected the tiles to the sea bed via tall anchoring pillars were long metal flagella disappearing below me. I swam between the tiles, looking for access back into Gideon. Fish zipped frantically away from me, interrupted in their hunt for pieces of trash that had been broken into edible, biodegradable clumps and dumped into the water. A couple of small sharks swam around, hunting for distracted fish. Ahead, a light pierced the darkness, the sign I'd been seeking.

The light was a marker for an access airlock into the bowels of Gideon, and I was pleased as I twisted the wheel on the small door open. Two minutes later I was inside and closing the outer door. Then I verified the seal, drained the lock and entered the chamber above. It was a maintenance room, one of the many that serviced the pipes and sewers. I didn't want to linger; I used to work here, a few years ago, and someone might recognize me.

A few hours later, I was back in my apartment, showering

the salt out of my hair. The risk I'd taken had been substantial, but I'd taken some precautions, so I should be safe. But deep inside, I didn't want to be safe. I wanted to be alive; not human-alive, but not this tamed half-death I was living. I wanted to be free.

But that had a price; was the price something I would pay?

CHAPTER 20

The next evening, I returned to work. I had the strange feeling that it should probably feel weird, but it wasn't until I was face-to-face with Mal that I realized *why*. It seemed ridiculous, but I'd forgotten about our fight.

"You're done avoiding me now?" Malcolm asked as I approached him, the start of a smile on my face.

That killed my smile. "I wasn't avoiding you," I said, but I sounded really grumpy, even to myself. "I had a hell of a day off, and I had to heal up from it." Mal looked at me, hard. His outward expression was anger, but I saw a hint of pain in there, too. "Come on, man...Let's suit up and I'll tell you about it."

His anger melted. He was still hurt, and probably would be for a while, if he thought I'd been avoiding him. "Misty, about what I said..."

I shrugged. "It's okay."

"You gotta learn how to be a girl, Misty," Mal laughed, and I grinned at the sound. "You can't let a guy off the hook so fast. You should let him finish."

"Well, maybe you were never on a hook in my head," I replied, and I got to watch the last of his hesitation fade. "Really, I wasn't mad. I was being stupid."

"God, I love you," Mal said, tossing an arm over my shoulder. "You apologize like a guy."

"Come on," I said, leading the way to the changing room and pushing his arm off. "You're not going to believe this story. Lemme change and then I'll tell you." I didn't worry about Mal breaking confidence—he'd rather have me there to tease than spread a story like this around. And he was my friend.

We weren't working on the nets tonight. Instead, Mal and

I were assigned to maintain the tethers, our usual job. It meant a long walk deep into the bowels of the concrete tile, where we gained access to the sea through an open pool. It wasn't that different than where I had gotten back into the city last night. This was a bit fancier. It was a door sealed with a closed-system pressurized room, meaning that one door had to be shut before the other would open. It wouldn't do to flood Gideon's maintenance tunnels.

I was a bit worried as I reviewed the details of the story to Mal in quiet tones on the way down. I wanted to believe it was done but couldn't quite; it didn't *feel* done. Mal shared my worry, frowning as the story continued. "Man, you have all the fun," he groaned as we entered the dive room. He was trying to cover his worry with humor, but I read right through it. "Chases, fights, two sexy women..."

"Two women?" I asked as I shrugged into my diving harness. "Where you'd get that from my story?"

"Well, you had two sexy men. I'd get sexy women." He laughed and I found myself laughing with him.

"Ok, fair enough," I giggled as I swung my legs over the wall of the pool.

He checked my diving harness and the safety line I'd already connected. "You're ready to dive, hon."

"Let's get going." I steeled myself to enter the water; just like with the nets, I had to fill my lungs with air and fight the sensation that I was drowning.

Mal waved as I sank out of sight; then I was alone under the city, in open water. I was weighted, so all I had to do was keep close to the tether itself and let gravity do the work. As I drifted downward, I checked the tether, examining it for wear. This was the easy part; I had to dive further to maintain the pillars. They had to be checked for wear and damage all the way around— unlike the tether, which could be assessed at a glance—as well as for barnacles on the sea floor. Gideon sits north of the Tropic of Capricorn and just south of the Romanche Trench, where the Mid-Atlantic Ridge comes close to the surface. It was shallower here than other places, but not so shallow to have an up-spur of land which could be claimed by another country. Both of these factors had been key in the location of Gideon; the depth was a reasonable concern and the lack of claimable land meant that no one could try to put a hold over the city.

Despite the moderate depth, it's still a long dive, something that I considered every time I did it. There's something unnerving, even to a corpse, about sinking into the dark water, with only a single cable connecting you to the city above. With the weights to lower me, it was particularly disturbing, like some insubstantial monster was pulling me downward into the water. Hydrophobia is fun!

But there is a sort of peacefulness down here; just me and silence. My only communication was through the small arm-mounted computer.

I worked at a steady pace, pausing only to read the messages Mal was sending me or to answer one before I returned to checking the massive tethers as thick as my wrist, and closely examining the concrete pillars driven into the sea bed. The currents can toss stuff against the pillars or press extra sand and silt against them. And there is always the random wildlife that can adversely affect objects, not to mention the constant deterioration from seawater.

The downside to telling Mal about my "thrilling adventures" was that I had to hear about it during the whole shift. Or rather read about it; the wrist computer was filled with bad jokes and terrible puns for most of the night. Even as I typed back exasperated messages telling Mal how silly he was, I was smiling. I had my friend back. But even that thought wasn't completely happy; it reminded me of Li. I hoped he was ok.

Toward the end of my shift, Mal sent me a message: *Ready-up?* That was his shorthand way of asking if I was ready to be lifted. I nodded instinctively while typing in the reply: *Lets go.*

I reached up and pulled my cable taut, making sure it wasn't wrapped around me. If it was wound around an arm or leg, I could lose that limb. It actually depended on how much speed the cable retractor had picked up by the time it had drawn in all the slack. They were supposed to have a governor to keep them to safe speeds, but those could break pretty easily. And as usual, there was no money allocated for repairs to safety equipment for vampires.

The cable snapped tight with no warning, and I was jerked

off the seabed. I crossed my arms on my chest so they wouldn't flap around and pressed my legs together. I veered upward—figures I got one without a governor. I probably wouldn't get hurt, even if I bounced off a tether a few times, but it was still unnerving.

I burst above the surface like mermaids and monsters do in the movies. Water festooned in the air, rising around me like the burst of a geyser. The cable retractor hung over my head from the ceiling; I dangled and simulated coughing, working on ejecting the water from my lungs. I could leave it in there, but I needed air to talk.

The retractor released a bit, dipping me back to the water until I could unhook the cable. As I continued to empty my lungs, someone cleared their throat. "Misty?" I heard Mal ask, and I twisted around to see what he wanted.

Li was standing next to him, and I stopped my forced hacking to stare at him. He was wearing a *gi* of some sort, though the pants were black, not white. Masako was in his arms. "Li?" I asked, or rather tried; the water in my lungs flooded my larynx.

"Hang on," Mal said as I shook my head and paddled for the edge of the pool. "She's got water in her lungs."

"I could never get used to that," Li said, watching me with his dark eyes. I avoided looking at him, but it didn't help; the room was full of their scents—his and Masako's. I felt that strange connection again as I pulled myself over the rim.

"She says you do," Mal said, leaning down to help me. I took his belated hand, then I knelt on the side of the pool and let the water drain out of my lungs. Mal stood over me and performed a Heimlich maneuver that would have been awkward if we hadn't been doing it for a while now. "I know this looks perverted, but it helps."

"I'm sure," Li said, a smile twitching the edge of his mouth. Masako watched me with her own dark eyes, but she looked so much better than the last time I'd seen her. That impression was probably helped by her lack of tears and screams. Babies are more attractive when they're quiet.

I coughed out the last of the water and said, "Li, what are you doing here? How'd you find me?"

"Your coworkers said you'd be down here." He glanced at

Mal. "I can't come see you?"

"She told me the story," Mal said, earning me a hard glance from Li. "You can talk in front of me."

"Really?" Li asked coldly.

I met his gaze as I sat up and started to unzip my wetsuit. "I trust Mal. He'd rather tease me about it than tell anyone."

"You're gambling my freedom on that," Li grumped.

"And mine," I agreed, "so chill."

Li visibly forced himself to be calm. "Fine. They attacked my home. If I hadn't left the dojo early, they would have killed my aunt and uncle, and taken Masako again. They're going to keep coming. This...it has to end."

"Sure, but how?" I asked, pausing with my legs curled under my body. I thought about Johnny's death, and knew with a cold certainty that I'd escalated the war. That was not something that I'd considered and I silently kicked myself. "I mean, I'm all for helping you with that, since I'm in the fire with you, but how?"

"I'm going to talk to Terada Hiroharu, Blond Johnny's boss. And really, you don't need to come. King Connor will protect you, which is why I want you...Misty, please take care of Masako, if I don't come back. I don't...I can't..." The admission had hurt him; his dark eyes flinched with every word.

"I can't care for a baby, Li." My eyes widened with shock and not a little fear. "I don't have a mothering instinct! I'll...I'll... I'll eat her in my sleep!"

Mal started laughing at me; my outraged glare only made him laugh harder. "It's just a baby, Misty," he gasped. "You're terrified of a year-old human."

"Shut up," I growled, crossing my arms and starting to feel like a petulant child. I attempted to sound like a reasonable adult as I said, "Li, I can't take care of a kid. The best thing I could do for her would be to put her into foster care. If you're going to try to talk to some boss, then I'd be more help with that."

Li hugged his daughter close, pain etched on his features. "Misty, I can't ask you to come. I may not come back. I have to know she's safe before I...go."

I stood up and put a hand on his shoulder. "Li, she needs you alive more than she needs you dead." He started to reply, and I cut him off. "Look, we did something pretty awesome at the club. And if we have to do it again, we will."

"That's so sweet," Mal said, his voice its usual mix of friendly and mocking.

I turned on him with a smart comment, but Li beat me to it. "If you want to help, you can watch Masako until we get back."

"What, are you serious?" Mal gasped, all humor gone.

"It's just a baby, Mal," I said, my tone sugar-sweet. "Are you afraid of a year-old human?"

It was Mal's turn to glare at me as Li snickered quietly. "You aren't serious," Mal said softly, his tone a bit too quiet.

Li shrugged. "It has the benefit of being out of character for me, which means that they won't look for her with you."

"I can't take care of a baby!" Mal said, his eyes going wide.

I had to snicker at him. "It isn't that hard," I said, smirking.

"You do it!" he snapped at me.

"I'm storming the...uh—"

"Symmetea Club," Li said.

I blinked and looked at him. "Symme-*tea?* What kind of club is that?"

"A teahouse, actually. It's Terada Hiroharu's favorite place to rest and relax."

"So we just walk in and chit-chat with him?"

Li smiled enigmatically. "Something like that," was his vague and disturbing answer.

CHAPTER 21

M al couldn't agree to take care of Masako without talking to Sarah, his wife, so it was off to his apartment. I'd met Sarah a few times. At first, I couldn't understand what Mal saw in her; she's not the loveliest woman in the world, with straight, dirty-colored brown hair, thick glasses that obscure her pale gray eyes and a figure that can best be defined as dowdy. She's also short, which makes her tendency to carry a few extra pounds around her waist even more pronounced. Mal's no physical catch, but he could attract a better-looking wife. Then I got to know her. Sarah has a quick wit, a big smile and a kind heart. She's easy to like, and easy to love. It was clear why Mal loved her.

However, her ability to love her husband was pressed to the breaking point at the moment. Standing in an oversized shirt with a bathrobe hastily thrown over her shoulders, she alternated between clear worry and outright anger at the three of us. I could understand. After hearing the condensed version of our story, she had to be wondering what Mal had dragged her into now. Of course, I should probably just consider myself lucky that she hadn't decided it was my fault he was involved.

Their apartment was much nicer than mine. It was roomier, as it was designed for a starter family. The main room was split into a living room and a kitchen by an open divider that added counter space to the kitchen without turning it into its own room. Large windows graced the other wall, though all one could see out of them was the building across the street; the curtains were drawn because there was a burning ball of light and death outside. There was a bedroom to the left with a small bathroom wedged between it and the closet. Everything was painted in bright, cheery colors, and it was all nicely and subtly decorated—clearly,

Sarah's touch, given the lack of soccer memorabilia. There was a tastefully framed picture of Andy Lebedev, one of the LA Galaxy's current stars, hanging on the outside of the closet door. Marital compromise at its best.

Sarah finally shook her head, pulling my attention back to her. "I can't get involved in this," she said, her voice shaking. I saw her eyes settle on Masako, who was sleeping peacefully and adorably in Li's arms. "I...crap."

"I hope you crap, sometimes," Mal rejoined immediately.

Sarah didn't miss a beat; she snatched a pillow off the chair and threw it at him. He caught it with a giggle, but it had its intended effect; Sarah was a bit less tense, at least for a few seconds. I quickly pressed, "Can you watch Masako tonight while we're out winding this up?"

Sarah sighed, but I could see we'd already won. "Yes," she muttered before shaking her head. "I'm going to regret this."

"Just like when you married me," Mal chuckled, curling his body around the pillow.

Sarah grimaced at him, but that was soon forgotten as she turned to glance at Li and me. "And you'll be crashing here today?"

I glanced at the clock, then at the glowing curtains. "I think I have to, now."

Sarah nodded, looking overwhelmed. Turning back to her husband, she said, "I have to get ready for work now, so you'll be in charge while I'm gone." With that dire statement, she turned and walked into the bedroom, shutting the door behind her.

"We're dead," I intoned dramatically to Li, who chuckled.

"You sound as though I've killed all my guests," Mal said, rubbing his hands together. "No one has produced any concrete evidence yet!"

"Is there someplace I can put Masako down?" Li asked softly.

"Take the bed," Mal said, jerking his thumb toward the bedroom door.

Li quirked an eyebrow at him and asked, "Shouldn't I wait for your wife to leave for work?"

Mal opened then closed his mouth. "Yes," he said firmly. "Yes, you should."

"Right," Li said, chuckling a little.

We fell silent, all of us worn and tired. Sarah came back out of the bedroom wearing a matching green skirt and jacket combo, with a dove gray shirt. Despite not having the greatest looks, she clearly took pride in her appearance, and did her best to dress up. "Guys, I had a thought. You're walking into a death-trap, right? I mean, the only way you're getting out with your daughter is if you give your life to them, right?"

Li nodded. "It may come to that," he said, his voice bleak but firm. "I have to erase Suran's debt, somehow."

"There might be someone else who could help you," Sarah said. "Your representative."

The hope that had blossomed with her first statement died with those two words. While in theory, going to the elected official who represented our interests in politics was a good idea, I couldn't trust that a human politician would have my best interests at heart—or Li's, either.

Perhaps the greatest roadblock to my faith in my representative's ability to help me was the requirement to run for the position: a college degree in the hard sciences. Without that qualification, you weren't even eligible to register for the ballot. That was enough for most people to mistrust their reps, but there was unspoken law that you had to have a pulse, so that was two strikes for vampires. It was one more sign of the secondary citizenship we—and by that I didn't mean just vampires, I mean all non-scientists—enjoyed in Gideon: we couldn't even be represented by our peers. Just because someone knew the periodic table didn't mean that they knew anything about me, or what I needed or wanted.

Li seemed to feel the same way. "With all my respect and thanks for what you've agreed to do," Li said, bowing his head to Sarah in a quaint gesture, "I have no faith in the government of Gideon. I have seen too much imbalance and disregard for human dignity come from this city. I will not place my daughter's life in their hands."

Sarah shook her head. "I know that you've seen problems, but every human institution has issues," she said, rubbing her hands together nervously. She didn't like fighting or disagreeing with people; I would have taken some heat off her by trying to be a moderate voice, but I didn't agree with her at all. "I'm going to see Representative Lila Asnayo today. Can I ask her—hypothetically, of course—what can be done here?"

"Why are you meeting with a rep?" I asked, feeling my eyes narrow with clear suspicion.

"That's part of my job. Didn't Mal tell you?"

Mal rolled his eyes, which I thought was a mistake. "Honey, we generally don't talk about your job at work," he said, his tone a bit condescending. I didn't add what Mal had told me about her job; that it was pointless and dull.

Sarah's eyebrows rose until they slid under her bangs. "Right," she said, and that one word held Mal's doom. Turning to me, she offered, "I work as a Blue-Collar Liaison for the GWE. It's ironic that were Mal a new immigrant, he'd be relying on me for work."

Mal's expression shifted into realization coupled with irritation. But Li was already speaking up, trying to defuse the tension. "Though to be fair, he relies on you for something far more important." Everyone chuckled a little at the bad joke, but I saw the bleak look creep into Li's eyes. That "something far more important" was an open wound for my unusual new friend.

"Anyway," Sarah said, drawing our attention back to the conversation. "I can talk to Asnayo; at the least, she can tell me who would be the appropriate rep for you guys to talk to."

"What's to stop him from turning us in?" I asked. "He'd just have to call the cops, and it would take care of a hell of a problem. He'd be a hero."

"Lila's a she, first, and second, she is very compassionate. She earned her degree after arriving here," Sarah said.

That was a strike in her favor; it meant that at some point, she'd been a plebian, one of the struggling working. She had once lived like we did now. Which doesn't mean that she lived in misery. It wasn't like the residents—Gideon's term for non-scientists—needed for anything, because we didn't. We had jobs, money, places to live, health care and more than enough food to eat. But we couldn't make the kind of money that the scientists did, even the ones who didn't work for the government, and we didn't get the same privileges. I couldn't enter the Citizen's Library, because I wasn't a citizen. I had another library, because

I was a resident. And in Gideon, the two were night and day.

"So she earned her lab jacket," I said softly, tilting my head. That suggested that she wasn't associated with the New-kuza; she couldn't have broken any laws or else she wouldn't have been awarded her full degree. The highest degree a convicted criminal can earn is an Associate's degree in the hard sciences, a law instituted to keep criminals from rising too far in the political structure. "So what gives her any particular sympathy to our plight?"

Sarah bit her lip and sank into her chair, clearly thinking. "You didn't kill anyone, did you?"

Li and I both glanced at each other, looking for the affirmative answer from one another. It was rather encouraging that we had to think about it. "Only one was severely hurt," Li admitted, "he may have died later."

"And the guards and the New-kuza at the airport were shooting at each other," I said, glad that my tells for lying and misdirection were more subtle now that I was dead. "We weren't directly responsible for any fatalities, but as a vampire, I get blamed for them sometimes." The "we" made that technically true, because only I was responsible for Johnny's death. Johnny had said Li killed his third, but that might have been a lie.

"I sometimes get blamed, as well," Li said, and stopped awkwardly. After a silence he finished softly, "Because of my criminal record."

Huh. *That* was interesting, but not unexpected after his near-confession at the airport. It could be useful to use his background as a shield by implying that possible charges were prejudice by an overeager police force. Then I realized that was the type of thought an elder would have, and I shut it down. My background wasn't exactly whitewashed and squeaky clean either.

"Well," Sarah said after a moment. She glanced at the clock, then stood up and grabbed her things. "I need to get to work." She glanced at us. "Should I ask her? I really think that she could help."

I looked at Li. I could go underground, change my name and squeak out a living in the darker corners of Gideon. So could he, I suspected, but it was no place for a child. We weren't fighting for ourselves, or rather not for our quality of life, but for Masako. Li had already come to this conclusion, because his eyes were full of pure love as he said, "If she can save my daughter, keep her safe, then yes. We'll talk with her. Or whomever. But they have to really help. If they want to deport Misty, then no way." I nodded my agreement, warmed that Li was thinking of me.

With Sarah's departure, Li took Masako into the bedroom. I had thought he was just going to put her down to sleep, but when I peeked inside, he was sprawled next to her, breathing deeply. Mal sighed to himself and, grumbling about losing his bed, moved over to the couch. Within a few moments, he was sleeping, and I was left to my own devices.

That was a bad place to leave me, something that my sires could attest to fervently.

I paced for a time, thought about sleeping, paced again and ended up watching Li sleep. Knowing that I was trapped here didn't help my level of comfort. Finally, I found myself on the Gid-Net, researching Representative Lila Asnayo. She was pretty much as Sarah had described her—a scientist for the people, as it were, tackling social issues that many in Gideon's government were only too happy to ignore.

I studied her picture—a serene, dark-skinned oval face was framed by a "professional" haircut: that strange, particularly styled bob that women in government had been choosing for decades. She was pretty, in a distant, you-can't-have-this sort of way. The gray power suit under her lab coat had a touch of purple in it, and her stitched name was also done in purple thread. Perhaps it was her favorite color.

She'd come to Gideon when she was twenty-six with her parents, three children and husband from Peru, attracted by Gideon's promise of jobs for those willing to come to the new city. She'd taken full advantage of the system, working a full-time job and battling her way into the university at the same time. Her husband died in a construction accident three months before she received her undergraduate degree in physics. She'd continued relentlessly, gaining a doctorate before running for office. Even before entering government service, she'd been devoted to the plight of the people of Gideon, consumed by the drive to improve the city that had welcomed her so reluctantly.

I think I kinda liked her, in that way that you liked someone who seemed to persistently buck for you.

Around 5:00 in the evening, after the humans had woken up, Sarah called. "Lila will meet with you tonight. She's agreed not to contact the authorities without hearing your side of the story."

CHAPTER 22

My watch beeped loudly, signaling sunset, and Li squeezed his daughter a little tighter. Masako wiggled, her eyes on the bright toy that Sarah had bought her. With a heavy sigh, Li set his daughter down. She promptly crawled over to the toy and started to play with it, not looking back at her father. She was too young to understand the gravity of the moment, but that didn't make it any easier on Li. I watched him silently for a moment before I touched his shoulder lightly. "Are you ready?"

Li drew in a deep breath and nodded. "Yeah," he said reluctantly. He stood up and followed his daughter, crouching to kiss her head. That at least earned him a gummy grin before she went back to the toy, turning it over in her stubby hands. Li reluctantly stood up and looked at me, nodding. "I'm ready."

Together, we shook Mal and Sarah's hands. "Good luck," Sarah murmured to both of us, looking confident. "I'm sure Lila can help you. And we'll take care of Masako."

"Yeah," Mal agreed. In addition to the hand-shake, I got an awkward hug from the red-head. "Be careful," he whispered in my ear. "I don't want to have to train someone to do your job. Training you was hard enough."

"Thanks," I muttered, but I was smiling as I stepped back from him, looking at Li. He was waiting for me to be done, looking strange in the thick flannel shirt that Mal had loaned him. He was also wearing Sarah's jeans, his belt pinched tight around his smaller waist. Mal's legs were too long to loan him pants, so Li had to wear woman's clothing. He handled it with the awkward grace that guys affect when something bothers them, but they won't show it.

Together, we left the apartment, moving through the

corridors and hallways with single-minded purpose. We weren't hurrying, exactly, but we were wasting no time or energy as we moved.

"Do you need to eat?" It was the first time I'd ever heard a human ask me that without tension or odd inflection in their voice.

I blinked at Li, wrestled with an answer and finally decided it was probably safest to just be honest. "No, I'm good for another night." I could go a night or two without feeding.

"But will you be at peak performance?" Li pressed. "When I don't eat, I get weak, sick. I need you to be on top of your game."

I glanced at him; his high, stark features were grim and unreadable. "We're just going to meet with a government rep," I said, watching his expression for clues. "Why the combat-readiness?"

"Because we may still have to fight tonight. After we talk to the rep, if she can't help us, then I'm going to talk to the Boss. Getting in to see him will be hard. And I'll need you on top of your form." He took a deep breath and added, "Don't worry—I just need you to get me in; I'll do the rest alone."

I reached out and caught his arm, forcing him to stop with my superior strength. "Wait. When were you going to share this with me?"

Li wouldn't look at me. "I wasn't going to tell you, because I wasn't planning on taking you all the way with me. Once we'd secured the way in, you're going to pull out and let me finish, alone."

A suicide mission. The stupid man was going to kamikaze himself for his daughter, and he didn't want to drag me down. "Do you really think that they'll just let their debt go if you're dead? They'll come get Masako, and this time, they may not sell her to some desperate couple. Who will save her then?"

"You will," Li said, reaching out and touching my face with his fingertips, lightly. It could have been sexual, but it was just a touch, another connection. "I know you will, when I'm gone."

"Li, I can't take care of a child." My voice was sad, sadder than I thought it could be.

"But you would make sure she's safe." Li's voice was full of hope and grief, the tone of a man who is ready for death and still knows optimism. He was going to die alone, a father's final, stupid gesture of love. "My aunt and uncle, they're her family, they will raise her and you'll make sure they can."

Anger roiled through me. What happened to living for his girl? Sacrifice was all well and good, but Li had options beyond that. My sires did everything they could to save me, but they had known that part of saving me was saving *themselves.* And they had been right; I had been afraid, being chased by mobs, hiding all the time, but I was never more afraid than when they were both gone and I was alone. I didn't want to share this emotional experience with Masako; I wanted at least one of her parents to live.

Strange, the emotions that run through us at times like this: I shouldn't feel on the verge of betrayal or abandonment, but I did. And I could feel them with a startling intensity, just like I did the night Daffyad left our hiding spot to attempt to save Aibek. Something about Li was drawing those emotions out, in a way that contact with a human shouldn't be able to accomplish. That strangeness compelled me to do something completely insane: test his scent. There had to be a reason for all of this.

Vampires can identify if they are related by blood by mingling and inhaling scents. There are many ways to do this, only a few of which can be done in public. This shouldn't work on a human, but so many things about Li worked when they shouldn't, so I tried in a desperate attempt to get some answers. I murmured to him, "Hold still for a second." He complied, even when I leaned forward, entering his personal space. He put his hands against my forearms when I nestled my face into his neck, and I could feel he was struggling to trust me. I stopped for a second, and the force in his hands eased, through he didn't lower them. I put my lips over his pulse, which jumped and began to hammer against my mouth.

I took breath into my cold, empty lungs and exhaled. It was something that I did every time I spoke, but it was still an alien action. Li shivered as I breathed room temperature air over his neck; his hands became softer, gentler as he murmured, "Misty... don't...please."

I wasn't listening. As my breath brushed his skin, I inhaled through my nose, drawing in our scents mingled together. It wasn't just our smells I was measuring; I was focused on the scent coming back, ignoring the part of it that said he was human and focusing on *him*. If you removed all the flesh, bone, and blood, what would remain would be the pure scent of a person. It's hard to describe what I was looking for; humans can't identify pheromones like we can and never created words for what I was doing. *Testing* and *tasting* are close descriptors, but still so inadequate. Some humans can smell and react to them, but only on a subconscious level.

Li should have had his own scent, a distinctive marker that would identify him no matter who or where he was. It would also have marked him as different from me. But he didn't smell singular; he smelled familiar. He smelled comfortable, like family.

I recoiled from him, pushing away more roughly than I had intended. What had just happened was impossible. He shouldn't smell like anyone but himself; he was human and shouldn't have borne the scent markers of my family. But he smelled like Daffyad, like Aibek, like my siblings. He smelled like he belonged to me.

"Misty?" He hadn't moved from where I'd pushed him against the wall. Smart man. "What's wrong?"

"You...I don't think we should talk about this." I shoved my hands into my pockets because I needed to do *something* with them. What was going on?

"All right," he replied, lowering his hands. "Are we going to see the representative still? 'Cause if we don't get going, we're going to be late."

"Yeah. Yeah, let's get going," I mumbled. "We should..." What? Talk about this later? What was I supposed to tell him? Could he understand, when I couldn't understand myself? "We should go."

He frowned at me as we made our way to the hub of the city. In addition to being the playground for the stupidly wealthy, the Inner Core was the center for government. Of course, given how much scientists paid themselves, it was easy for the lines between scientist, politician and the affluent to blur.

We were silent as we took the trolley across the Inner Sea, its black depths hiding everything beneath the rolling waves. I thought, once or twice, that Li was going to say something. He glanced at me occasionally, and the look in his eyes suggested that he had something to talk about. But he didn't speak up, and I was left to my thoughts.

Round and round I went in my head, going back over everything that had happened since I had met Li. Realizing that he smelled like family explained my willingness to help him, as well as my general comfort with him. It had taken weeks to build enough rapport for me to feel like I could joke with Mal; the ease with which I had slipped into Li's life and problems was unnatural. At least I had a reason now for my actions, but not a reason for why Li exhibited an inhuman trait.

Dear God. My new friend was a mutant. What next, a set of claws and laser eyes?

"I just wanted a new life," Li said softly. "A safe place to raise my daughter, to have a family."

I studied him for a moment, noting his regret. "You...you've been involved, in the New-kuza or the Yakuza, on the mainland, right?"

Li sighed, looking twice the twenty-three years his ID card had claimed. "It was a mistake." At my doubtful expression, he growled and added, "I was young and dumb. And now I'll pay for it forever."

"No, Suran paid," I said before I could shut my damned mouth. Li flinched, his dark eyes closing so I wouldn't see how much that had hurt, how close to home I'd hit. "Yeah, I probably didn't need to say that."

"Not really," Li agreed, his voice tight.

My statement killed conversation; the rest of the ride was silent. When we got off at the station, I said, "Sorry. I'm just pissed that you're considering this suicide run. Masako needs you alive, more than dead. I..." There went those pheromones again. I know that among vampires, it enforced societal ties among solitary predators. But when you made it so that a human, our prey, evoked those reactions, it changed everything. It made your food your friend; not something you *owned* but something that was a part of you. *"I* want you to be alive." Crap, even when I knew why, I was still bound to act on the prodding of my blood.

Li gave me a quick smile. "Thanks," he murmured, a flush tinting his cheeks a little. "I...I just don't know what to do if the rep can't help—I mean, our options are pretty limited at that point. I wasn't even sure what I was going to do before Sarah brought up this idea. I mean, the teahouse idea was pretty lame." He was quiet. "What about King Connor?"

I thought of Gregor and swallowed. "I think they would save me, but you and Masako would be out of luck."

"Damn. Then I just don't know, Misty."

I sighed. "I don't know either. If you have connections to the New-kuza, or even the Yakuza, then can't you do anything? Call anyone? Pull a rabbit out of your ass?"

"Maybe, no, and ouch, no," Li answered with a hint of a chuckle in his voice. We walked a bit further in silence before he added, "We'll figure something out."

Yeah, sure. I didn't really need to say that was what people said when they were in over their heads. We both had a good idea exactly how deep we were.

The Capitol Building in Gideon was one of the few buildings in the city that looked like it belonged in most towns in America. It had the Neo-Classical columns and boxy front that are common in government buildings, particularly those over two hundred years old. It even had the ubiquitous dome on top of it. This building was done in white stone, or something that *looked* like white stone—how would I know? All I knew is that when the lights shone on it, the building glowed in the night. I've been told it's pretty during the daytime, too, white and unspoiled under blue skies.

The cold wind gusted sharply as we walked up the wide stairs, pushing on the door that Li tried to open. The building was open until midnight, so that we—the undead we—could conduct official business. Li wrenched the door open against nature's desires, holding it for me.

I shivered at the sight of the open door, suddenly uncertain. It felt like a trap, but I couldn't say why. I only knew that I didn't want to enter. *It's just your imagination, your phobia of authority,* I told myself. I knew that was the reason; my rational brain could see the source of my fear. But that animal voice in the back of my head, the one that warns about dark alleys and strange men, wouldn't shut up.

The guard, stationed more as a reminder of the authority of

Gideon than an actual guard, glanced at us and nodded. The red flag flew up again in my brain, the animal squealing louder still. Why had he nodded? Why had he noticed us? I choked back my paranoia, feeling the urge to flee.

Li took my hand; I hadn't realized I had stopped. "Come on. We'll do this together, right?"

I nodded and stepped forward; he dropped my hand as we moved deeper into the building. This was the main entrance; there were offices with people entering and exiting, going about their business. The tang of vampiric pheromones hung thick in the air; this was our prime time to interact with the human authority. The black and gray marble tile floor stretched away in four directions: back to the entrance, left and right to the administrative offices, and straight ahead to the representatives' offices.

I pulled out the paper with the directions that Sarah had given me that afternoon. We went straight before winding through the hallways, sorting through the maze of offices that twisted through the Capitol. It took about fifteen minutes to find Representative Asnayo's office, which was buried in the further portion of the Representative Wing. "Ready?" Li murmured. When I nodded, he knocked.

"Come in." The voice was a woman's, but it wasn't what I'd imagined Asnayo to sound like. It was sterner than I'd expected, lacking the warmth that I'd assumed a crusader for the people would have. It didn't bother Li, but he hadn't researched her like I had. It made me nervous, because I had felt like I'd known her and this revelation took that feeling away.

The door opened when Li turned the knob and pushed, the dark wood gleaming in the soft overhead lights. Asnayo was standing with her back to us, looking out her window. I was surprised to find that we'd walked to the other side of the building. With all the backtracking we'd had to do, I'd gotten completely turned around.

"Welcome," she said, her voice muffled by its bounce off the glass. She didn't turn around, not even when she spoke. The animal voice in my skull raised its urgent mutter to a full-out shriek, and I grabbed Li's arm. He turned to glance at me, and at the same moment, I caught a glimpse of the woman in the reflection of the glass. It was not Asnayo.

I jerked Li backwards into the hallway, ignoring his yelp and hoping I hadn't pulled his arm out of its socket. It was a worthless gesture; both ends of the hall had filled with goons of a distinctly New-kuza stripe. It was Li's turn to react and, since he was still halfway inside of Asnayo's office, he jerked me back into the room. I stumbled in and spun, slamming the door closed with a well-placed kick.

"No one's going to hurt you, so stop that," the woman said chidingly. She had finally turned around, staring at us with a smirk. She'd be very pretty if she'd just smile, but the sneer on her Asian features twisted her pretty pink lips and large almond-shaped eyes into an ugly mask. As we stared at her, she peeled off the lab jacket and draped it over the back of Asnayo's chair. "The Boss wants to see you, that's all."

"So you lied," I said, "because you should have said, no one's going to hurt you until you get to the Boss. With that in mind, I'm going to say no thanks."

She smirked at me, then looked at Li with enough intensity to telegraph that she was now ignoring me. Nice. "Li, don't you want this cleared up? You can keep running and fighting us, but we'll catch you, and your child, eventually."

Li raised a hand to cut off the insult working its way out of my mouth. "I know," he said, his voice full of pain and regret.

"What? No!" I snapped, stepping between them so that Li had to look at me. "If you're just going to give up, then what have I been risking my life for the past few days for?"

Li winced. "I'm sorry, Misty, but I can't run forever. I thought I could…but I can't."

I shook my head quickly. "No, no…there has to be some-thing we can do." A thought poured through me, and I spun to look at the woman who had pretended to be Asnayo. "I take his debt."

Chapter 23

There was a moment of silence, then Li shouted, "No!" He grabbed my arms, his fingers squeezing with a surprising amount of strength. "No," he repeated, shaking his head, but I ignored him.

"I'm a vampire. That's got to be worth something," I told the woman over my shoulder, trying to keep the sick, roiling motion in my stomach off my face.

"I won't allow it!" Li said, stepping past me to address the woman directly.

I turned around to face her as well. "It's my choice," I said hoarsely.

"Well, well...two people willing to pay the piper," the woman smirked. "How...entertaining." A knot of tension in me eased; surely she would have mentioned Blond Johnny if they were going to take that personally? Did they know?

"Shut up," I snapped. "Look, you guys just want Li dead—I know that I'm worth more not dead. Well, more not dead."

"Who said we wanted to kill him?" She tilted her head like an inquisitive bird.

"I...uh," I glanced at Li. "Didn't you tell me that?"

Li frowned, troubled by this turn of events. "It's usually how they do things," he muttered, glaring at the woman.

"Yes," she said, drawing out the word gently. Her pale eyes, their true color obscured by the dim lighting, darted between my face and Li's. "But sometimes we believe that the person can actually overcome their debt, and so we give them a chance to do so. Of course, that's something you need to discuss with the Boss. Especially since you're making it a duet."

"And if we don't go?" I asked.

"Then you'll hardly be able to claim that you want to repay your debts." The woman arched a perfect black eyebrow.

Debts? "So I take it that you're accepting my proposal?" I hoped that's what it was.

"No," Li said again. "My debt, my responsibility."

"Actually, I seem to recall that you inherited the debt from another," I grumbled.

"Well, actually, you both were involved in trashing the Tiger Club and what happened to Blond Johnny. You both owe us something now." Her dark eyes lingered on me for a moment. "And in truth, I'm not sure that the Boss will accept your proposal." She spread her hands in a gesture of resignation. "That's not my decision."

My stomach lurched again as I said, "Then I guess we have to go see him." Li looked at me, staring in disbelief. "Hey, you wanted to talk to him anyway."

"This is different," Li muttered.

"Why?" I hissed back. "Because you aren't riding to a martyr's death?"

"No," he snapped, grabbing my shoulders. "Because I'm putting my friend in danger."

"How touching," the woman said, cutting into the argument.

We both yelled, "Shut up!"

Her delicate eyebrows rose in annoyance and she took a step back, pulling out her phone. For a moment, I wondered if she'd have us killed anyway. But she merely said, "I'll let you two talk while I make the arrangements." She turned her back to us and opened the phone, typing something on the stupidly small keyboard.

I looked at Li and softly told him, "I can't stand by and watch you walk into something alone. We're friends, right? Right?" I grabbed his face, cupping a cheek in each hand and catching his eyes when he looked at me in surprise. "Or are you going to tell me, to my face, that what we've done together means nothing?"

Li dropped his eyes. "That's why I don't want you to take this from me. I'd never let a friend take my burden."

"Would you take mine? Hey, look at me." He did, and I said softly, "Would you?" He dropped his gaze again, this time while muttering under his breath, and I knew that I had him. "You would, and now I'm taking yours." I gave him a smile I didn't feel. "Don't worry—we'll work out a repayment plan."

Now he looked at me, anger making his eyes snap, but the look was also colored with relief. He'd been afraid, worried to go in alone. As much as he hated that I was going in with him, he was relieved that I was, too. "You're such a pain in the ass," he grumbled to me, his hands sliding to rest high on my waist.

Our faces were close, and I leaned my head forward until our foreheads rested together. "Always," I muttered back. We were winning. We were going to make it out with our lives, and we'd get to keep Masako. We were going to be ok, as long as we watched each other's back. This camaraderie was instinctual on my part, but no less powerful for being manufactured. That thought sobered me up. Just because we were getting out of this mess didn't change the fact that I still had to deal with Li's scent issue. I'd be inclined to believe that only worked for me, but I remembered the gleam in Gregor's eyes, and I tensed. A soft growl slid out of my throat at the thought of him trying to take Li from me.

"Misty? Is there any reason you're growling while trying to squeeze my head off my neck?" Li asked with shocking suddenness.

I relaxed my grip, then forced myself to release him. I had a second to decide if I was going to be honest with him, or lie so that I didn't have to explain what was going on in my brain. "No, no reason," I said, ignoring the urge to be honest to blood. "I'm just nervous." I'd tell him later. One problem at a time, thanks universe.

"Me, too—"

The woman—who still hadn't bothered giving us her name—snapped her phone shut violently. "Come on," she said, and all of the condescending mockery from earlier was gone, replaced by an intense urgency. She marched to the door and wrenched it open, telling the goons in the hallway, "Something's wrong at the teahouse. We have to scramble."

Before we could react, she'd twisted to look at us. "And you two—you're coming too."

"This doesn't sound like our problem," I said, feeling a smirk twist my face. Li nodded, adding his own smug expression.

"It wouldn't," the woman answered, "save that before you got here, your friends and daughter were rounded up and taken to Symmetea, to be used as incentive should you fail to be cooperative. They are in the heart of what is going on there, right now."

"You damned—"

"Cursing at me will not help." Her words cut off Li's angry exclamation. "We'll figure it out later, but for now, I'd suggest coming with us."

Her words were hard to argue with, and we joined the rush of goons down the stairs to the street. Two aeros idled in front of the Capitol Building, and we were pulled into the first one, with the woman. Li moved to slide in the forward-facing seats, but a goon grabbed his arm and pushed him toward the rear-facing seats. I quietly followed, squeezing into the narrow seat next to him and eyeing the goons with us. Two were a matched set of burly men with Asian features; the third, who was actually sitting on the floor because there wasn't room, was petite, blonde and female. One of these things is not like the others. When the sharp scent of vampire floated into my nose, my eyes naturally fell on her though the car was too crowded for me to be sure without blatantly sniffing people. The New-kuza took in anyone that the Yakuza wouldn't, but they also weren't fond of hiring mini-Barbie. Women in the business were either dangerously good or dead. The smart money was on her being the dead one. Settling back into the comfortable seats, I was content to watch her for any signs of danger and ride in silence, but Li had other ideas.

"So who are you?" he asked, crossing his legs and looking at ease. He was addressing the woman who had pretended to be Asnayo.

"I'm Khamla," she said, smiling a touch. It wasn't a nice smile—it reminded me of a cat's. So far, she'd only seemed capable of two expressions: authoritative concern and annoying smugness.

"Laotian," Li replied with a smirk. At the nod of her head, he added, "I thought you were."

"Only a quarter," Khamla shot back. "I'm as muddled as you...Iwao."

Li stiffened next to me. "That's not my name," he stated, his voice way too flat to be truthful.

"No, it's not, but it was once." Her smirk grew to the point that I wanted to smack it off.

"Since you seem to have all the answers," I interrupted, compelled to come to Li's aid, "how about telling me how you arranged all this?"

"All this?" She looked truly confused for a moment; a new expression! It quickly cleared and she nodded. "We have friends in high places," she non-answered, with a full return of the smug. "It was easy to catch wind of what you were doing and change your arrangements. Representative Asnayo was all too willing to cancel an unwanted evening meeting so she could spend time with her family." Khamla grinned, her lips twisting cruelly. "That's why you should make your own meetings—makes it harder for other people to revoke them for you."

I wanted to smash in her face, a rising tide of anger I could taste on my tongue. I swallowed that rage and the destructive desires, forcing myself to remain calm. I even managed to remain calm when she chuckled at us, as we sat silent and still; otherwise, I'd rip her arms out of their sockets. She was wise enough not to push us further, and the goons riding with us remained silent.

All the anger was forgotten when we rounded a tall building and Khamla began to curse softly, staring past us out the window. Li and I twisted in our seat to see aeros parked on the street in front of a building. It was a pretty teahouse, set at the end of a cul-de-sac decorated like a Japanese garden. Or it had been before someone had parked aeros all over the yard, using them as cover. Men and women knelt behind the machines, their backs to us, firing into the building at the end of the cul-de-sac. Our own aero swung around sharply, then came in low to hover over the last open area in the yard.

There was a moment of shock, then Li reached for the door. Khamla stopped him. "Not so fast; the aero is bullet-proof. You're not, Iwao."

"Is my daughter in there?" At her reluctant nod, he said, "Then I'm going."

"Wait." My voice stopped him; that was trust. "Let me go out and clear the way."

"You and me," the blonde said, and we gave each other The Nod. It was a simple gesture, but it acknowledged all that we shared, just by being of the same people. "The undercarriage?"

"Perfect," I agreed. We could get out without risking someone shooting into the aero—well, without risking anyone but us, anyway. "Misty."

She knelt and popped up a plate in the floor with a swift, sure twist of her arm. A dull thud hit the outside of the vehicle, echoing a gunshot. We'd been seen, but she answered me with a careless smile. "Heidi." She flipped blonde hair out of her face, looking way too pleased about our situation. "Fifty says I put down more than you. I've got the left."

"Wha—?" Before I could finish the word, she was out in a low, scuttling run that sent bullets soaring around her. While they were focusing on her, I dropped out of the aero, rolling right and away from the barrage going after my peer.

One of the gunmen reoriented his sights on me quickly, and I felt the snap as a bullet slipped into my skin. I ducked behind an aero before leaping over it, landing ten feet away behind another one. I dashed forward from vehicle to vehicle in a zig-zag, faster than a human, and harder to shoot. The poor guy couldn't get a bead on me, though he came close. Once I was inside his range, two quick blows took him down.

To my left, Heidi threw someone down the street, sending them to a rolling stop. He didn't get up again. Any curiosity I might have had about his status was subsumed by another bullet thumping into me. I whirled and saw another shooter aiming at me. I dashed to him and spun into a fast kick, knocking him down and onto his back. He shot me again without getting up, more luck than skill, and I answered with a quick stomp on his chest. As he rolled on the ground and considered a life with broken ribs, I leapt past an aero to tackle a running gunman, ramming him into the aero he'd been trying to enter. He rolled into a ball and started to moan as I landed on my hands and feet.

The lack of gunfire was like an auditory slap; I looked around, hearing the groans of the conscious wounded. Running footsteps echoed on the pavement, and I looked up to see Khamla, Li and the Goons rushing to join us. "All clear," Heidi called, waving from her stance on top of an aero.

"So I see," Khamla replied, crouching behind a vehicle for cover. She peered over the transport at the building while Heidi walked boldly on the roof of the vehicle, stepping over the still rotors. I crouched like everyone else, content to let Heidi take all the bullets if she wanted them.

"Do we go in now?" Li asked.

"Heidi," Khamla stated, and the vampire dropped off the roof, running at the building single-mindedly.

Li turned to me. "Are you going with her?"

I didn't trust Heidi, so I nodded and moved to follow. She had reached the door, and I called, "Hey, wait for me."

She turned and smirked at me. "You'll catch up." She opened the door, still smirking like this was a stupid game, and the building blew up.

Was it wrong of me to have enjoyed that?

The blast threw me backwards; I probably would have gone ten feet, but I'd only been about five from the aero behind me. I slammed into its side panel hard enough to rock it, but I didn't notice. All that filled my mind was the desperate need to preserve my life, despite the fact that the bomb had already detonated. I had to pull myself out of the dent I'd created in the panel, but I did so as quickly as I could and scrambled behind the vehicle. Smoke was thick and heavy, and my face felt numb and waxy. I touched it, and found that the skin was soft. The heat from the fire had started to melt my epidermis. That is what you call way too close.

My ears were filled with a static roaring. The immediate concern for my own well-being faded and I remembered where I was, and what I had been doing. That awareness caused me to sit up behind the aero's tail, and look around.

Li was rolling to his feet, hands to his head. He staggered as he moved, clearly dazed. Khamla seemed better; she was standing, her face slack as she stared at the building. And Heidi...

My eyes fell on the pile of charred flesh and bone. It had stopped burning, so she'd live. The blast had melted flesh and exposed bone, but the force of it and getting thrown through the air had put her out. As I watched, one of the human goons stumbled over and stared at her body, horror on his features.

I glanced at the building. My belief that it had blown up wasn't entirely accurate; the front was mostly intact, through the windows were gone. Smoke rose from the back, and a little drifted out of the shattered windows. Flame flickered in the windows, a dangerous beacon. "Oh, god," I heard myself whisper. *Mal. Sarah. Masako.*

Someone staggered out of the building and fell in front of it; I could hear them coughing and hacking. Too tall to be Sarah, but I realized it could be Mal, and I leapt over the vehicle. I'd only taken a few steps before I saw how dark his hair was, and I knew it wasn't Mal, but I didn't slow down. Kneeling beside him, I growled, "The child. The two people you brought in! Where are they?"

"He's not one of ours," Khamla said, standing beside me. I glanced up at her, realizing that I was still having trouble hearing, and I saw that she had a gun in her hand. She pointed it at him; I saw her squeeze the trigger.

I snapped a hand out and shoved her wrist to the side; the gun bucked and roared, and a chunk of pavement fractured next to the man's head. "Wait!" I shouted. "Just wait!" Khamla quirked an irritated eyebrow at me, but I was ignoring her. I turned to the groaning man and picked up his hand. Some might have seen it as a moment of tenderness, but that illusion was shattered when I broke his pinky finger.

He screamed, the sharp pain pulling him back from the stunned fugue in which he'd been caught. "Where is the child?" I screamed.

He jabbered something in a language I didn't understand, but Khamla smirked. "He said, in the basement. There's a secure room down there—they would have pulled back to shelter there until help could arrive."

"So they're okay?" I asked.

Khamla sighed, looking pensive. Yay, another expression! We were up to four. "Maybe. The fire will slow help, and the blast might have threatened the stability of the shelter."

"How do we get there?" I asked, making no attempt to hide the intention in my eyes.

Khamla smirked. "Through the kitchen and store room, then down to the basement. Look for the hidden door by finding the stars carved in the bricks."

I nodded, abandoning the man at my feet and striding toward the building.

The gun barked again, but I didn't care. That was Khamla's sin to bear, not mine. Li staggered into step next to me, and I gave him a smile. This is what I could trust—him and myself. Together, we'd get Masako back.

CHAPTER 24

The building was burning as we eased over the threshold of the front entrance. The remnants of tables and chairs were scattered all around, burning or smoldering. The body of a waiter—distinctive in the green uniform—lay smashed and broken under a counter. It looked like he'd taken refuge there only to have it collapse on him. Smoke hung thick in the air, and Li started to cough. Hearing running water, I pointed him to it, and watched as he ripped the bottom off of his borrowed shirt. He moistened it in the water trickling from a burst pipe and wound it around his mouth and nose. With a nod, we moved forward again.

Voices behind us were ignored by me; Li glanced back, his face torn between relief and disgust. I didn't care that they were there, so long as they stayed out of the way. I peered through the dim light, trying to find the door to the kitchen. Li was the one who spotted it; we were almost all the way to the back of the room when he tugged on my arm. Still hacking and choking, he pointed at a door marked "STAFF ONLY."

I stepped forward, indicating to Li that I would go first. He nodded and I pushed open the door. Soft, choking puffs of sound were accompanied by flashes of light, and I blinked as bullets smacked into me. There was a second when the shooter paused to see if I would go down; when I didn't, he shot me again. Growling, I stepped through the door, fighting the backwards push of the bullets. The shooter was crouching behind an overturned cart, next to the center island; the lighting was horrible, but I could see his strangely misshapen head. When he stopped shooting, I heard him say, "Vampire." His voice was muffled and distorted by electronics. *Face mask.* Li could use that.

I bounced forward in the haze, leaping on top of the cart. It was careless; as I gained my balance on the metal frame, another person rose from a squat behind a counter. This one also had a mask—he had that lovely mechanical respirator sound—and a machete. The blade hissed downward, slicing at my torso, and I jumped sideways onto the counter, landing on food I'd half seen. The machete opened my arm from shoulder to elbow, but it cut with the grain of the muscle, and didn't slow me down too much. Hanging pots and pans rebounded off my head and shoulders as I tried to stand up and get some kind of defensive stance.

The machete wielder was swinging again, but I ripped a pan off its hook and used it as a shield, saving my knee from a sideways chop. The shooter fired in the next second, aiming not to kill, but to knock me off my feet. It almost worked; the bad footing among the implements on the counter, my own inability to stand straight up and my dodging weave all left me off balance. I tumbled to one knee as the machete cut where it had just been, opening a rent in my stomach. My erstwhile shield disappeared into the darkness, dropped when I'd fallen.

I'd had no balance on two feet, but now I was a tripod. I planted my hands and kicked with my free foot, connecting with my assailant's head. The glass in the mask cracked but held, and the guy tumbled backwards into the stove behind him, then slumped to the ground.

There was no one shooting at me. I twisted to see the gunman and Li struggling, the gun pointed upward between them. I turned myself around and crawled back to Li, scuttling on my hands and feet. The shooter saw me coming and jerked his upper body to one side, forcing Li between us. That slowed me for a second, as I had to reorient. In that heartbeat, while I was starting to shift to a better position, the gun fired and both men fell.

No, not that gun, I realized a second later; that one hadn't been silenced. I glanced at movement in the doorway, and saw Khamla lowering her gun. "Are you done playing around?"

Li flailed on top of the guy he'd been fighting, trying to get to his feet. I caught his arm and lifted him, giving him the leverage to get his footing. "We aren't playing," I growled as Li pulled himself together, scraping the guy's blood off his face with a grimace of disgust while trying to replace his mouth covering. "And the next time you shoot into a fight that has one of my friends in it, I'll kill you." The statement rolled off my tongue without hesitation or thought. In a second, all the trappings of civilization that Gideon had beaten into me were stripped away, and I knew that I could kill her.

"Let's just go," Li said, his hand wrapping around my forearm.

I swallowed my anger and resolved to deal with her later, if necessary. "Right."

"Russians," one of the goons said softly, but loudly enough that we all heard. I glanced at him, seeing the wallet in his hand. For a horrible moment, I thought we'd just killed Basil. The man on the ground was too slight, and I tried to tell myself that Basil was not a foot soldier, that he wouldn't be in this fight. I hoped it was true. The New-kuza may have been in Gideon first, but they weren't the only Underworld element that wanted a piece of Gideon. The Russians and Italians both had been stepping up the war, with rumors that the Triads were looking this direction, too.

I looked deeper into the room, using my better eyesight. "I see a door marked 'Storage,'" I reported as I dropped off the counter and walked toward the door. I could hear the others following. I wondered if we'd be facing more shooters when I opened the door.

We weren't. We were facing a drop into the basement and the night sky. Whatever had exploded had done so here, peeling the walls back and putting a massive hole in the floor. The fire was stronger here, fed by the cold night air and the organic matter in the store room. I shivered at the dancing flames for a moment, watching them burn far too close to my head for comfort. I forced my gaze away from them, swallowing hard, and looked down to see what was below.

Corpses lay below us, blackened and twisted. I couldn't tell if they'd fallen through to the basement after the explosion or if they had been in the basement. I didn't know anything about explosives, and I couldn't tell if the blast had come from here or from beneath. Below us, two bodies shifted lazily, making me freeze with surprise. After a second, I relaxed. "We need to move," I said. "The basement is filling with water."

Li cursed and moved to jump down. I caught his arm. "Let the vampire," Khamla said coldly. "That's what they're there for."

Li spun on her. "Shut up!" he shouted. "She's my friend." He reached for her, to hit her. I should have stopped him, but I was angry at her, too, and I didn't think it through. But I did see the guard reaching for him, and I reacted, grabbing the thug by his shirt front.

"Hands off!" I shouted, pushing him back. He shoved against me and I twisted him to the side and past me. Even as the goon caught himself, I heard Li shout and then fall, landing with a splash below us. Rage pounded through my bones, hot and furious. I had to lash out, and I already had a target. With a roar I picked the goon up and tossed him through the hole in the wall, throwing him onto the sidewalk behind the building. Faster than a viper, I turned back and grabbed Khamla, pulling her close. "You touch him, or one of your goons touches him again, I will finish you. No jokes, Khamla. Li is mine, and I kill for what is mine."

She was trying hard to remain calm, but I saw the stark fear in her eyes and the way her chin trembled. "Put me down, vampire." Her voice was shaking. "I suggest you remember why you are here, and who I represent."

"I suggest you remember that the man you pushed down there and the captives you have are the only people I care about and that your pet vampire is incapacitated," I snarled, pulling her close enough that I could feel her warm breath tremble over my face. I released her abruptly as my hunger surged; she was too close and I was too angry at her. I couldn't kill her, not at this moment, not before getting what I'd come for first. I cast another scathing glace upon her and dropped into the hole.

I saw Li an instant before I landed on him, and it was just enough time to spread my legs and not come down directly on him. The shock of the landing was cushioned by what he was lying on—a half-submerged body. He groaned as I crouched over him, looking up at me with glassy eyes. "You okay?"

"Ow," he gurgled and took the hand I offered him. "That was dumb."

"No kidding," I said, glancing around the basement as I pulled him up. Above us, I could hear voices arguing about who was going down next, which made me wish I'd thrown her down here anyway. The room was dark, filled with water, smoke and shattered bricks. The basement had been lined with them, giving it an old-fashioned look. But one wall of bricks had come down and revealed a steel wall. Set in that wall was a door of the same, but it was gaping open, torn and sundered. Li and I exchanged a glance and moved forward, leaving Khamla and her still-arguing men behind.

The stairs went down, and as we paused at the doorway, we could hear shouting and gunfire. We leapt to the attack, rushing down the steps toward the noises. The stairs opened onto a landing, and a body lay there; I stopped when I realized it was vaguely familiar. "Sarah?" I called as I knelt next to the woman, reaching for her face.

Li cursed behind me, then knelt next to me, his hands going to her neck. "She's alive," he murmured, sounding relieved. He took off what was left of his shirt and draped it over her form. "We need to hurry, though."

As he spoke, I sniffed the air. "I smell Mal, too, here not long ago," I didn't mention that the scent was full of pain and agitation. If he'd been dragged away from Sarah, that was under-standable. And she was only alive because she was absolutely unimportant to them. They'd left her behind, like trash, and I felt anger. Sarah was mine, damn it—not my family, but mine, because Mal was mine. I heard myself snarl, and saw that same anger reflected in Li's eyes.

The stairs continued after the landing, but where they had been metal, they were now a red wood, polished and gleaming in most spots. The fighting had taken its toll on this area, because the fine wood paneling was scraped and wounded. We found another body, a stranger's, slumped over the steps, which we leapt over without pausing.

The stairs opened to a landing; I could see a railing at the edge. I lengthened my stride and was several steps ahead of Li. It was intentional, and a good thing I'd done so; the man hidden behind the door hit me in the throat with the butt of his rifle. It would have killed a human; it crushed my vocal chords and larynx.

Li took in the situation immediately. He stepped around me

and grabbed the guy's head. Before he could react, Li had pulled his face into his knee. The man's nose burst and he tumbled backwards falling against the wall. I grabbed him and tossed him over the railing. Then I checked to see what was below us.

Armed men hid behind overturned tables at the far end of the long room, facing off against other armed men. I wasn't sure who was on our side, until Li gasped and grabbed my arm, pointing. I followed his finger to see Mal curled behind the far line, hiding in a corner. There was something small and wiggly in his arms, something he was wrapping his body around protectively.

I hopped over the railing and dropped, landing on the guy I'd just thrown. He screamed, a sound that didn't come close to being heard over the warfare going on around us. I glanced up at Li, to find him scooping up the dropped gun and aiming on the men with their backs to us. He was pointing left, so I went right.

The first couple of guys were easy. They didn't have a chance to hear me coming, and I was careful to hang back and take one that was mostly behind his buddies. I simply grabbed his chin and jerked his head back, revealing his neck to me. I caught a flash of wide, startled brown eyes before my teeth sank into his throat. Fresh blood poured into my mouth, and had my family not been in trouble, I would have stopped to feed. But my desire to save my family was greater than the desire for blood, and I only tore open the man's throat.

Conflict surged as I released the man, dropping his dying body to the floor. Part of me wanted to eat. Part of me was screaming about assaulting a human. But the largest part of me was alive: awake and aware as I hadn't been since I had lost my sires. It was more than the instinctive joys of fighting and hunting and chasing; it was doing it with and for family. This is who I was supposed to be, the hunter drenched in blood, fighting with his pack.

Only one of his buddies saw me; as I dropped the dying man, he tried to scramble away from me. I pounced on him like a cat, snapping my hands around his lapels and jerking him toward me. He managed to get his handgun up and pointed at me, but I pulled him to me, muscling past all his resistance. I bit deep, swallowing what blood entered my mouth.

Hands grabbed me from behind and tossed me through the

air. I tumbled until I hit the wall, rebounding and slamming into the floor. I popped to my feet, sparing a glance up toward Li; he was now lying flat on the landing, shooting down at our opponents. They had spotted him and were starting to shoot back, but I was more concerned with the small black man stalking toward me. His speed and his grace meant one thing.

I sniffed the air, and he slowed, stopping, letting me scent him.

He was a vampire all right, and he was older than me, by at least a century.

CHAPTER 25

The vampire moved again, standing close enough that I had to smell him. "I am Robert Sanders, born of flesh in the Town of Sac, in the Golden Land. I am the second child of Molly the Slave, of the line of the Lion-Eaters in the Nation of Heaven. I am the second child of Nochhuetl, Priest of the Sun, and Son of the People of the Seven Caves. I am Lion and I am the Sun, respectively." He finished with a little bow.

Great, my turn. "Nice heralds." Fighting back the urge to sigh heavily, I recited, "I am Misty Sauval, born of flesh in the Big Easy. I am the third child of Daffyad, of the line of Pendragon of the Blessed Isle. I am the fourth child of Aibek, Son of the Line of Bab-ila-on. I am Oak and Fire, respectively."

"I am honored to fight you," he answered and rushed me.

He was too fast. I was immediately thrown off guard, jumping backwards and forgetting that there was a wall there. I slammed into it as he brought up his arm, pinning me to the wall with a forearm in my throat. In a second, I was trapped as his other hand drove into my stomach, his fingers digging and writhing against my skin. He was trying to force his fingertips into my flesh.

I kicked my feet up and slammed them into his thighs, using my bracing against the wall to put my full strength behind it. Robert fell back, and I fell down, unable to get my feet back under me. I flipped back up to my feet, just as Robert did the same and rushed me again.

"This is getting old!" I screamed as I dodged. He bounced off the wall in a beautiful display of physical prowess that used his momentum to continue his attack. I'd have been envious if I'd had the time to do anything other than scramble madly out of the way. And it was a mad scramble; he was moving so quickly that I had no time to act offensively. I was screwed if I couldn't slow him down.

The gun shot tore through his shoulder, wrenching his upper body back with enough force to make him stagger. *Thank you Li.* I turned it to my advantage as best as I could; I leapt forward, landing both feet on his right knee. Even a century-and-a-half old vampire needs his kneecap in place for his legs to work. For the first time, his stoic demeanor slipped, and he snarled. It had actually hurt him, which was a good sign. It meant that the knee might be too injured to use.

He still climbed to his feet, but he was slower. The shot to his shoulder had torn up his flesh, but not enough, because he raised both hands. I wasn't sure what he was doing until he hopped forward, graceful and deadly on one leg. I hadn't expected that he'd be that strong with one leg.

Robert's hands closed over my face and elbow; lightning fast, he began to pull my arm from its socket. I kicked up, knowing that unless I was knocking him over, I wasn't doing much to him, but needing to try, needing to take him down. I caught him between the legs, which was worse than useless; his knee was hurt but his thighs were fine, and he pinched his legs around my ankle. I jerked and twisted, trying to get my foot out, and only succeeded in knocking us both down. Before I could turn this to my advantage, he was on top, pinning me with an arm, my free hand pressed between us. My face was released, but the pressure on my arm was increasing.

A shadow loomed over us; I had just enough time to see the gun pointed at my face to turn my head and hide under the man I'd been trying to wiggle away from moments ago. The explosion of the gun firing was loud enough to make my head ache, and I felt a sliver of the floor slice across the back of my head. At the same moment, the muscles in my shoulder finally tore, disjointing and immobilizing it in one step. I screamed, my voice broken from my crushed throat; I couldn't help it. The pain in my arm was sudden and intense, bad enough to tell me that I was seriously hurt.

I gained a tiny moment of respite; the person who had fired at me collapsed, dropping onto Robert's back hard enough to make him grunt. With a growl, the vampire rolled the body off, and I could see the hole through the corpse's chest; he'd taken a large-caliber bullet. Better him than me.

Now I was done being nice. I was probably about to sign my death warrant; using your teeth took a fight to a lethal level, where your opponent was justifiably less inclined to merely stop you. It's the baseball bat/gun principle; the guy with the bat may kill you, but his intentions feel less fatal. If he pulls a gun on you, it suddenly feels like a very different fight. So when I turned back to Robert and sank my teeth into his throat, it was a threat to him, personally.

He roared with pain and reared back, but my life depended on keeping my teeth in him. I followed him, trying to bite to his spinal cord and do enough damage to it to immobilize him. It was a race, and I was pretty sure I couldn't win it.

Robert's fingers tangled in my hair and pulled me back; I made sure to take a bite of flesh with me as I was pulled away from his neck. His other hand twisted my arm sharply, spinning it and pulling even harder on it. I was about to lose an arm. But twisting it off wasn't fast enough; he dipped his head to my shoulder and began to gnaw through the cords of muscle.

The gnawing drew another scream out of me; I thought that I heard Mal replying with his own shout. I let myself scream, but I didn't lose my mind to the pain. Instead, I eyed his neck, noting how close it was, yet far away. *I need longer hair. Or no hair. No hair it is.* Decision made, I lunged forward, ripping my hair out of my head and his hand, and I got another bite into him. This one scored the side of his neck. More importantly, as his dead, inedible blood was squeezed into my mouth, he was shifted a bit more to the side, and my trapped hand was free.

I began to rake at his eyes, trying to blind him. Robert jerked back from my bite, howling as I removed another chunk of flesh. This chunk joined the other one on the floor as I spat it out in a lurid display of gore. He screamed an obscenity at me, but he didn't paw at his gaping throat as a human might. Instead, he put his hand on my face and pressed it back to the floor, while giving one last inhuman pull to my arm.

It pulled away from my shoulder with an audible shredding noise, like meat being put into a wood chipper. Screaming seemed like a really good idea, but even as I indulged in another throat-ripping shriek of pain, it wasn't enough. I'd never had this kind of injury before; they say that the first time is the worst. I believed in that moment; I couldn't imagine anything hurting more.

Robert was sitting on me, holding my arm up. The light of victory shone in his eyes, all signs of civilization, human or vampire, stripped away to show me how much he'd enjoyed maiming me. And I replied by filling my own eyes with my rage and pain.

I snarled and pushed up with my legs, tipping him forward onto me, but this time, it was okay. He came down, and my now-freed hand came up, my first two fingers pointing at his eye. He fell into it cleanly, and I growled like an animal as I dug into the eye socket, straining to do the same to his brain. Robert howled and ripped himself away, leaping to one leg. Then, with nimble brutality, he began to smack me with my own arm. Each slam was accompanied by a shouted curse, damning my heritage, mental faculties and personal hygiene.

I huddled for the first few blows, too shocked and confused to do more than cower. Then I grabbed blindly for the arm, hoping to catch it so that he couldn't flog me with it anymore. To my amazement, I caught the arm, grabbing it securely in one of the luckiest grabs I'd ever managed. Even better, the sudden change in his swing loosened his grip, and the arm shifted inside the sleeve. A quick twist and it was mine. Again. Kind of.

Robert dropped on me again, and I rolled to the right frantically. He got an arm around me, but most of his bulk landed to the side. As he rolled back to his feet, I began to hit him with my arm; when his hands came close, trying to grab me, I snapped at him with my teeth. That stalemate lasted a few seconds before he limped down to my ankle and began to grab for my feet. I kicked and struggled, but it was only a matter of time. He was stronger and faster than me. At least my question had been answered: age really does make a difference.

When he had an ankle, he took a hop, spun, twisted and used his momentum to fling me across the room. I dropped my loose arm and spread my attached arm, trying to control my tumble, but all I got was a broken wrist when it smashed into the edge of a table. Groaning, I clambered for my feet, knowing that my advantage was that I had two working legs. My knees were so weak that I wasn't sure about that "working legs" idea, but I managed, standing up shakily.

Robert was steadily advancing, hopping and limping determinedly at me. "God," I muttered, wanting to just lie down and die. Again. Kinda. "Can we call a truce?" I mumbled. "Sit down? Take a nap?" Robert slumped against a table for a moment, then stood up and tossed it away with one arm. "Guess not."

I dodged to the right as he tried to close the gap between us. It would be a bad idea for me to let him grab me; I'd probably lose the other arm. He seemed fond of that maneuver, at least with me. Seeing the over-turned table gave me an idea; as Robert came at me again, I grabbed the end of another table and slammed him with it. It was heavy and had a nice momentum, once you got the hang of swinging it. With only one working leg, the table slapped him sideways and sent him flailing to the floor. I swung again, throwing my hips around to add momentum to the table and tried to pancake him to the floor. I managed to hit him, but I had reached the limit of the table's endurance. It shattered in several pieces, leaving me with a leg attached to a perpendicular shaft of wood, sharpened naturally into a jagged blade. It was far from perfect, in either weight or balance.

I didn't care.

I over-handed the remnants of the table, swinging it like the misshapen hoe it now resembled. I again threw my body into the swing. He saw the blow coming and scrambled backwards with two arms and a leg, hissing like an enraged cat. My blood-lust rose; hissing was defensive, and regardless of whether it was actually true, made me feel like I had the upper hand. I got in a second swing, not bringing it completely behind my back this time. I snarled joyously as it cut into his body.

Something pushed into my flesh and shoved me backwards; the noise of the gun only registered after I was tossed to the ground. I tried to flip to my feet, but without both my arms to push off with, I was unable to do it. It took a second try, and by then, Robert was rolling over and coming up on his good knee. I was so screwed.

I quickly scanned the bad guys, trying to see if the one

who'd shot me was going to do it again. To my surprise, they were pulling to one side of the room, trying to call all their people over. I pointed to them, shouting, "Hold up! Looks like your table is leaving, Robert of Lions and Suns." My voice sounded like I'd gargled gravel, but it worked.

"Will you let me walk out?" He asked the words calmly, but there was a definite tension in his voice. He was afraid I'd say no. I wasn't sure why; I'd done pretty well in this fight but he'd have won.

"There are only so many of us left," I said, giving him a little nod. I also really didn't want to fight him anymore. "I'll let you out—walking, running, skipping, crawling. Just go."

"We may meet again." Was he warning me? I searched his eyes, his face, and I knew. If we fought again, he wouldn't let my mercy today stop him.

"Whatever," I grumbled, waving my remaining hand. "Just go. I'll worry about fighting you again later."

He nodded and bowed his head. "Misty of Oak and Fire, there will be teeth when we fight again."

Hey, great. He was telling me that the next time we scrapped, he wouldn't play around to start. He'd go straight for my throat, so to speak. I shrugged. "That's your choice." I nodded across the room. "Your ride's leaving."

I watched him limp over to where they were staggering out, using a back exit I hadn't noticed earlier. There weren't that many of them left; Li was a good shot.

Speaking of—I scanned the room for my friend, and found him catapulting over the barrier, hurrying to Mal's side. Mal had been hiding Masako, and I sighed with relief as the again-crying baby was given over to her father. Mal didn't stay; he scrambled over the barricade with far less grace than Li, but no less hurry. He came straight to me, his eyes filled with pain at my condition. "I'd stay and help—"

"We saw Sarah. Go. I just need to find my arm." I had about two hours to attach it before it started to disintegrate and I would have to regrow it from scratch. That would be a long process, and annoying. Best to avoid that outcome.

I retraced my steps in the fight, following the shattered

table to the gun-shot crater in the floor. Other humans were in the room, men wandering around checking the dead and helping the wounded. I ignored them, looking for my arm, which was somewhere between the table and crater. Grumbling to myself, I put my head down and began to hunt for it. I flipped tables over, feeling a false exhaustion. My body wanted to sink into a deep slumber and start to regenerate. I'd thought that I'd experienced it before, with the glass in my back and other injuries I'd incurred, but I'd been wrong. Those urges to sleep were nothing compared to the desire I had right now. It was a good thing, as it allowed us to fall into a healing hibernation when we were badly injured, but this was the first time I'd felt how hard it dragged at you, whispering soft pleadings to sleep. It was like being mortal again for a time. My sires had warned me about this. I thought it was just a warning about getting injured. There was more to it than that. It was a total fugue; I was having trouble thinking about anything other than sleep.

The backdoor opened again and I snapped around expecting to see a force of returning thugs, coming to reverse the retreat. But all I saw was a hand tossing out a small silver ball, sending it rolling into the room.

Grenades used to look like pineapples, but they don't roll very well. So hand grenades have gotten progressively smaller and rounder, becoming more ball-like. I hadn't grown up with them; the silver ball didn't send an immediate shiver of fear down my spine. But once my brain remembered what that ball was, the shivers started.

I think I shouted. I don't remember. I dashed forward, scrambling with one hand. I couldn't kick it back, because the door had swung closed. I managed to get it, and drop it, and got it again. I didn't know how long the fuse was going to burn. It could blow up right now.

I clamped it against my body, cuddling it like a football. I almost smashed down the door, but we'd need that door to stop the explosion. I levered the door open with my hand, finding a hallway beyond. I could see the running backs of the people who had left the parting gift. I felt a wicked grin crossing my face as I opened my arm and kicked it down the hallway. I even managed to ping it off the back of someone's head as my own parting shot.

But I didn't manage to get the door closed before the bomb went off. I saw fire and light before I was blown into unconsciousness.

CHAPTER 26

I woke up in a hospital, still hurting. It was a struggle to remember what had happened. But my current pain wasn't as bad as the memory of having my arm ripped off. That thought made me look to the side, my eyes falling on my left arm to see how much of it was there. A three-inch stump was connected to my shoulder. If it had grown that much, I must have been out for a while. A quick test rotation of the joint and a couple of pokes with my other hand confirmed that it was my arm.

I looked around, seeing the brightly painted walls that were so common in today's medical centers. Designed to cheer up living residents, it only made me miss the clean, white simplicity that had once been typical in hospitals. I sighed and shifted slightly, making the bed rattle. That noise was followed by a familiar moan from the floor.

I sat up and leaned over to confirm what I'd hoped—Li was rolling upright, grinning up at me. He'd been stretched out on the floor, waiting for me. I had to grin back; it was damned good to see him. Then I realized that Masako wasn't here. "Where—the baby?"

"She's with my aunt and uncle," Li said, moving up to the chair. He was a little stiff, and he had the occasional bandage sticking out from under his clothing.

"Is that safe? Why are you here?" I asked, manipulating the bed controls so that I was sitting upright. I still wanted to sleep, but I wanted to see Li more.

"It's safe now," Li said, and I could see the strain that statement caused. "I made a deal." His dark eyes focused on me, equal parts apology and relief.

"A deal?"

"Yeah, I had to," he said softly. "I wanted to wait for you, but the doctors said you'd be in a healing sleep for weeks."

"How many?" I asked, dreading the answer.

"Three. Your, uh, boss is kinda pissed."

"No doubt," I sighed, pressing a hand to my forehead. "He's been here?"

"A couple of times."

I eyed him. "How long have you been here?"

"As much as I could be. Mal's been here a lot too and your case worker, Rick. We've all been worried."

"Mal's just worried about breaking in a new partner," I snorted, but I smiled at the warmth behind the words. A second later, I stiffened. "Sarah?"

"Full recovery, aside from nightmares," Li quickly assured me.

I nodded, relaxing. "Anyway. The deal?"

"Well, first, you and I are a gang of associates," Li told me, leaning back in his chair and crossing his feet at his ankles.

"That sounds like it means something, but I'm not sure what."

"It means that we're not individuals. Our debts are all kind of lumped together, and we're getting treated like a collective— no individual jobs or anything like that. We're a gang, separate from the New-kuza, and by calling us associates, that just means we're not part of *their* gang."

"Okay, that sounds good," I said softly. "There's got to be a down side."

"Yeah, our collective debt is somewhere in the seventy thousands."

"What?!" I shrieked, my eyes flying wide. "Suran only borrowed twenty!"

"The damage done to the Tiger Club was added to our bill," my human friend sighed. As I sputtered, he added, "Thankfully we aren't accruing interest, though."

"Oh, and that makes it okay?" I snapped, trying to cross my arms before forgetting I only had one.

"No, that means that we have a chance of paying our bill down before we die, otherwise, they'd have it at twenty percent interest, compounding hourly or something. Basically, it'd mean we'd never be free of them."

"God... Li, how long will it take us to work that off?" I asked, feeling a pit of unease in my gut.

"Depends on what jobs we do," he said softly, looking discouraged. "A while, Misty."

"What about forgiving the debt entirely?" I grumped, sounding bitter. "I mean, I did toss away that bomb, and I seem to be *missing an arm!*"

"That'd be a sign of weakness," Li shrugged, nodding at my irritation. "And if we refuse their generosity, then they just keep coming after us. They also kept the police away from us. You and I were meeting someone at the Symmetea when a gas line exploded."

I rubbed my eyes, missing my other arm. "So you honestly believe that this is the best deal?"

"The best we're going to get that doesn't involve being on the run for the rest of our lives. Oh, and we have a contact that will be in touch with us soon."

"A New-kuza contact," I mumbled. "Perfect."

"He seems pretty clean. I wouldn't expect him to be New-kuza by his appearance."

"So when do I get to meet him?"

"Later, when you're better," Li said, grinning. He stood up and bent over me, kissing me on the forehead. "I'm glad you're awake. They said you'd been healing, but it's good to talk with you. I've been worried about you."

"Me, too," I told him, and got a laugh in return. "But I'm glad you and Masako are all right."

"Yeah, we are, thanks to you." He paused and glanced at the clock. "Aw, I need to go. Masa's preschool will be letting out soon. You'll be all right? Mal's supposed to be here in a couple of hours."

"I'll be fine," I lied. I wasn't fine. I owed the Japanese mob more money than I'd ever dreamed of making, and I still hurt a lot. "Go on."

Li bent down and kissed my forehead again. "I'll be back, promise. I'll bring Masa, too."

"Poor thing. I think she's scared of me," I said, grinning. "I only show up when there are lots of bad things going on."

"She just needs to get used to having you around," he assured me, his dark eyes sparkling. "And when she's older, she'll get to hear about all the crazy things we did for her."

"Yeah," I agreed. I kept the smile until he had left; then it faded. Sighing, I thought about sleeping, but noticed I had several vases of flowers. "Huh," I said, reaching for the call button. When the nurse showed up, I asked her to bring me the cards.

The first was from Gabe, or at least he'd sent it. It held fairly standard sentiments of recovery and I set it aside. It also offered the implicit statement that my job was preserved. The next card was simple, almost bland, and bore one handwritten line: *I have not forgotten. R—* It took me a second to remember Robert. "Oh, well that's *great,*" I sighed unhappily. I didn't expect him to forget, but there was not forgetting, and there was taking the effort to remind someone you weren't forgetting. It was very troubling, and I put that aside too.

When I opened the third card, I had to smile. Rick's card was very simple, but his message was nice: *Misty, I heard you got hurt in an accident. The police had told me that your legal troubles are clearing up. Oh, and I've managed to keep your apartment for now, but you should probably get better soon. If you do lose it, I'll help you find another one. Yours, Rick.*

The last was the most interesting. Aside from the usual wishes for my recovery, there was a hand-written note: *Ms. Sauval, I heard about your accident. My condolences. I wished to inform you that you have been cleared of suspicion in the death of Suran Assawaroj. I thought you might wish to know that you needn't worry about that anymore. Sincerely, Det. P. Benoit.* "Huh," I said again, feeling my eyebrows rise. "That's interesting. Why would *he* send a card?" The stiff paper held no answer, and I was forced to leave the mystery alone.

My thoughts turned to my life. It seemed to be in a shambles. I owed the New-kuza a ridiculous sum of money. I was now working for them to pay off that sum. I'd been badly injured, and would miss who knows how much work. I'd be fed blood while here, but I might find my government-subsidized apartment had been given to another and I had been relocated to something smaller. Mal and Sarah had been hurt—I wondered if she'd ever talk to me again. I wouldn't blame her if she didn't. What a mess.

But it wasn't all bad. I had friends, I have my health and so long as I was willing, I had work. Gideon would ensure that a job would always be waiting for me. I may be doing something else than I was, but the release from the hospital held the promise to return to my old life. But after some consideration, that wasn't all that comforting. I was associated with the Underworld, I had broken the Vampire-Donor laws of Gideon, and I had felt that rekindling of my blood. I had been asleep, a monster in sheep's clothing, but now I was awake, and the costume no longer fit me. The old ways, subsuming what I was behind a wall of obedience and conformity, wouldn't work for me anymore. I could feel it, burning and hot in my blood.

The truth was, I was going to have to find a new balance, a new way of living. But they say you can find anything, for the right price, in the City of Promise.

❀ ❀ ❀